Hurricane of the Heart

Sunshine Gulf

Oil Platform No. 6

Farley Dunn

THREE SKILLET

SUNSHINE GULF: OIL PLATFORM NO. 6, Dunn, Farley L

First Edition

Hurricane of the Heart, Book 3

 THREE SKILLET

www.ThreeSkilletPublishing.com

Cover design by Farley L Dunn

ISBN: 978-1-943189-32-8

Sunshine Gulf

Oil Platform No. 6

Chapter 1

THE WATER was calm as far as Louinda Reinhardt could see, but the rotor wash buffeted her, threatening to tear her safety helmet from her head. She didn't need this man who was about to come aboard Sunshine Gulf Platform No. 6, and with God as her witness, she'd see that he was gone as soon as she could drive him away. He'd be off her rig before that weather disturbance on the other side of the Gulf could brush anywhere near this oil production platform. She'd rather deal with *it* than him, if she had to choose.

Her eyes blinked behind her safety glasses, and the tears that threatened to come were forced back to their hiding place behind her rough bravado. Her Tracy had been taken from her, she'd found safety here, and this world was hers, no matter what this man had to say.

The reports were on her desk, though. It was that sign on her door that made her stand here and wait for this man to step into her life. *Rig Safety and Training Coordinator.* She'd worked hard for her position on this rig. College. More classes after that. Even before applying for her transfer to Sunshine Gulf, she had earned her BOP certificate. Blowout prevention was the jewel on her wall, too. She was also well-versed in offshore safety procedures, well control, and a variety of other safety training courses. Then there were her much practiced interpersonal communication and organizational skills. Without those, she'd still be land based. She'd proven she'd acquired those, and that she was good at them. Today, however, they would be put to the test.

Other than Tracy—who had been too forgiving with her, her sisters claimed—her family roasted her as sharp-tongued at times, but her brusque manner worked well with these roustabouts and roughnecks who filtered out to these offshore rigs. Only with the more prestigious jobs on the rigs was she able to relax her barbed tongue. They usually had more to lose if they were kicked off, and they exercised more restraint in their behaviors and mannerisms.

Thank God Ben Tosh had been here her first week on the rig. Several of the roustabouts had gotten drunk and seen the new girl as an opportunity. She'd fought and clawed, bloodying noses and blacking eyes, but they'd gotten her clothes half off before Ben showed up. Those ruffians were gone the next day, and Ben had taken her under his wing ever since. Lou loved Ben, just not in the way she'd loved Tracy. She'd hardened up since then. She'd never find another one like her Tracy. In his place, Ben was all she had.

However, she missed Willie. She'd raised her brother for ten years, from the time he was two, even living at home while attending college to make sure he had the assurance of a solid home life at the most critical stages of his development. Then, at twenty-five, she'd married, and she and Tracy had continued to live with her father to help out with Willie. It was when her husband was killed the next year that she took her first job at the oil fields up near Tulsa. Although it had rankled at first, under her father's very good advice, she'd hired on under her maiden name. The oil field workers were a bit rough, sometimes, and he felt it added a measure of privacy when she was home. He didn't want her pursued in her time away from the fields. The job had been perfect for her. She could return home to help with Willie and his two older sisters for two weeks, then her father could take his turn for the two weeks she was gone. Although her father struggled in dealing with a twelve-year-old boy, the parishioners at his church in Oklahoma City often stepped in to fill the gap when Lou was gone. When Willie finally graduated high school, she had been ready for more adventure, and she had fled offshore.

This man arriving on the helicopter, though, was a threat. He wanted her job. He wanted the whole rig shut down. She *knew* it. She also knew Rampart Oil had deferred maintenance on this rig for long before she had shown up. She had been able to jerry-rig the more urgent repairs, but it hadn't been easy. Especially those two escape pods. Parts had been on back order for them the entire time she'd been aboard. Now that the company had gone into receivership, her time for improvements had slipped through her fingers, and with it, her job security on this rig. A growl grew in her throat at the thought of that. She was well aware how many hours of her life would be thrown away. This man's visit was surely tied into the takeover bid linked with the pending bankruptcy.

The moisture whipped from the rotor's wash as the aircraft drew closer, and it stung her face. She was glad for the safety glasses that kept her eyes clear. Still, the needle-like pinpricks of water focused her thoughts. She would be polite to this Chad Dickson, if barely, and she would escort him immediately to procure supplies for his safety equipment. She would even see that he received his green helmet. *Green.* Everyone would know he didn't belong. All the regulars would be in white, and he would be wearing green. *Rookie* green.

She reached a hand to place it on top of her helmet to keep the torrent of wind from blowing it overboard. She groaned at the thought of having to go through this man's luggage. He probably had a cell phone, cameras packed full of batteries, and even matches, just waiting to blow up her rig. Sometimes she thought only boys made it out to these rigs, kids ready to set a match to the world just to watch it burn. That's the one thing that would cause her to walk away, to head back to shore in a heartbeat. She'd put up with anything else. She already had, even that assault that first day, but a careless kid? No, she *wouldn't* put up with that. Not even when they paraded as adults. A kid and an oil platform were a deadly combination, and she didn't intend to risk her life on this job. *Rig Safety and Training Coordinator*, right? She was there. She knew safety, and nothing was more dangerous than a kid, matches, and petroleum byproducts, no matter how grown up the kid pretended to be.

Then the sun flashed off the helicopter's canopy, and in that moment, she caught a glimpse inside. She felt the hair on her neck prickle. If she weren't mistaken, there was an extra person inside. She had been told to expect only Chad Dickson, and she'd set things up for him accordingly. She'd had to swap a few people around to do it, too, and not all of them were happy. Dickson needed a workspace. A *workspace!* This whole platform was a workspace. No, he needed one in his *room.* She'd done it, though, rearranging bunk and room assignments, and getting this man the *privacy* he demanded. It only had one bed, though. One bed and a private workspace—actually a closet door bolted horizontally into a corner. The second bed had been removed, and it was in storage. This was an old rig, and not the largest in the world. Sunshine Gulf was lucky to have a pool table and a theater room. Most workers bunked four to a room, and there were even two six-bunk rooms. When she patrolled the rig on safety inspections, they appeared more like sardines in a closet. At least the men could be scheduled on opposing twelve-hour shifts, alleviating some of the crowding. This man, Dickson, had a private, though. Even she barely had that.

Her mind roiled with who this other person might be. She didn't know what she'd do if she had to put up another person somewhere. Outside? Could this interloper sleep outside? She didn't think so. With all her heart she hated this sudden not knowing, these curves management back ashore liked to throw at her. She began to click off options and possibilities. There was a spare bunk in the medical section. Also, she thought she might fit an extra body into the cook's quarters. Cookie wouldn't like it, but if it were temporary, he might not grouse too much. Maybe, she hoped, just maybe the extra person she thought she saw was along just for the ride out, just to say he or she had been to an offshore rig. Maybe. It was a long way out just for someone to say he'd been here, though. Somehow, she expected this extra person was not a good omen for Sunshine Gulf.

It was more, however, besides simply an extra person. More than just the possibility of making additional room arrangements on the rig, if she truly had to accommodate another *guest*. Lou's chest tightened, and standing there waiting on the approaching helicopter, her eyes began to burn. She'd just gotten back yesterday after being gone two weeks. The trip home had been hard this time.

It was her father's birthday, and the entire family had gathered at her sister's lakeside home. They'd had a barbecue around the pool, and Lou's younger brother, Willie, had been in his board shorts. He'd climbed out of the pool, and when he stepped up on the diving board to do his trademark jackknife, he'd paused for a moment. He was so young and yet so grown up. He'd shot up in the year since graduation, and he was very slender. The Buttless Wonder, they'd always called him, and now it was certainly true. He smiled and jumped on the board, kicking himself up into the air. The sun flashed from his moisture-dappled skin, and he pierced the water with barely a ripple. However, he did leave one thing floating right there on the surface. His trunks.

Jelwin, Lou's sister just older than Willie, shrieked in delight, grabbing them and flinging them out of the pool. Willie had come up at the other end with his hands on the side, pushing himself half out of the water, fully prepared to leap onto the concrete deck, to spring out in one mighty thrust, landing with both feet directly on the side. His arm muscles had been tensed to leap, and that was when he realized he'd left his suit behind. Frantic, he turned to search for it, only to see that someone had already hung it on the fence, far from his reach.

The family, including Lou's father, roared with laughter at his predicament, as Willie pleaded for his shorts. Lou finally took pity on him, spitting sharp-tongued barbs at her siblings as she plucked the shorts from the fence and tossed them back into the pool.

Her sisters booed as he pulled them on. Her father and brothers-in-law laughed as Willie finally crawled from the water, red-faced with embarrassment. Lou knew it was all good-natured, but she had felt a third wheel, and it hadn't been a good moment.

In that instant, surrounded by her loving family, she'd missed her husband Tracy so very much. She had him for that one year, and then he was gone. He was the one who'd softened her sharpness, who'd made her into the person she'd wanted to become. She'd been nicer with Tracy and had become bitter without him. Now, she was the extra person in her family. No one expected Willie to be married, but both her sisters were, and happily, too. Razor-edged Lou was truly the one who no longer belonged.

Back on the rig, Lou stood straighter. This man arriving on this machine didn't belong, either. That went double for his companion. They'd figure that out, and it wouldn't take very long. She fingered the earplugs in her pocket. She always carried an extra set for herself, and today she had a set for this man. They'd want them, too. At least they would if they still wanted to be able to hear anything once they got off the rig.

With a clunking vibration Louinda felt rather than heard, the helicopter was down. She stood for a moment to let the blades grind to a stop. Many people, she knew, didn't mind ducking to walk underneath them. She wasn't all those other people, and the pilot wouldn't be gone for another two hours. There was no rush that required her to dash under the moving blades as they spun overhead. Waiting was a better option. It also set the tone for her opinion of this new arrival. He wasn't welcome, and she wanted it made clear she wouldn't grovel at his feet.

Peering through the reflections scrawled across the helicopter's canopy, she could see the second person—a man—sitting on the opposite side. That was a small consolation. She knew how well a woman would be received. She had lived that. So, she had two men to juggle. Perhaps she could manage.

One of her files on her desk had a photo of this Dickson person. With his blond hair, he had to be the one closest to her. The identity of the other was the mystery. She knew nothing about him, and anytime she didn't *know* something, it ate at her. The next time something like this happened, she'd let the toolpusher push himself on out here to take care of this sort of business. After all, he was the general manager of the rig, and he could earn his pay doing this little reception duty. Just because he was over her didn't mean she should be shouldered with this. He should review her job description and let her get on with it. Greeting these men had little to do with either safety or training, and that's what her job was all about: safety and training.

Then, the rotor was still, and the side of the aircraft began to open. Louinda stood back. She intended to be officially polite, but welcoming was simply too much. She would greet this man and his companion when the pair walked up to her, and then she would simply apologize that there was no bed for a second visitor. When she inquired whether the visitor intended to return to shore with the helicopter, she was sure her hint would come across loud and clear.

She turned for a minute as the end of a long boom suddenly flared in an unexpected burnoff. She hadn't remembered they were scheduled for one of those, but she enjoyed them whenever they happened. More surprising was that it stopped almost immediately. She shrugged. If they were being shut down by this Chad Dickson, burnoffs would soon be a moot point, anyway, so why worry about it? Still, it rankled not to know.

Turning her head back to the helicopter, her heart caught in her throat, and she felt sudden silence fall around her as everything slowed to a halt. In that moment of recognition, she floundered. It was Tracy, again. The motion of the flags overhead became rigid cardboard, and the steps of the roustabout unloading a black leather bag were frozen. Even the clouds in the sky hung motionless. The clanking of the giant drilling clamps, as well as the

15

deep thrumming of the myriad motors all over the rig simply ceased. The only thing Lou was aware of was the man who exited the helicopter and his crystal blue eyes looking right at her. Her heart jumped—My God! Those eyes!—and then he looked away, the Tracy she had seen in them gone. With a jarring sensation, she felt the world around her snap back into motion once again. However, just for that moment . . . . Then, with horror, she focused on the second man still inside the machine that had invaded her world.

ACROSS THE HELIPAD, Chad Dickson looked around the landing area. His mind had been in observation mode as the helicopter drew near the drilling rig, and he knew how many sets of steps they had to walk down to get to the main level. About four floors, and he saw nothing that looked like an elevator. Safety flaw number one. His eyes were peeled for anything that was amiss on this outdated offshore platform. That's why he was here. How would they evacuate injured personnel, up four flights of stairs? The Ways and Means Committee hadn't been able to correlate the reports that had been presented in their inquiries with the facts that had been dug up on Rampart Oil. One of the major expenses listed on the company's spreadsheets was the expenditure for infrastructure and safety upgrades on this rig. With what he could see already, he suspected the books were being used to hide certain facts the company didn't want anyone to know.

A man in a white helmet ran up to the helicopter, darting under the spinning blades as he exited. When the helmet motioned to Chad, pointing to the two bags in the back, Chad just nodded. Speaking would have done little good. Not only was the spinning rotor over their heads whacking the air to shreds, this old oil rig was atrociously noisy. He wondered if any one piece of machinery here had been greased even once since the thing was built.

He considered his companion with some trepidation. He hadn't intended to bring him, and his official paperwork from the Ways and Means Committee made it clear he was supposed to be here alone. He would be, too, if his ex-wife wasn't so determined to make his life a living nightmare. He'd told her he couldn't take the boy during August. The good old U.S.A. was sending him offshore for however long they needed him. It would be at least a month, he had explained with no lack of clarity. She had laughed. "He's your son, too, Chad. You can't wimp out on every one of your responsibilities. Besides, it's mine and Chip's second anniversary. We'll be in Hawaii for six weeks. For the first four, Chaddie's yours, buddy. We're leaving the last weekend in July. You figure it out."

Up until this morning, Chad had thought he could get Diana to change her mind, maybe take the boy along to Hawaii, or perhaps set him up to stay with a friend. When he hadn't shown up already, he'd decided she had done just that, made other arrangements without telling him. It would be like her, once telling the boy he could stay with a friend from school, and Chad only finding out after a worried night and repeated unanswered calls. The boy had enough of them, friends, that is. It seemed he had formed friendships with everyone in his junior high. As a ninth grader next year, he'd probably befriend the entire high school campus. Surely someone would want him for a month.

That hadn't worked out. After catching the Forecast on the Fives, the meteorologist telling of a low-pressure system off the Florida coast, Chad had stepped out of his townhouse this morning for his last early morning jog until he returned, and he nearly tripped over the boy. He'd been sitting on the stoop with a portable video game in his hands, contentedly waiting for his father to come out the front door. Then, the boy had smiled and given Chad a hug he hadn't wanted, as if that was what sons did, showed up unexpectedly on their fathers' doorsteps with a suitcase as an armrest. When questioned, the boy said he'd sent his dog to Dallas to stay with his great-grandfather, and his mother had put Chaddie on the bus to Fort Worth the night before. It was twelve hours from Boulder, and Chaddie hadn't wanted to wake his father. He grinned and said he hadn't minded waiting outside with his video game.

When Chad had shown up at the airport with an extra tagalong, he thought that might be the end of his son's vacation adventure. His trip was at government expense, the travel, anyway, he explained. Out on the rig, his expenses would be covered by Rampart Oil, just as was everyone else's on the platform. It wasn't an all-inclusive resort prepared to cater to family and friends. Chaddie might very well be on a flight to Dallas to stay with his great-grandfather, Wally. Chaddie's face had fallen—and yes, that stirred Chad's sympathy—so Chad had suggested to his Rampart Oil liaison that if they wanted to comply with the government mandate, there was no choice but to let him bring the boy along. The rig personnel would just have to accommodate the extra person. It was amazing how quickly an extra airline ticket had appeared.

As they traveled down, Chad was irritated to learn that his son had indeed received offers to stay in Boulder. However, he'd refused them all. He wanted to spend his vacation on an oil rig. When would another opportunity like this come along? It was the coolest way to end his last summer before high school, he'd bragged to all his friends. He also said it was his month with his father. Then the boy had laughed just before he'd gone back to his video game. Chad just caught his final words, ones he didn't think he was intended to overhear: "Plus, there you can't get away from me, Dad."

As he stood on the helipad, Chad was surprised to see a woman wearing a white safety helmet, glasses, and coveralls. He was amused, too. He knew women worked the rigs in the Gulf, but somehow he expected them to be big, burly Amazons who could wrestle a collar into position without a second thought. Yet, standing before him was a petite brunette who might even be beautiful without all her gear. That caught him off guard. Still, however attractive she might be, Chad knew one thing. He'd already been put through the grinder with women: chopped up, stuffed into a chili, thrown onto the grill, and fed to the dogs afterward. His ex-wife had burned him on all things female. He wasn't interested.

Besides, this woman was probably just a roustabout, the lowliest of all the rig workers, here to direct him to his quarters. She'd go back to mopping floors, chipping paint, or some other menial task when she was through with him. He wouldn't see her again except as she slaved away, and she wouldn't remember him except as another of the mundane tasks she was forced to perform on a previous day.

A flag far above his head snapped in a sudden gust of wind, catching Chad's attention. A surprising yet welcome coolness brushed his face and quickly receded, fading with the warmth of the summer sun against his back. He let his eyes rove the structure as he waited for his son to disembark the helicopter. The rig was enormous, although not the largest in the world by far. It was all one big machine, tubes, pipes, and catwalks, standing starkly against a faded blue sky, with the ocean as far as the eye could see. Production Platform. That's what his papers called it. And the *noise.*

He shook his head at the cacophony of sounds from all around him, and he turned to the copter at his back to see Chaddie still on his video game with wired earpieces trailing across his chest. Irritated, Chad stepped to the door and reached across. Grabbing the wires with one hand, he yanked the earbuds from his son's ears. His son looked up and grinned.

"Yeah, Dad? Are we here?" When he saw his father frown and point to his ears, Chaddie looked around and leaned forward to peer outside. He cupped his hands around his mouth, repeating, "Are we here, Dad?"

"Out, Chaddie." Chad slapped the boy's leg with his hand and motioned. His own words were called just as loudly. Part of that was the noise. The rest was irritation. Then he turned back to the woman.

Off to her side, the man who had come for their bags was disappearing down a set of metal steps that dropped off the side of the helipad. Glancing back to see his son finally unbuckling his seatbelt, Chad took a deep breath and prepared to meet this woman. Placing what he hoped was a congenial look on his face, he allowed a smile to play at his lips, and he strode forward with his hand outstretched.

When he reached her, instead of returning his handshake, she stood with her hands in her pockets, and she glared over his shoulder as if he weren't there. When Chad turned, there was his son climbing out of the helicopter. The boy stretched, holding his arms high over his head, and as he yawned, his gaze roved all around the place he'd come to stay. Not only did his teenage frame reveal his true age, he also revealed the video game still in his hand. At last his sparkling green eyes found his father and the woman standing at his side, and his face broke into a sunny grin of excitement.

Chad took a deep breath and turned his head back to the woman he'd stepped forward to greet. That was his first inkling of trouble. There was no excitement on this woman's face, no interest in greeting either him or his son, and certainly no welcome to Oil Platform No. 6. If this woman's looks could drive a fiery stake through a man's heart, then someone would be dead already.

It embarrassed Chad to find that she was looking directly at his son, the daggers in her eyes shooting his direction one after another. He knew bringing the boy out here would come to no good, and Chad closed his eyes and hoped for the sudden throbbing in his head to go away. Maybe, please, God, he silently prayed, let this be the only time we must interact with this woman. He took a deep breath. He wondered if his son had enough games to keep him inside his room and out of her way their entire visit.

Then he felt the metal under his feet vibrate, and he opened his eyes to see the woman striding angrily towards the helicopter and his son. With lightning fast speed, she snatched the video game from the boy's hand and flipped it over. With a sure motion, she opened the case, extracted the batteries, and dropped them into her pocket. Then she held the game out to return it to the boy.

As she came back to Chad, she hissed, "What is he, thirteen? He might look older, but I know thirteen when I see it. Did you bring him here to blow us all up? Batteries on an oil platform can do that, you know."

Then she reached back into her pocket and brandished two small plastic bags in her hand. Holding them out, she waited for Chad to take them.

"GO AHEAD," Lou said, and she made sure her words were brittle. She wanted them to sting. "You'll want these. Take one pair for the boy, too." One set was her extra pair, and it galled her to give up those—They were hers, after all!—but she could get more. She set her jaw hard, grinding her teeth. What little politeness she had left was just about used up in those words.

Lou recognized her irritation was more than just the boy, and that's part of what galled her. That blond hair and those crystal blue eyes. How could this man have stepped onto her rig? Except for his height and his chin, this could be her Tracy all over again. How had she not seen that in the picture attached to his paperwork? God, how could she not have seen that?

Her heart pounding in her chest, she wondered why this *man* had to be the one to come aboard her rig, and even worse, why did this *boy* have to come with him? The fire she'd spat at them was more than just the batteries and the extra set of earplugs she'd handed to him. It was her heart catching in her throat, and the sudden pounding in her chest over this man's resemblance to someone she had loved. No, not had loved. Loved, still. This blond-haired man was the enemy, and yet, just for that first brief moment, there had been a vivid response to his blue eyes. Intense feelings had quickly swept through her body. The only thing was, she couldn't admit an attraction to this man. She simply couldn't. She didn't know him, didn't *want* to know him. Just because his appearance triggered a gripping flashback, reminding her of her Tracy, didn't mean anything. Not now, anyway. Maybe never, either. No. She didn't mean that. It was never, period. This man had no connection to her Tracy. Chad Dickson was simply an intrusion that needed to be expelled as quickly as possible.

She averted her eyes to the clear blue skies, searching. She didn't like to admit it, and would have denied it if asked, but it was God she looked for; and her eyes narrowed in a flash of irritation. He was someone else she wasn't happy with, but there was nothing she could do about Him. He was just there, and He was ignoring her. It was just as well, she thought. If He paid her any attention, she would just rail at Him, too.

She looked at the man standing on the metal landing platform with her. She knew then it was not his looks that had made her think of the only man she had ever loved. Yes, her Tracy had been blessed with those blue eyes, ones that a woman could fall into and never be able to find herself again. His hair had also been that sun-drenched blond just like this man's. However, it was neither of those that had made her think of her Tracy. It was the fluid way he moved, that masculine grace that only the supremely self-confident could assume. She also knew from her own Tracy that this man was surely not aware he possessed that grace of movement, that leonine majesty that was only found in supple jungle cats living in the wild.

As she took a deep breath, forcing herself to focus, she reluctantly replayed the events that had just slipped past her. The hated and unwelcome batteries had been no more than an excuse, a reason to react in order not to admit what really troubled her. From that first moment she had seen this man standing outside of that helicopter, she had felt herself turn inside out. Her heart had raced, and the oil platform had disappeared from around her. For that one brief moment, there had only been Lou and this man in front of her. She'd felt her legs go weak, and she had known she wouldn't be able to resist this man like she had all the others.

Without even knowing he had done so, in his first steps onto the metal surface of the helipad, this man had reached into her and tapped his fingers against her heart. Then, he'd presumed the audacity to lean into that helicopter, and another figure had also climbed from the craft, only he had been no man. He was as tall as his father, but a thinner, more youthful version. His hair, longer, was that same sun-shine gold, although his eyes were crystalline green, just for trapping some young girl who happened along and fell inside. He looked sixteen, but Louinda knew better. She had raised her brother. She knew sixteen, and she knew thirteen. This boy wasn't sixteen, not by a long shot, and he had come bearing *batteries!*

In those final moments, with a sudden anger, she had stridden forward and taken them with no explanation. Batteries on an offshore oil rig needed no explanation. They just needed to be removed, and feelings could not be considered. Now, calmer, and with her emotions reined in, she offered her hand to shake. Her eyes once again found the man she was speaking with. Yes, his eyes were still that crystal blue, but she wouldn't fall into them, no matter how much they made her heart pound. He was the enemy, and this boy was not yet gone. She raised her voice over the rig's noise when she spoke.

"I'm Louinda. You must be Chad. Is this your son?" She tossed her head at the boy who was putting his earplugs into his ears. At least the kid hadn't been belligerent with her. He'd just smiled and slipped the game into his pocket.

Thank God for small favors, she decided.

CHAD TAPPED his ears at her muffled words. Wearing these would take some getting used to.

"Chaddie," he called out. "His name is Chaddie."

"Louder, Chad. Earplugs, you know." This time Lou tapped her own.

He raised his volume a notch. "That's my son, Chaddie. You're good. He *is* thirteen. I had hoped he was staying with a friend, and then he was on my doorstep this morning when I headed down." He smiled in apology at the unexpected surprise he'd brought with him. He was embarrassed, too. The boy was an unwelcome intrusion, even to his father. "He wanted to see the rig."

"So, he wants to see where his father's staying? He only has two hours, and he'll have to wear safety gear while on the rig, even if he doesn't stay. Have you told him that? I think we have time to give him a quick tour. And I see you brought two bags. Both are yours, I assume." Lou nodded her head towards the boy, who was now hanging off the edge of the helipad, looking down at the ocean nearly a hundred feet below. "How's his balance?"

He glanced over and just shook his head. "Better than mine. The kid knows no fear. He won't fall, though, and no, I haven't said anything to him about safety gear. I didn't even know he was coming. Surprise, surprise, to both me and you."

He did offer a smile at that, covering his irritation over having to apologize for his son. It wouldn't do to get off on the wrong foot, even if this woman was only here to greet him as he exited the helicopter. He had to do his job, but he didn't have to be rude about it. Even a lowly deck-hand deserved to be treated with respect.

LOU CAUGHT the smile, but she didn't return it. She'd listened for the clue she needed to hear, and this man hadn't said the magic words. She needed him to say the boy wasn't staying, and she hadn't heard that.

She hoped that didn't spell the need for that extra bunk, because in spite of the fact that she *could* pull extra bunks from various quarters as possible locations for this boy, she knew both the cook and the medic must be kept happy if at all possible. She'd hate to ask, and their spare bunks were the only ones not filled. God help her, but this was

26

likely to be a mess if she didn't get an answer soon. This helicopter would be leaving within two hours. She took a deep breath and tackled the problem head on.

"Your boy. He *is* returning with the helicopter, is he not? Space aboard the rig is tight." She looked at the man next to her, her eyes narrowing within the safety glasses. "Very tight." She snorted her emphasis, willing the man to understand what she was suggesting. *Send him home!*

With those words, she strode quickly to the boy and grasped his shoulder, pulling him back from the edge. No matter that his father claimed he wouldn't fall, this thirteen-year-old would have to be restrained, or the death count on this rig would go up. She wouldn't be able to stop it. It would be this visiting *safety inspector's* fault, that and his son's. It would be because he had brought a *boy* onto the rig, but it would still reflect on Louinda. *Rig Safety and Training Coordinator.* That was what it said on her door. She was the one ultimately responsible.

"Chaddie? That's your name?" She turned to glare at the teen's father, but quickly turned back to the boy. The enthusiasm in his energetic response surprised her.

"Yes, ma'am. This is so cool. Have you ever looked down the side? The ocean is right *there.* Has anyone ever fallen off? I bet you could high dive off this thing, except if it was windy. Then you might blow into the side. I know wind forces. Even cliff divers in Mexico don't dive when it's windy. Have you ever been here in a storm? Like a hurricane? That's what I'd want to do, stay here then, right in the middle of a hurricane." He grinned, as wide as his face would allow.

Lou's irritation began slipping from her grasp. This

boy was certainly thirteen, and with his words, she remembered how Willie had been at that age. Everything had been new and possible to him, and he had wanted to know about it all. This boy had that energy, and her heart softened. How could she hate thirteen? She hadn't hated her Willie at that age. She had loved him dearly. Her next words to this boy still carried an edge, but her tone was gentler.

"Yes, yes, no, and no you don't. This is a small rig, and it's old. Almost everyone evacuates during a hurricane. If a big storm blows up, you will, too. Did you know even batteries can explode the fuel vapors on this rig?"

"BATTERIES?" Chaddie's hand went to the video game in his pocket. He looked to his father, and he saw him standing across the helipad watching the conversation disinterestedly. That was his father since his parents' divorce. Beaten. Civil, but distant. He pushed everyone away. Especially his family. He had become a cardboard image of himself. Chaddie loved his father, and he knew the man he worshipped was in there somewhere, hiding just below the surface. He had to find him again, make his father come out of wherever he had disappeared inside that shell of his. He would, too. He had him trapped out here for a month with nowhere to go.

He smiled at the pretty woman, offering, "Does that mean you want my cell phone, also? What about my iPod?" He felt his pant pockets until he came up with a small case. "It has batteries, too."

He held them out to her.

LOU RELAXED inside, and without thinking, she smiled. His face was so innocent. He might have his father's height, but this *boy* wanted to please. She didn't know but what she could grow to like this young man. However, there was still no room for him on the rig. He needed to return with the helicopter.

"I think you can keep your iPod and cell phone. Only use them in approved places, though. You can use your video game, if you use the power cord." She looked to see his hand still holding the music player out to her, and she pushed it back. "Keep that. Put it in your pocket, then please come with me. As long as you're with us, you have to wear safety gear, even if it's only for two hours. You and your dad, both. Come along." She took his arm and started to walk towards the steps, only to have him stop after a few feet. When she turned to him, he had a look of astonishment on his face.

"Two hours?" Then he grinned, his expression shifting with the fluidity of youth. "I'm here with my dad. We're bunking together." Then he yelled across to his father, "Aren't we, Dad?" His father, unable to hear, just waved, pointed to his ear, and shrugged. Chaddie yelled, "I'm staying, Dad, aren't I? The whole month." He was pleased to see his father smile and shoot him a thumbs-up sign.

He turned to Louinda. "See? Let's get me suited up. I'm ready to be a part of the team." With those words, he dashed off to slap his father on the back, giving him an enthusiastic one-armed hug, talking to him as he pointed to various things around the rig.

Lou was left with her mouth agape. How could she argue with that? Now she had to find some way to accommodate this boy, and he thought he was rooming with his father. She knew the extra bunk in Chad Dickson's room was now a workspace, and this boy wanted a bed of his own for a whole month. God only knew what she was going to do about that. Cookie wouldn't be happy tolerating anyone's company for that long, and neither would the medic.

In spite of her reservations, she would have to work this out. She just wasn't sure exactly how at the moment. Gathering her energy, she took quick steps over to the stairs to join the two men. They seemed preoccupied with the things the boy was pointing out across the rig. Not two men, she corrected herself. One man and one boy. One thirteen-year-old boy. Just a skinny kid with blond hair and those green, crystal-clear eyes.

She paused as she stood behind them. His father had that same build, she saw with interest, even if she would refuse to admit to it, except there was something not the same. Her mind didn't want to face up to it, but her emotions did, and that was what was causing the frown on her forehead. Her heart knew this man didn't have the same build as his son at all. This man had a sturdiness about him, a strength, a masculinity that the son had yet to grow into. The boy's look, his height, and his unconscious grace even at thirteen were the same, but he wasn't there yet. His father was, though, just as her Tracy had been. She shook her head to clear her thoughts. She was on an oil rig. She *wanted* to be on this platform in the middle of the Gulf, out of sight of land, and out of sight of anything and anyone she had ever known. It had been an escape for her, a place to run. That's why she'd come here. It was a way not to deal with her husband's death, and in her subsequent loneliness, her family's cloying closeness.

This man standing with his son in front of her was not the answer to the emptiness inside of her, the longing that she hadn't been able to find a way to satisfy. This man was a thorn in her side, and she'd be smart to realize that, to *remember* it when she looked at that golden head of hair and felt herself falling into those clear blue eyes. That was why she had stomped across the metal surface of the helipad, snatching the boy's batteries from him. She just as easily could have asked him to turn the device off and requested that he remove the batteries before turning it back on. "Plug it in when you want to use it," she could have said.

No, she hadn't been able to rail at Chad, to vent at this man, because he had reminded her so much of her lost husband. She hadn't known anything resembling real love since those years when Tracy had been alive. Her actions with the batteries and her words to the man afterwards had been to hide the connection she'd felt.

She was still hiding it, too, and she would continue to do so, if it meant being cruel to both these visitors. Even the boy's charm wouldn't keep her from doing that. She could do it, too, be cruel. She was confident in that. She could be as cruel as it took.

As she reached and slapped her hands on the two shoulders just in front of her, one fully mature and the other still on its way, it was just to get their attention, she assured herself. Even so, her slaps were much harder than necessary, and when she squeezed the two shoulders firmly, the squeeze was much firmer than needed, too. In that action—very objectively, Lou told herself—she noted how the two shoulders felt very much the same, from the muscle underneath the clothing to the bone beneath that. The two shoulders were indeed very much the same.

The part of her that refused to admit what she was doing said not exactly, though. The boy's shoulder, trim and athletic, revealed his youth. The man's, however, was the firmness of manhood already in full flower, a masculinity that made her knees weak and her stomach turn over.

Then she felt both men shift to look her direction, one man and one boy, turning to her at exactly the same time. One set of blue eyes looked at her questioningly, and one set of green danced in impish curiosity. Lou felt her face flush, even in the warmth of the Gulf sun. She would have to be cruel to fight this. That she knew for sure.

Dropping her hands, her voice was rougher than even she intended as she lashed out at them, "You're blocking the steps, both of you. If the two of you want to get along out here, you need to learn to keep out of the way. We have a business to run, and we can't do it with useless people just standing in the way of those who have jobs to attend to. The first thing we have to do is get you safety gear. Follow me."

She stepped through the pair, forcing them to move aside. As she did so, she made sure she turned to face the father. The space was tight, and there was no question she had to go down the steps ahead of them. She must, in order to be first. And that she had to do, be first. These two rookies would likely go the wrong direction even with her clear instructions. If that meant she had to brush against this man, then that meant she had to brush against him.

She did, too, touching his arm lightly with her hand to steady herself as she tried to make it appear she didn't want to touch him at all. She brushed across his torso—she made sure of that—and through his clothing, he was firm to her touch. The fabric of her coveralls slid against the cloth of his shirt, and even after she was past him, she could still feel warmth lingering where she had pressed against him.

There was one other thing she was aware of as she walked down the steps ahead of the pair. There were tears in her eyes, and behind the safety glasses she wore, the air couldn't dry them. How was she going to deal with this man? How could she fend him off until she could send him away? He was here for her *job,* to shut this rig down. She was certain of that, and she should hate him. She would have to work very hard on hating this man and his son. She suspected that doing so would be very difficult. As she stopped at the first landing to let them catch up, she silently cursed this rig she was on. She never had before, but now she had reason. The reason for her curses was just behind her, following her down the steps, and she had to live with that reason for two more weeks. At least then she could look forward to being home in Oklahoma City for two weeks. They would be gone by the time she returned. She had been promised that.

Yet, even as she thought of leaving them behind, with a sudden tightness behind her eyes, it seemed as if that distant two weeks was an unknown pit of nothingness, an emptiness. She might need to hate this man she had just met, even be cruel to him, but for five minutes, the five since he had stepped off that helicopter, Lou had felt alive again, alive and vibrant. She had felt love was once more possible.

She straightened her back as she led the way, because she knew one thing for certain. A future was not something she would allow herself, not with this man. Not *this* man. This man was a nuisance. His son would obviously be so, even if, for the first time in many years, she had felt unexpectedly vibrant, simply because Chad Dickson's way of moving had reminded her so much of her deceased husband's.

When she paused on one step and closed her eyes for a moment, she pictured Chad exiting the helicopter all over again. That sudden, overwhelming feeling of life and longing and something she would never admit to flooded her body once more, and she took a deep breath to steady her next few steps down the walkway leading to the pipe deck. To get there, they still had two flights more to go, and this alluring, sexy man was walking right behind her. She could not afford to trip and fall just because he had those infinite blue eyes and that masculine, firm shoulder.

Ooh, she thought with a harsh, angry fire boiling through her veins. *Ooh, ooh, and maybe even double ooh!*

Chapter 2

CHAD FOLLOWED his son and their guide into the rig's supply room. Quieter, he could finally think. Glancing around, he was relieved to see at least a modicum of safety supplies filling the shelves or hanging on hooks on the walls. Louinda slipped her safety glasses in her pocket as Chaddie grabbed a green helmet out of her hand and grinned at his father.

"Dad, this is cool. I get to wear one of these, just like I'm a real roughneck." He turned his eyes to Lou. "That's the right term, isn't it? Roughneck?"

She stood amid the safety equipment in the supply room and chuckled. "Not for you. Roustabout is what a rookie gets called."

"Roustabout? Oh, I remember reading about that back

home." He turned to his father. "Dad, are you wearing a green helmet, too?"

Chad looked at his son, attempting not to see him there. He sighed. He could tell that the boy planned to be a continuing distraction from the real business on this oil platform, and it wasn't as if this was the first time today, either. The truth of the matter was that the question irritated him. The *battery* thing was still eating at Chad, as if he had gotten off on the wrong foot with this woman—Louinda Reinhardt, per the name stitched on her clothing—all because of Chaddie and that video game.

The boy was his son, though, even if the kid reminded him entirely too much of his ex. Chad also knew the young man was more like him than he'd ever be like his mother. Other people saw it, so it must be true. Chaddie had become his father 2.0, just like Chad had been all those years ago.

Chad desperately hoped not.

Although it had been three years, he could still remember before the divorce when he and his son had still been close. Bungee jumping, hiking, and *video games!* Video games had been their passion. Since the breakup, Chad had no interest, anymore. In anything.

Still, he couldn't sit and do nothing, and he'd found busy was better than misery. So, there was running every morning, and endless sit-ups when he was bored by television. He was grateful his job kept much of his time so occupied that he couldn't think. It was how he'd survived the dry years since.

That's all it was, though, busywork to stay occupied. Interest and enthusiasm had faded long ago, and that was why he had no patience with Chaddie's boisterous eagerness in everything, especially not here on this rig.

Chad glanced down at the helmet he was holding. It was also green. He looked up to see their host had on white. He cleared his throat. "Um, Ms. Reinhardt?" He hesitated to use her first name. She had introduced herself with her given name earlier, but there had been no friendliness in anything she'd said or done.

An answer quickly snapped back at him. "Lou. And it's Miss. That feminist Ms. is for aggressive men-haters. I don't hate men. I just want them to keep their distance. It's not Missus, either. It hasn't been for five years. That's part of my life back home. I don't bring it here. So," she stopped and glared at him, "what?"

Chad was taken aback by her burst of information. It was like he'd stuck a lance into a festering wound, and rotten pus had spewed out. However, he wouldn't let this woman wear on him. He couldn't afford to. He was here to do a job, and this lowly *roustabout,* to use her own term, couldn't be allowed to get in his way. He wasn't here to step on toes, but he would perform his duties.

"You have a white helmet on. Does the green indicate a certain position on the rig? My son isn't here to work, you know." He glanced at the boy. Chaddie was here because there had been nothing else for his father to do with him. He didn't know how he would keep the boy occupied and do his job, also. He would need to figure something out. "Should he have white, too?"

He smiled in his best imitation of good manners among courteous business associates, certain she would clear things up and he could get about his business with no further delay.

LOUINDA LAUGHED at the man's naivety. She really couldn't fault him for it, and it actually made him seem a bit more approachable, someone who could actually make a mistake, instead of someone who had the ultimate power to shut the entire rig down. Even still, she put a bit of a bite in her response.

"Mr. Dickson—"

He interrupted, "Chad, please," as if he intended to match her brusqueness tit for tat.

"—this is a special color green." She heard the snappish tone, and she smiled before she continued. It was a smile of satisfaction, and not one of pleasantry. "*Rookie.* We call this color *rookie* green. That way, when the two of you are out and around the rig, everyone will know to watch you closely. Out here, we like to stay alive, and it wouldn't do for someone who doesn't know the ropes to screw something up for an experienced hand. Accidents on oil production platforms can kill."

Chad frowned at the sharpness of the response, but his son just grinned.

"Hey, that's great!" Chaddie turned the green helmet over in his hands. Looking up, his eyes jumped back and forth between his father's and Louinda's. "Not the killing part." He held up the helmet. "Green, just so everyone'll know I'm a rookie. That's so cool. Then they won't be surprised when I don't know anything. I'm going to ask lots of questions. What else do I need before I go exploring?"

Louinda's smile softened at the boy's response. She

knew she had to be sharp and cruel to keep these two at a distance, but she couldn't fight this boy's enthusiasm. Not well, anyway.

"Safety glasses," she said, handing him a pair. "Also, coveralls. Let me find you a pair that might fit. I'm good at guessing sizes." She pulled a pair off a shelf and laid them out for the boy. "Boots, too. Steel toes. Never be outside without them. However," and she looked sternly at both the man and the boy, "you must also never wear any of this in the mess hall. No safety gear is allowed there. Rules, you know."

Her words had become less harsh, and that somehow surprised her. She knew the boy had done that. He was a charmer. The father? That remained to be seen. Strong and muscular with blue eyes that she could sink into wouldn't dampen her resolve to keep him at a distance. Besides, this man had a son. That meant there was a wife.

With that thought, Lou felt her heart involuntarily sag. A wife. A family. One that she couldn't be a part of even if she wanted. Her eyes found the man's face, and she could see him looking inside his helmet as he worked to adjust the straps to fit his head. Then she glanced at the boy who was already slipping inside his coveralls, his enthusiasm written in each of his movements. In half an hour, this boy had charmed her, and despite her determination, this man had done even more. Now that she realized he had a wife, she could admit that she had found him attractive. These two were inaccessible, and they would return to their family life on the mainland once they left this rig. That knowledge made it easier to keep the relationship a professional one, emotionally circumspect, and for that she was grateful.

As Chaddie pulled on his boots and slipped his safety glasses on, Lou pictured him out and about on the rig. Even at thirteen and slender in the coveralls, this boy had the height of any worker on this rig, and he would blend in. With the helmet, glasses, and coveralls, he could easily pass for an official Sunshine Gulf roughneck. A roustabout, at least. Only the green would give him away. Now, if he'd just get those coveralls good and stained with the lifeblood of the rig, then he'd really look like one of the hired hands.

She felt a twinge of envy towards this man with his son. She missed her Willie at that age. She guessed this boy appealed to her because thirteen was when she'd loved her brother Willie the most. Not most. She couldn't say that. She still loved him just as much as she had then, but thirteen was when she'd been most wrapped up in the burgeoning man that had been exploding inside the boy he was leaving behind. This man in this room with her had that in his son, and she envied him.

When Chaddie waved and grabbed the door, he was suddenly gone, and she turned to pull down supplies for his father. She stopped when he cleared his throat.

"Green, huh? Newbie green. I guess that sets me in my place." His voice was deep and resonant, and as she turned to him and caught his eye, he looked quizzically at her. "You don't like me much, do you?"

"*Rookie* green, Mr. Dickson." Lou felt her neck flush. He'd gotten her message, and, it seemed, very clearly, too. Obviously, this man was no dunce who had to have information drilled into his head before he caught on. She felt the flush push into her face before she could turn back to the shelf. "Thirty-four waist, right?" Her voice cracked, and she knew he heard it. "I have one in a tall right here."

She turned to hand it to him, only to find him standing right there. Her breath quickened with his proximity and the masculinity he paraded about in his every movement. With determination, she told herself her feelings had nothing to do with him as a person. It was the way he moved that reminded her of her Tracy. That was all.

She held up the coveralls as a shield. "Your boots. Thirteen. Thirteen narrow. Right?" When he didn't move, she looked at his chest, afraid to catch his eyes again. She might completely crack.

There was another problem threatening to dismantle her carefully constructed blind. Her body was also prompting her to step closer to this man, and that was something she absolutely must not do. She could see him breathing. His shirt rose and fell, sliding across the muscles in his chest. Directly in front of her, she could see a silvery button move in its buttonhole as the fabric of his shirt shifted with each indrawn breath.

She couldn't take her eyes off that button. In her thoughts, she could see it slipping from inside the stitched opening, sliding smoothly through the thread-wrapped buttonhole. The shirt would pull free, and just inside she would see a glimpse of chest hair that was the same sunburst blond as on the top of his head.

She heard him clear his throat, and guiltily, her eyes yanked to his face. When she saw him lick his lips, she didn't know if it was to question her or kiss her, and she panicked at the latter. She thrust the coveralls directly at him, pressing them to his chest, talking in a sudden torrent.

"Here. Take these. You can put them on after I show you your assigned quarters. You'll need to wear your safety glasses and helmet when we step outside. I need to get you your steel toe boots. They're on the shelf over there. If you'll take these from me, I'll get them for you, and we can be on our way. We need to find your son, too, and there's no fraternization on the rig, and certainly no kissing people you don't know, no matter how attractive they are."

When she realized how she'd phrased that final sentence, she froze, horrified. She also knew her hands were still holding the coveralls, and the tips of her fingers were firmly pressed into this man's chest. She could feel his warmth, his breathing, and even his heartbeat. If anything, she was certain it had increased in speed and intensity just as hers was doing. She couldn't tear her eyes from his.

This day had become a disaster, and she didn't know how she would extricate herself. Dear God, why had this man come aboard her rig? In the name of all that was good and holy, why, God, indeed?

She felt tears burning in her eyes, and she couldn't speak.

CHAD BROKE the silence with a resonant whisper. "I have the coveralls. You can let go, now." He fought a smile as he continued. "I would like my boots, too. You may get them, and Lou," he winked at her, "I don't intend to kiss anyone while here on my assignment. You and everyone else are perfectly safe from my advances."

He turned away with the coveralls in his hands, and he

immediately began to unzip the front. If his son could don them in this woman's presence, so could he. Anyway, he desperately needed something to distract him. In spite of her earlier antagonism, he could feel the sparks flying with this virtual stranger. He had to steer clear. Chaddie's mother had taught him that. Steer clear of all women. Like rabid dogs, they always came back to bite him in the rear, and Chad had experienced enough of that for a dozen lifetimes.

However, he couldn't help but smile in amusement at the woman's words. She'd stumbled over herself, and then he'd thrown his barbs at her. He couldn't imagine what he'd done that she thought he might be preparing to *kiss* her. The idea of doing so brought back something he'd noticed earlier. With her protective eyewear removed, she was as beautiful as he had thought she might be. More, even.

It hit him what he'd been doing when this beautiful woman had erupted all over him. He'd been moistening his lips to ask her a question, and it was in that moment that she'd spewed her angry torrent all over him. Perhaps he gave her a nauseous stomach, butterflies, as some would say, and that was why she had to get all that out. He wasn't sure. To remember the unexpected torrent was humorous, though.

He looked to his side as a pair of boots appeared. When he turned, his reluctant guide for the day was already back at one of the open shelves, rearranging supplies.

Slipping the boots on, he called out, "What's your assigned job here? You have a white helmet, so you can't be a rookie. However, I can't decide what job would give

43

you enough free time to baby-sit two greenies you'd rather not have on this oil platform."

He didn't want to insult her, but he didn't think management personnel on this rig would take the time to deal with him. He didn't expect that his assignment was a popular one for those stationed out here. It hadn't been popular back ashore with Rampart Oil. They had tried to prevent him from coming. However, there was something to be said about working for the U.S. Senate Ways and Means Committee. Rampart Oil had to comply; they just didn't have to be nice about it. They hadn't, either.

He watched the woman in the room with him. She still had her helmet on, and she looked like she was waiting on him. He stood, stamping his feet in his new boots. They fit perfectly, and in a moment of inspiration, he put all the events of the past half hour together. This must be her job. Supply and requisitions. That would explain her skill at guessing sizes, both for him as well as for Chaddie. He decided this could be his way to make a sort of peace with her, and he smiled.

"You're good with what you do, do you know that? I'm impressed. You didn't even measure, and these fit perfectly." He used her own terms to compliment her. "I'll bet you haven't been a roustabout in a very long time. You must be, what did you say earlier? A roughneck?" Obviously not a worker on the pipe deck with her clean coveralls. He made another attempt to compliment her, and he grinned his much-practiced witty smile, trying to be playful. "I suppose if you have an 'office' job," and he stressed the word "office" to make this room seem more important than it probably was, "that you could still be called a roughneck."

She chuckled at that. "You're right about the first part. It's been a while since I've been a roustabout. Let's get you to your assigned room. I understand you must be anxious to get busy. After all, you've only got four weeks to cover the entire platform." Standing, she moved toward the door. "Safety, first. Don't forget your helmet and glasses, *Chad*."

He was amused by the emphasis on his first name. He guessed she wasn't quite through being irritated with him just yet. However, he couldn't fix that, not in his first half hour on the rig. If he couldn't make amends with this woman eventually, it might make his job here more difficult, but not impossible. He was used to people not liking him when he came to investigate their jobs. He could live with that. Still, while on this rig, he wondered what it took to see the real leaders, those with titles on their doors. Should he start with, *"Take me to your leader,"* in order to get access to the real movers and shakers? Would that work? He didn't know.

So, he'd bide his time and ply the waters. It would all work out. Besides, he had a month, and how big could this oil rig be? It was offshore, and there were only so many nooks and crannies. Surely he would meet someone with real authority before the month was up. This *Miss* Reinhardt couldn't keep him squirreled away forever.

Chad walked forward, positioning his safety gear in place and putting the expected congenial smile on his face. "All right, *Lou.* Let's head to my quarters. Let's see just where Chaddie and I will be sleeping."

Lou smiled, although Chad didn't understand why.

What could be funny about him and his son needing a place to sleep? He shrugged it away as another odd thing that he would probably never understand.

LOU SLIPPED her protective eyewear on and opened the door to the riotous noise of the oil rig. The surface of the sea churned dully in the background, occasionally slapping at the legs of the massive rig with a surprisingly loud smack, while closer at hand, the structure of the oil platform groaned in metallic protest. The thumping of machinery and the whining howls of tortured motors screamed danger. She turned her head to Chad and tapped her ears, yelling, "Earplugs!" When he smiled and reached into his pocket, she remembered how Tracy used to reach into his own pocket in just that way, and her heart jumped. It was just that this man's movements were so like Tracy's, she insisted to herself. She wasn't attracted to this man. It was all about Tracy, and this man would just have to understand and live with that.

However, she had also seen his third finger, and she'd noticed something. He wasn't wearing a ring. Married men usually wore wedding rings, didn't they? Her Tracy had. He had worn his every day during that year they had been married, even when he was on the road. She knew, because he'd been wearing it the day he died. He still had it on when he was found.

This man, however. Her thoughts wandered, and she was unable to keep them contained. Widowed? Divorced? He had a son, and that meant there *had* been a woman in his life at some point. She wondered if he could have adopted the boy. No, this man and his son were too much alike. Still, there was always artificial insemination, a surrogate parent providing a baby. It was certainly within the bounds of conceivable possibilities.

In any case, after seeing that bare finger, Lou's heart felt lighter, and her fingers actually tapped at the railing as she walked along the catwalk. She didn't need this man, and really wanted him gone. That was a fact. It was the change in the weather. That's why the air smelled fresher to her, and the day seemed full of possibilities that hadn't been there before. Certainly not because there was no ring. That was coincidence. That's what her mind tried to convince her. Cause and effect? No way, no matter what her heart tried to say.

FOLLOWING LOUINDA down an open, railed catwalk, Chad was startled at a sudden, oppressive weight on his shoulders, and he stumbled, barely catching himself before going down. Grabbing the handrail, he found his son's arms wrapped around his neck. In exasperation, he latched onto the boy's wrists and twisted out from under him. Turning, he found Chaddie's eyes sparkling as his chest rose and fell in wheezing gasps.

"What, Son? Is this knock-Dad-off-the-rig day?" Chad's eyes caught Louinda's, and he saw a glint of amusement there. He'd been certain he'd made a positive step with her back in the supply room just a moment ago. Now, this boy was throwing a wrench into his professional relationship once again. When his son yanked his arms free and wrapped them around his father, Chad repeated with greater force, "What is it?"

"Dad," Chaddie was breathless, "sorry, I had to catch

my breath. You have to see the recreation area. Game consoles. They have game consoles all over the place. You've got to see this. There were men down there playing games. With headphones on! *Games,* Dad! We have to go." He twisted around to stand in front of his father and looked him full in the face. "Dad, say you will. Please."

Chad felt irritation well up inside. This was a working trip to this oil rig, not a father-son gaming session. Now, this woman who clearly didn't want him here was probably laughing at him. He ground his teeth, and he couldn't bring himself to say anything.

LOU WATCHED the scene unfurl, and she was very amused. Both these visitors were six solid feet of golden hair and leonine movements. Seeing these two was observing a graceful dance being acted out, as the father and son parried with each other. It was obvious Chad wanted his boy to back off, and the boy was determined to pull the father into whatever activity he currently found interesting. Father and son. Two peas in a pod.

Almost, anyway. She wondered where the father's enthusiasm for life had gone. The boy had it in excess. Surely this father who was so similar in physical appearance and manners hadn't always been so disinterested.

At the apparent stalemate between the two, she stepped in. She knew there were other priorities to get out of the way first. No matter what the boy wanted, and no matter what the father agreed to, they wouldn't be seeing the recreation area immediately. In fact, the boy shouldn't have been down there, yet. Lou could get reprimanded for that. She cleared her throat. When she got no response, she remembered the earplugs they all wore and realized they'd been talking in sharply exaggerated voices to each other just to be heard above the rig. She would need to do more than clear her throat.

"Men!" She waved her arms to get their attention. "We need to take a tour before anyone goes anywhere else on his own. You, Chaddie," she pointed, "need to stay close. Don't run off again until I'm through with you. Otherwise, I'll put you on that helicopter even if you have to sit on shore for the next month waiting on your dad. Capiche?" She narrowed her eyes at him to make her point. "We have to show you the alarms and drills. There are several muster points you have to be aware of, also. What if the wellhead blew out as we're standing here? Would you know where to go? Of course not, and rescue teams would only look for survivors at the muster points. They'd assume all other personnel were lost. If three blasts of the air horn sound, what does that mean? Do you know? Of course not. Well, after today you will. Follow me." She slapped the boy on the shoulder and turned to walk off.

"Three blasts? They really do that?" Excitement filled his words, and he hopped backwards beside her, one hand bouncing along the rail, as he attempted to speak to her face-to-face. She smiled at him. Stopping, she placed her hand on his chest.

"Chaddie, turn around. Not only do you look silly to your father, but if you back into any unseen steps, you might fall down them. If you went under the pipe rails and over the side, it's a long drop to the sea. Then, I'd be the one to think you look silly. Silly and very possibly dead." She turned her head just enough to see the boy's father

49

looking at her, watching what she was doing. She was sure he could hear her words, too, in spite of the noise and the earplugs. She was used to talking quite loudly when on the outside walks on the rig. "Now, walk beside me and listen to my explanations. You just might learn a lot of new information."

As she pushed him to the side, she reached with her free hand and wrapped the boy's fingers into hers. There was something else she had to remember. He was thirteen, not sixteen as he appeared. This was still truly a *boy* beside her, and he needed clear-cut, adult supervision, especially here among the dangers on this oil rig.

As they walked, she pointed out things, explaining where and what, giving the boy time for any questions he might have. He seemed genuinely interested, and she quickly understood he hadn't been joking earlier with his comments about his green helmet. Everything she pointed out, he had more questions about than she knew the answers to.

As they walked, a second line of thought wove itself among the words she spoke aloud. She knew she had no interest in this boy, even as she held his hand in hers. He was just that—a boy. However, he was a mirror image of his father, and she was very aware of the feel of the hand resting in hers. It was muscular, with long fingers and an easy grip.

Just as Chad's would probably be.

She breathed in deeply, almost wishfully. It was simple for her to imagine the arm it was attached to as belonging to someone else, someone the same height as this boy, with the same golden hair. Of course, he would have blue eyes, instead of green, ones she could fall into, and when she pointed out a piece of equipment to explain all about it, he would look at her and smile. Then, rounding the corner to stand in one of the few nooks on the platform that afforded actual privacy, he would take her in his arms. Her safety helmet might fly from her head to the sea below, but she wouldn't care. He might brush her glasses from her face just to peer into her eyes, and she wouldn't notice as they fell to hang around her neck. She would breathe in the smell of his cologne, and he would whisper to her—

She jumped at a hand as it gripped her shoulder. A sudden, resonant voice called to her, "Louinda! Miss Reinhardt! Chaddie just asked you a question. Are you feeling all right today?"

She jerked, startled to find the boy's father questioning her. It was his hand on her shoulder, and his touch was the fire of a lightning storm as it burned through her. What had she been thinking, daydreaming of this man? She was also appalled at her carelessness. She had lectured them about safety, and she hadn't been paying attention, at least not to where she was walking. With the pressure of his touch on her shoulder, all she could do was nod.

Then, the hand was gone. Her eyes glanced at the boy next to her, and she realized his fingers were still entwined in hers. Squeezing them, she smiled, but it was hard. How could she have done that, slipped into a dream world of her own out here in this very dangerous place? What was this man doing to her? If this continued, this man and his son would be the death of her, yet. She'd thought she would have to save them from themselves. She took a deep breath, considering that maybe it would be the other way around.

"Yes, Chaddie? You have a question?" She attempted to make her voice strong, cringing as she heard it break, but it was a relief to hear her words. She had been unsure whether she could speak at all.

He glanced at his father and then at her, and a grin grew across his face. "Sure. Under the helipad, were those the air conditioning units for the entire platform? I saw them when we arrived. I thought you might know."

She turned her head to look out across the water before answering. That knowing look she had seen on the boy's face. Could he possibly understand what had caused her to blank out? Could he even imagine what his father's hand had done to her as it rested on her shoulder? Just the thought that this boy might read her so easily made her stomach churn.

"Well?" the boy continued. "Lou? I can call you that? I can read my dad's lips, and he's telling me I have to ask." He snickered, as if he found this game fun. "Is Lou all right?" She refused to look, but when she nodded, he pressed her. "The air conditioning? Is that for the whole platform?"

She nodded again as she kept her eyes out to sea and began walking. She felt the tall boy next to her as he leaned very close to her ear until their helmets literally bumped. Her blood burned in humiliation at the words she heard him speak.

"It's okay. I really like my dad, too. I'll share him with you. Then he'll have two fans."

When she turned to glare at him, she was surprised to see him looking right at her, and through his safety glasses, she was certain she saw the boy wink. She looked away immediately. *Surely not,* she thought. He couldn't have seen her emotions that clearly. My God, surely not. If so, God help her! If he told his father, she would push this boy over the rail, and she would blame it on a hurricane, even if there wasn't one anywhere in sight.

Then the boy squeezed her hand twice, and in that reassuring touch, she knew she was in love. The only thing was, she was in love with a thirteen-year-old boy, one who was charming her with abandon, and the person she found really interesting was the father who was walking right behind them.

However, *interest* was a two-way street, and besides, she didn't even know him, only that he moved like her Tracy. Her eyes burned once more. Tracy was gone. He wouldn't return just because she needed him. If that were possible, he'd have returned a long time ago. Lonely or not, she would need more than someone who moved like the man she'd loved to fall in love all over again.

Yet, in the back of her mind, and perhaps in the depths of her heart, and most certainly in the pit of her stomach, she knew. There was more to this man than just his walk. There was that golden hair and those infinite blue eyes that she could feel herself falling into. She would have to ward this man off like frostbite in the depths of a blinding winter storm, or she would be lost for sure.

Chapter 3

STEPPING FROM the walkway into the accommodations block, Chad brushed carefully by the brusque woman leading them around the oil rig. He knew his presence here on Sunshine Gulf Platform No. 6 wasn't exactly welcome, but this woman had shown animosity toward him from the onset. Yet, he could have sworn her tone softened by the time they stepped to the door of the mess hall, even though she insisted they remove their safety gear to enter.

"Boots, too?" he had asked, amused.

A smirk had pulled at the corner of her mouth, and she said his boots could remain on. His coveralls, too. However, the helmet, glasses, and earplugs must come off. In fact, she told him, he wasn't required to wear them anywhere inside the accommodations block. Make sure to wear them outside, though, at all times.

She removed hers at the same time. It was the first time Chad had seen her with her hair free, and in that glance, he cursed his ex-wife. No, he backtracked, gears shifting in his mind. He didn't curse his ex-wife. He hated her. Rather, he hated what she'd done to him, playing with his emotions, his mind, and his willingness to open up to another woman. She had also played with his ability to open up to other *people,* even his own son. He recognized that, was even convinced sometimes that Chaddie understood what had come between them. His boy was perceptive, if somewhat overeager. Chad would give him that.

Keeping his distance from women didn't mean he wasn't aware of them. Far from it. When Louinda pulled her helmet off as she stepped inside, reaching an arm to select an item from the shelves, in that movement, her coveralls tightened across her chest, and her waist, alluringly trim beneath the flexing fabric, was all he could see. Then, without thinking, she reached her fingers into her hair and worked them in. When she lifted her thick mane of dark tresses and pulled it back, she unconsciously tilted her head, and the smooth skin of her jawline caught the light, just where it slipped into her neck to disappear underneath her collar. Then, she released her hair and shook her head.

In a moment of tantalizing weakness, Chad's heart stopped in his chest, and he felt his face warm with sudden longing. This woman was beautiful, more so than he could have guessed with all her gear hiding her looks.

Afterwards, moving into the mess, he stepped forward to slide around her. The doorway was narrow, and when he slipped past, he tilted his head down just as he brushed her body. Her hair, the smell, it swept over him, connecting him with memories he preferred left dead and buried.

Outside earlier, when they had brushed, the odors of the equipment and the sea and all the things that happened on an offshore rig had assaulted his nose, protecting him from his past. Now, inside, those odors were gone. He smelled her hair as he moved close to her, and it contained the creamy smell of coconut, one that told of beaches filled with golden women lying under the sun, Fourth of July picnics, and holidays at his grandmother's house. It especially reminded him of being on the Baja Peninsula before Chaddie was born. The marriage had still been good then, brand-new, in fact, and during that week, they had enjoyed a private pool off their villa's patio. Clothing had been optional, and the doors had remained opened the entire time. That week, the sea air had blown across their bodies, and life had felt good.

Even in the disillusionment that came later, Chad could still be pulled back into that week, if he wasn't careful. That was why he kept it pushed to the back of his mind. He had held onto the Baja pictures, even when he'd thrown out all the rest of his ex's things. One was of their pool with the beach in the background. The ocean sparkled in the distance. He was the only one in the photograph, and he had just returned from a dip in the warmth of the sea. He had joined Diana in the pool, and after a time, she had climbed out, dripping water all over the villa's tile floor as she searched for the camera. He remained in the water, the sun thrusting deep fingers into the pool, and it glistened on his shoulders. The water around him was still and crystal

56

clear. He stood on the far side with his elbows resting on the coping. His hair was wet, and the water obscured the lower part of his body.

For others, the picture was just him in a pool, his skin browned and his smile bright. For him, it was much more. After a time, he began to hide the pictures away.

On one long weekend after the divorce, when bad weather had trapped Chad and his son inside with nothing to do, Chaddie found the pictures. When his father tried to take them, Chaddie begged and wailed that he had no pictures of his father, that his mother had cut them all up. Chad relented, although in retrospect, he wished he hadn't. He should have gotten a camera out and told the kid to have at it. Take all the pictures he wanted.

As he brushed by Lou, he was yanked back to that time. All that week, Diana had bathed with the most alluring coconut soap, and each time he'd buried his face in her hair, the smell of coconut had overwhelmed him.

That was what Louinda's hair did for him. When he stepped past her, and the smell of coconut wafted up to him, he was back in that picture once again. Once past her and inside the room, Chad closed his eyes and stood still just for a moment. He couldn't do otherwise. He drew in a ragged breath as he tried to regain his self-control. He could not want this woman. That week with the coconuts and the pool was fifteen years ago. Fifteen *years!*

His eyes opened with the awareness that he was entering a space that also contained his thirteen-year-old son. As he blinked his eyes to clear his vision, he looked around the mess hall and caught his son grinning at him. What he saw there sent an icy shock through him. The boy winked at him. Then his son looked to the woman who was still standing at the door and back to his father again.

To cover how transparent he felt, Chad pivoted to inspect a safety poster on the wall. It was framed in metal and covered by glass. The display seemed to be permanently attached to the wall, one that could be updated with an interchangeable insert. His eyes saw it, stared at it, but he wasn't really reading it, wasn't able to focus on it. He just wanted this room and these people to be gone from him, to let him pick up the emotional detritus that he felt had just been thrown into the room and shattered across the floor for all to see.

Then he felt an arm wrap around his neck from behind, and from the pressure and the closeness, he recognized his son. He froze, and the next words he heard shook him to the core.

"It's okay, Dad. I like her, too." Then Chaddie tightened one arm against his father's chest and released him, slapping his father playfully on the shoulder. "Come on, Dad. The galley's this way. Lou told me it's called that. Snacks, you know. Wait up, Lou!"

Then the boy was gone. He glanced around to locate their host, this roughneck with the something-or-the-other job that Chad had no idea about, only to find she had moved past them and disappeared while he and Chaddie were having their "father-son moment." Whether she had gone on to give them a bit of privacy, or simply because they wouldn't keep up, he didn't know. He was glad, however, for the breather. The flashback caused by Lou's coconut hair had left him jittery, and in disappearing, she'd left him unsure, also. He wasn't certain if his jumpy nerves were just nerves, or the remnants of those teenage adrenalin surges he remembered so strongly from his youth. He didn't envy his son over the next few years.

"Dad, come on!" Chaddie's head poked from the door across the room. "You're missing it. There's a refrigerator in here we can use whenever we want. The cook puts leftovers inside, and we can snack anytime." Then the head was gone again.

Chad looked around the mess hall, already evaluating. The dining space was spartan but clean. He understood only about sixty men were on this platform. Half of those actually worked on the drilling operation, with the others in support positions. Other rigs might have thou-sands, but not this one. About a third of them could eat in here at a time. While the items he could see appeared to be very clean, he noticed that several of the lights didn't work, and he noted the fact as a lack of maintenance on his inter-nal checklist. It would go in his report later that evening, but for now, he was satisfied to check it off mentally.

Stepping through the door into the galley, he didn't find Chaddie or Louinda. Their voices, however, drifted in from another door at the other end of the room. The galley was old, but very clean, and small with all stainless steel finishes. The sounds of the voices drifting in carried excep-tionally well against the metallic surfaces.

"So, Chaddie," the woman's voice began. "Your dad says you're thirteen. You must be starting eighth grade next year."

Chad heard excitement in the reply.

"Ninth grade. I'm a year ahead. I'm on the student council. I really like spending time with the other kids in school. On the student council, we get to do all sorts of projects, raise money, and even sometimes help out at the middle schools."

A year ahead. How had Chad not realized that?

Then a laugh filtered in to Chad, and it was from Louinda. Chad noted that while she had been little more than brusque with him, she seemed to have a very pleasant manner when speaking with Chaddie. He liked the sound of it, too. He wondered how his boy had managed to connect with this petite woman, and he, Chad, had only managed to irritate her.

"You mother will miss you being out here for a month. I'm surprised she let you come for four whole weeks." That was from Louinda. Chad stood very still waiting for the boy's reply.

"She didn't want me to. I came anyway."

Came anyway? That caught Chad's attention. Before he could interrupt, his son barreled ahead. Chad paused and waited, needing to hear this.

"Mom said I should stay with Gramps. He's actually my great-grandfather, but I just call him Gramps. My dog's already there." That was news to Chad. When he'd talked to Chaddie's mother, her version had sounded very different, indeed.

With an amused tone, Louinda's voice prodded the boy for more information. "And you came anyway. Your mother and grandfather do know where you're at? This is the middle of the ocean." It was really the Gulf of Mexico, but from their vantage point, the difference was moot. "You did tell your mother and your grandfather? A month is a long time out here."

60

Chad wanted to hear his reply. It had seemed odd that he'd just shown up on the front step that morning without any warning. His son was scheduled to be his for the month, but when he hadn't arrived on any sort of respectable timetable, Chad had hoped alternate arrangements were in place. Still, with their plans never finalized, he had accepted his son's explanation. Perhaps he had wanted to. It kept him from needing to speak with the boy's mother. Diana was often capricious, so it had at least seemed plausible that his son was supposed to be with his father for the month—even if it was on an oil rig.

The boy had yet to answer Lou's final question. That was odd. Usually he was a motormouth. Not answering meant he was assembling his words carefully. Surely his ex's grandfather wasn't supposed to be keeping the boy. If the old man already had Chaddie's dog . . . . Chad groaned inside. He couldn't see the old man consenting to keep the dog without his "grandson" along. He might be wealthy and well able to board the dog in a kennel, but he was a bully. A rich one, to be for sure, but a bully just the same.

The answer he heard his son give was not the one he really wanted to hear.

"My mom's out of town. My bus ticket was to Dallas to spend the month with Gramps. When my stepdad took me to the station back in Boulder, I told him the wrong time, so I'd miss the bus. Then, I exchanged the ticket for one to Fort Worth to meet up with my dad." There was a moment of silence that was more pronounced than the first. Chaddie's next words were in a near whisper, and his father had to step closer to the door to hear. "I shouldn't have told you that. My dad doesn't know. He thinks my mom sent me down here. I wanted to come, though. I really did. Please, Lou. You can't tell him. He'll send me to Gramp's for the month."

Louinda's reply was almost as soft. "Chaddie, we have no choice but to call your mother. I think you know that. She must be told where you are."

"But—"

"No buts. What if something happened? An emergency, and she needed to contact you? Your dad should be the one to contact her, of course—or I can, if you want, I suppose. How about your grandfather? Don't you think he should know, also?"

At those questions, a hint of amusement began to color the boy's words. "My mother's in Hawaii with my stepdad. It's their anniversary. They won't be back for six weeks. My grandfather lives on the golf course. What would he care? There's not anyone else to call."

"Your father's wife?"

Chad was surprised to hear that question. Wife? He didn't have one, and for three years hadn't wanted one. His son's answer, one that mirrored his own thoughts—at least at first—surprised him even more. The boy's final words jarred him sharply.

"My dad? Oh, he doesn't want one. He thinks he doesn't need a wife. I'm working on that, though. He's lonely and just doesn't know it."

Chad knew instantly that this conversation had gone far enough. With a sharp rap, he knocked on the wall and strode through the doorway. He was in a supply pantry for the galley, and his son and this woman were facing away from him, leaning on a chest-high shelf with their arms under their chins. Their heads were turned towards each other, and they seemed to have become confidants of a sort.

"Chaddie," he called out, walking up to slap his hand on his son's back before sliding it up around the nape of his neck. Squeezing, he remarked with false good cheer, "Our quarters await us. Miss Reinhardt, er, Lou, here, must have other things to do. Floors probably need mopped, or paint needs chipped, or people might even need new coveralls. Let's see if she'll take us to our room, so we can let her get on with whatever it is she does." He turned to the woman at his son's side. "Lou, will that be acceptable to you? Our room? Or do we need to know more safety measures, so we don't fall off this rig? Three blasts to catch the falling government worker before he crashes into the sea? Anything like that?"

He smiled broadly, but his eyes were burning. He knew his words had run on, slathered with an awkward dose of embarrassment, saying things that were surely stupid or even incoherent. However, he had just been waylaid by the smell of this woman's hair; and now his son had made two major gaffes. He had let his father hear that he wasn't supposed to have come here, and even worse, he'd described his own father as lonely, and to a stranger. How could Chad endure that?

There was nothing to be done except escape from this woman as quickly as possible.

LOU STOOD and reached to a shelf to give herself something to do. This man couldn't be allowed to see her smile at what was happening. This boy and his father had danced earlier, and now they were sparring. It seemed they weren't on the same page, and she had been drawn in right in the middle.

She also suspected this man didn't understand her position on the rig, either. She'd picked up on several of his references, and she also realized it was her fault for misleading him. When he'd shown up, she hadn't wanted him here—hadn't wanted to speak with him at all—and for that reason, she hadn't introduced herself thoroughly. She had given him her name only and not her title. That had been wrong of her. Despite that, she wanted to laugh, although it would sound pompous to correct his references to her job description at this late point.

However, she *had* finished her tour, or as closely as she needed. They hadn't made it to the recreation room, but the boy had found that on his own. She suspected the father would never want to go there, and so that would work out just fine.

Stepping away from the shelf, returning the items she'd been examining, Lou put her hand to her mouth as if in thought, although in actuality, she was merely trying to keep her smile off her face. She wasn't sure it was working very well. However, she couldn't help that, could she?

"Okay, let's get you to your quarters. Let me grab my gear from the dining area, and we'll be on our way. You won't need earplugs this time. We'll remain inside."

She walked past the sparring partners and headed through the galley without looking back. If she had, her amusement would have been obvious. She couldn't keep the laughter from her face forever. All she could do was try for it not to be heard out loud.

CHAD STEPPED to the door to look in his lodgings for the next month, only to have his son push past him.

"Hey, Dad!" Chaddie threw his helmet off his head and landed on the bed in one motion. His hands reached to unzip his coveralls as his voice continued with excitement, "It's comfortable, too." He patted the bed, grinning.

Chad stood at the door and looked around the small room. There was a table bolted to the wall in one corner, although it seemed to be more of a door turned on its side. Surely not. There was a small closet, and it was open to the room. He also noted that the table seemed about the same size as the door that was missing. There was only one bed.

He turned to speak to Lou, who was standing outside the door. "A trundle bed? I don't see one underneath the one my son's on. Is one being delivered later?" He gave her a hopeful smile, and then he let it quickly fall away. There wasn't even a frame for a trundle under the bed. He prompted her further, "I don't think we can share one bed."

She stepped in and cleared her throat, as she removed her safety glasses and helmet. "Well, Mr. Dickson," and she quickly changed her term of address when she saw him frown at her, "Chad, my apologies. You can see there's definitely only one bed. As I mentioned earlier, space is at a premium. This rig may seem large to you, but it's very small, indeed, for the number of people on board. We fill every space with machinery. When we've done that, left-over crevices get filled with people." She paused before continuing. "You need to know just what your allocated space means to the other men on the rig. Two people had to be relocated to make this space for you. A bed was moved out so you'd have your required private work area. You're lucky to have this, and there's nothing else anywhere aboard. An emergency bed in the medical section, maybe. That's all." She didn't mention the extra one with the cook. The crew needed Cookie to be kept happy.

Chaddie sat up with sudden concern on his youthful face. "This isn't your bed, is it, Lou?"

She laughed aloud at that question, then she replied with a smile, "Not mine, Chaddie. I get to keep mine."

"So, I don't guess I have a place to sleep, do I?"

Louinda cleared her throat and looked hard at his father. "I'm working on that."

"I don't, though, do I?" His face had taken on a very distraught cast, and he looked at his father with reddened eyes. "Dad, I guess I should really go back. I wanted to be here with you, but maybe Gramps could . . . I guess I could stay with him if he's home." He glanced at Louinda and then quickly back to his father.

"Is your grandfather expecting you?" Chad spoke up, taking this chance for the boy to own up without being directly reprimanded. The boy's eyes told him he was. However, Chad had seen a helicopter taking off as they were entering the accommodations block, and at this point, he suspected his son was stuck here.

When Lou cleared her throat a second time, he turned his gaze to hear her response.

SHE RAN her fingers through her hair before she stepped to take the boy's hand in hers. Thirteen. At thirteen, she knew, boys had abounding enthusiasm and quick solutions to insurmountable problems. She had raised Willie, after all. She also knew how hard a thirteen-year-old could crash when those solutions didn't work out. She had already surmised that this boy had devised his own plans for the time his mother was to be away, and they didn't follow any of those proscribed by the adults responsible for him. His plans were now evaporating all around him, and he was out of his depth. She had more unwelcome news to tell him, too. At least it might be unwelcome. There was a slim possibility he would be glad to hear it; she couldn't be sure.

"Chaddie," she began, looking into those sparkling green eyes that were now rimmed in red and filling with tears. "I think the time for that solution has come and gone. The helicopter to the mainland left nearly an hour ago. Now, if you want to swim . . . ." She was relieved to see a hint of a smile gather at the corners of his mouth.

She turned to his father, hoping to further rescue this situation for this charming boy. "Chad? What do you think? Is your son that strong a swimmer?" On an impulse, she pushed the boy's sleeve up and exposed his arm. With her hand, she felt the muscles in his upper arm. "Maybe," and she smiled at him. She paused as if making a decision. "I think there's enough muscle here. Okay, I'll tell you what. I think Ben has an extra pair of swim trunks. You look about thirty-one in the waist. We might have to get you a piece of rope to tighten Ben's trunks up, though. As big as you are, he's bigger, yet. It'd never do for you to arrive on shore, and for your trunks to still be floating miles behind you. Trust me, without a rope, you'd lose Ben's. They'd come off as soon as you hit the water."

She released him and turned to his father. "Now, Chad. You might want to call someone in Galveston. Anyone.

Have them turn on a light or two. I'd hate for Chaddie to miss and wind up in New Orleans. Bus fare from New Orleans to where his grandfather lives in Dallas is a lot more expensive than it is from Galveston." Then her eyes riveted the boy's face. "Unless, of course, you arrive late, miss your bus, and manage to exchange it for a different destination."

At those words, Chaddie's eyes dropped, and his face flushed a brilliant red. It was obvious her words had hit home, he knew exactly what she meant, and he probably suspected that his secret was about to come out. However, Chad laughed, and Chaddie looked up to see an expression of amusement on his father's face.

AT THIS POINT, Chad didn't know whether to like this woman or hate her. On one hand, she was constantly curt to the point of harshness with him, and on the other, he'd been intensely drawn to her in that moment when he had entered the mess hall. He listened to her quiz his son about his own marital status, and he heard his son tell her incredibly embarrassing things. Now, here she was handling this boy's tears like a pro. With just a few words, she seemed to be guiding him out of whatever had suddenly eaten at him. Surely she wasn't old enough to have raised a family of her own, yet she knew just what to say to this boy whom she'd barely met.

In a rare moment of teasing, rare for the past three years, anyway, Chad went along with Louinda's premise. "Chaddie, you know money is impervious to water. That means waterproof—"

Chaddie interrupted, "I know impervious, Dad." He

frowned at this new direction in the conversation.

"So," Chad smiled, "don't worry about the bus fare. I have some cash, and I'm sure Lou has some duct tape to fasten it to your leg. Or your arm." He winked at his son. "I guess anywhere you'd like it taped would be fine, Son."

Chaddie's frown grew deeper as he listened to his father, and he opened his mouth as if he wanted to speak. Then, in a burst of thirteen-year-old frustration, tears ran down his cheeks as he tried to put his hands in impossible-to-find pockets on his unfamiliar coveralls and couldn't locate them. His words tore from his throat, "I just wanted to be with you, Dad." Then he was gone out the door, and his safety gear lay on the bed without him.

Louinda glanced at Chad, and he looked back at her wide-eyed. The boy had seemed buoyed by Louinda's story, and his father's few words had torn pain from him. He ran his hand over his neck and chuckled.

"That didn't go over well." He stepped to the door, peering down the corridor, then back at his host. "Maybe we should go find him."

LOUINDA GUESSED otherwise. She guessed his *father* should go find him. However, she was already growing attached to this boy who reminded her so strongly of how much she had loved her own brother at that age. She also knew this thirteen-year-old had run from the room without his safety gear, and even if his father did think she would soon return to mopping floors when she was done with them, she knew otherwise. This boy's safety was her responsibility, and doubly so because he was thirteen. That's why he shouldn't be here. If he ran outside the accommodations block, he could be injured.

She also now knew that the boy's presence wasn't this man's fault. Oh, in a way, it was, but not really. One way or another, though, he would be spending the night, and that she had yet to arrange.

She walked up and slapped Chaddie's father on the shoulder, and she slapped him hard. She was gratified to see him wince as she began to speak. "I think we should go find him, *Dad,* and I'll carry his safety gear just in case he went outside. I think we'll find him easily enough. After all, this is a drilling platform. How far can he run?"

She laughed loudly at her joke and stepped past him. She didn't look back, but she heard his footsteps on the metal treads under their feet. He was following, and she was walking fast, too. He'd better keep up. This was *his* son.

Chapter 4

THEY FOUND him in the recreation room. Tables of two and four were scattered about the low-ceilinged space, and light-blocking shades covered the windows. One was half-way up, casting a rectangle of sunshine on the floor. A big-screen television, dark, was pinned by several loungers, with video game controllers tumbled about. The lights were off, leaving the perimeter of the space in shadowy dimness. Chaddie sat in a corner with his feet pulled up in a chair and his arms wrapped around his legs. His forehead was pressed firmly to his knees, and all they could see was his tousled head of hair. Lou let Chad go in first. She had raised that brother of hers, and she knew how this might go. This boy, so full of charm and enthusiasm, could easily come out of this with a few well-chosen words. He could also drop deeper into his despair if this blundering father bungled this. It was the opposite side of thirteen. In boys this age, emotions ran like wildfire, both the good and the bad. She had loved her brother most at this age, and he'd also been more volatile at thirteen than at any other time.

Against her earlier misgivings, she felt sympathy for the boy's father. Whatever job he had to do here, and Lou was certain it was to shut them down, he wasn't just a government official out to harass Sunshine Gulf Platform No. 6. This man was also a parent, divorced and single.

With a sudden frown of determination, she knew the single part wasn't important to her, and she didn't know why she'd earlier asked the boy about his father's wife. A feeling of relief had flooded through her when Chaddie said his father didn't have one, but Lou told herself she was just relieved that there would be one less person to call to straighten all this out. She didn't care if he was married or not. She just wanted him gone. Yes, that was it.

However, she put that aside for now. This boy needed a father, and it seemed the one he had was foundering. For the boy's sake, she might be forced to help.

"SON," CHAD started tentatively, "you can't run away like that." He hadn't spent enough time with the boy in the past three years to be sure how to step around this mess that seemed to suddenly be swallowing the day. He was still very aware that he was here to do a job, keep very busy, and remain disentangled from all things emotional. He hadn't actually pictured it in those terms, especially the disentangled-from-all-things-emotional part, but the feelings were there, nonetheless.

Then, there was this woman, Louinda, who was right here observing him wallow in all of this. He must look a fool in front of this female whose coconut hair had yanked him back fifteen years. Immediately, he had wanted this woman as he hadn't done with any other female in three years—more if he counted the final few years of his marriage. Those last years hadn't been all that great, not in the bedroom sense, anyway.

"Chaddie?" When the boy didn't respond, except to wrap his arms tighter about his legs, Chad turned to look at Louinda, and he shrugged his shoulders and held his hands out, palms up. He had no idea what to do, and he hoped to heavens she would please step in and help him out.

AS SHE watched, Lou didn't see a fool. She saw a man who was just that: a man. In this botched interaction with his boy, this younger twin who looked so much like him, this man, this Chad, this loathsome visitor to her beloved oil rig, had changed on her. It was that frog thing, the one from the fairy tale where the princess has a revolting amphibian she must confront.

Lou was amused to picture herself as the princess in the story, but that was the part she had taken on. This man was the slimy green creature from that enchanted tale. Even his hat told that. He'd been odious to her when he first arrived, just something to be rid of.

"Back to the stinky swamps, warty frog!"

She'd thought that, too. No, she'd *said* it. It had come out in her actions and the tone of her voice. He had seen it, also. She remembered his words as they stood in the supply room.

"Rookie green. I guess that sets me in my place. You don't like me much, do you?"

She knew what made the difference in the way she saw him now. It wasn't the kiss the princess had bestowed in the fairy tale. She had imagined this man taking her in his arms just a short while ago, but no, she didn't really want to kiss him. His lips might be sensuous to the right woman, and that strong shoulder she had touched might cause another woman's heart to melt. Another, weaker woman might even fall into those blue eyes, never to climb out again. A different woman, not Lou, one who didn't have iron in her blood, might feel the need to be close to this blond tower of masculinity.

Lou steeled herself with determination and fortitude, telling herself that she wasn't some other woman. This man wasn't affecting her, causing unwanted feelings, and keeping her heart beating faster than was good for her. No, with the door open, it was hot in this room, and anyway, there had been the excitement of this man's son running from them in torment. They had rushed after him, and that had caused her elevated heart rate and temperature. That's all it was. The tenderness she felt? It was for a situation that reminded her so much of her brother, not softness towards this man who didn't know the right words to say to a boy he should intuitively understand how to parent.

She let the door shut and set her helmet and safety glasses in a chair. Stepping to Chad, she touched his arm to ask him to step aside. When she was jolted with electricity from the touch of his arm, it was only the intensity of taking over for this inept father. That was all it was. There

74

was no roiling in her stomach at his touch, no butterflies. Her knees didn't go weak, and not for a moment did she feel queasy. No, this man wasn't affecting her at all.

As she stepped forward and placed Chaddie's helmet on the chair beside him, she glanced over at his father. The *kiss* given to the frog, the one starting that fairy-tale transformation into a prince, had been simple. This man had shown himself to be human, to have faults, and to be unable to deal with them. He had let her see that he needed help, that he was more than a government godling that carried limitless power in his thunderbolt, ready to lash her poor oil rig with devastation until it fell into the sea. He might still do all those things, but he was also very, very human, and for that, she'd let him touch her heart. She didn't think of it quite that way, but despite that, she had let him in, anyway. Something else that hovered at the edge of her thoughts was just how hard it might be to get him out again.

Turning to the boy in front of her, she spoke very gently. "Chaddie, I brought your gear. You left it on the bed." She smiled when he refused to look up, simply waving one of his hands to tell her to go away. She tried again, kneeling down and placing her hands around his shins. "Have you eaten?" He shook his head no, and she continued, "I haven't, either. The cook will be back in the galley in about half an hour, and I'd like to have dinner with you."

She looked over at Chad and smiled when the man gave her a thumbs-up. Things might be improving, but she still had to deal with the sleeping arrangements. That was what had thrown the boy into this state of despair.

"Chaddie?" Her fingers moved up to wrap around his calves, and she massaged the muscles there. She quickly dismissed her curiosity when the thought occurred to her that his father's legs would feel very much the same. Then she saw the boy's eyes look over his knees into hers. They were such a beautiful green. She thought she saw gold flecks inside, too. It was that sparkle, she knew. Either the sparkle made them seem to be flecked with gold, or the gold flecks made them seem to sparkle. One way or another, they were beautiful.

"Chaddie, do you ever get hungry at night?" He nodded his head, and she smiled at him. "So do I. And you know, I was thinking how hungry I've been all day. Well, as hungry as I am right now, I might decide I want a snack tonight. Getting the snack is easier if I sleep down in the cook's extra bunk."

She glanced sideways at a shift in the lighting to see the boy's father had moved up beside her. She continued, "Just for tonight, no one will be in my room. Would you like to stay there? I put clean sheets on just this morning." She'd put them on yesterday, actually, or two weeks ago when she'd packed to leave. She'd slept on them one night, but thirteen-year-olds usually weren't especially concerned about the cleanliness of the bedding they slept on. She knew that from her own Willie.

Chaddie's eyes looked to his father, and he reached the backs of his hands to wipe the straggling tears from his face. "Dad? Can I stay one night? I have a place to sleep, now." He sniffled and turned his eyes back to the woman who was offering him her bed.

Chad glanced at Lou and reached to put his hand on his

76

son's shoulder. He smiled and said, "Chaddie, I'll do you one better. I'll let you have my room, and I'll borrow for the night. How does that sound?" He spoke to Lou from the corner of his mouth in a loud stage whisper, "They do have laundry facilities on the rig for washing the bedding afterwards, right? We might need fresh sheets when everyone returns to their proper places tomorrow night." He leaned in to whisper more privately, "You don't know how grateful I am. Your touch with my son was magic. You spoke a few sentences, and the boy is perfectly fine. Thank you."

She stood and let herself smile. Men. A father and his son. She also searched quickly for the sharp responses she was known for, and at the moment she couldn't find them. In that one moment of his tenderness toward his son, this man no longer seemed a frog. She didn't quite think he was a true prince yet, but he'd at least become human. Turning a frog all the way into a prince took more than a bumbling father who didn't know how to deal with his son. She knew. It had been one of her favorite tales from her childhood. Her mother had told it to her over and over again when she was small. The princess must kiss the father, er, the frog, and she must do it with true love in her heart. Only then could the frog truly change into a prince.

That wasn't going to happen, at least by her. She would never kiss this man. It was enough for her that he had become human. A prince? She didn't need one of those. Princes were for fairy tales, and fairy tales didn't happen on oil rigs, especially on Sunshine Gulf Platform No. 6.

What she said aloud was entirely different. She clapped her hands together in the manner of a genie that was granting the first of three wishes. Or, perhaps this was the second or third for the day. It wasn't important. Her words told the magic she'd performed.

"A bed for everyone! Clean sheets, also!" She cringed at that one. Chad wouldn't *exactly* have clean sheets. She'd only slept in them the once, though. Also, Cookie's extra bed didn't have any sheets just yet. However, these visitors didn't need to know that. She grabbed her safety gear and held it in her arms, motioning to Chaddie to do the same. Then, the genie in her stepped to the door to lead them back to their princely chambers.

It was when they opened the door from the recreation room that they noticed the weather had changed. The door just outside of the mess was still open, and Chad's gust of cool air from earlier had become a stiff breeze. It was a very cool, stiff breeze, and off in the distance, a dark bank of clouds hovered. It actually felt very good to the three people standing on the rig in their coveralls and holding their safety helmets, and in that moment, they were grateful.

Chad remarked on it. "It's August, Lou. Does it always cool off in the afternoon like this?"

She laughed. "Not likely. A thunderhead will cool us down sometimes, or maybe there'll be a storm coming in from the Atlantic to push some moisture our way. August is pretty safe, though. You can bet it'll heat back up before long, and any rain will pass far to the east. *That,*" and she walked to the door and pointed to the darkened horizon, "is hundreds of miles away, and it's going to hit the Florida Panhandle. Count on it, buddy." She hoped so, anyway. She chuckled and reached to slap Chaddie on the shoulder.

"Come on, young man. We have to get you to your room. You get to kick your dad out for the night. How does that sound? You get a *single* with a *private bath* and your own *workspace*." She caught Chad's eye and smirked at him. "Your father gets a girl's room, all pretty and pink and fluffy. How does that sound?"

The boy grinned at her, and Chad smiled. As Chaddie walked ahead of them, Chad leaned in to her. "I was sure you had magic in your words earlier when you spoke to him, but I don't think that any longer. I *know* your words were magic. That boy is actually enjoying all this. God help me, I think he's actually reveling in it, especially the part about me sleeping in a pink and fluffy room."

She laughed his remarks off. She had something new on her mind. Once again, she hadn't been exactly upfront with the two men she was leading to their rooms. Her intentions were certainly aboveboard, and she didn't mean anyone any harm. However, pink and fluffy? Her room looked just like the one that had been assigned to Chad, except smaller. It was designed as a single, and it had a tiny workspace, not one the size of a closet door. Also, those clouds weren't headed towards the Florida Panhandle. Obviously, these men weren't meteorologists, or they would have caught what she'd said. For the clouds to reach Florida, the winds would have to be from the southwest. Those cool winds that had felt so good to them just a few moments ago were not from the southwest. They were from the northeast, and that meant something entirely different.

Those clouds were headed directly toward them. Of course, weather was the science of estimation, seasonal averages, and patterns. Maybe the storm that was gathering those clouds to itself would veer north or south. Maybe it would just peter out altogether. Maybe it would rain butterflies and gold doubloons, and pink cotton candy would fall from the sky. It was obvious to Lou that this storm just might pass them by. That was why she hadn't said anything. It just might pass them by, after all.

THE TELEVISION chattered its weather lessons, telling of the most powerful hurricanes that had ever accosted the United States Gulf Coast. Watch out, it decried. The season has returned, and the storms are on their way.

In an overstuffed easy chair, an old grandmother dreamed of a much-loved granddaughter gone to sea, as well as of a younger brother named Willie. When the thought of Willie crossed her mind, a smile ghosted her lips, and the dreams became pleasant. Willie was her project, a young man she intended to fatten up with as many peanut butter sandwiches as it took.

On the screen across the room, the announcer began the *Forecast on the Fives*, telling of the upcoming heat wave sweeping across the Oklahoma plains. Before he could finish, the television clicked off, the sleep timer having used up its allotment of available minutes.

Out front, a car started up, and its wheels spun on the gravel driveway as it darted for the road. A skinny boy, one barely out of high school, was at the wheel, and in his hand was the remains of a sandwich, one that looked and smelled very much of peanut butter. He left behind an empty jar on the kitchen counter and a plastic bag that contains the heels from a loaf of bread. The crumbs scattered everywhere and the knife not quite licked clean tattled on his hunger.

It was okay. Granny Reinhardt already had it on her grocery list. Willie could have all the peanut butter he wanted. After all, what better way to keep his shorts on when he was diving into his sister's pool? Yes, she would buy all the peanut butter the boy needed, and he needed a lot.

DINNER WAS a loud, noisy affair. The tables were filled, and it seemed this evening had a Chinese theme. Chaddie had reminded Lou that she promised to eat with him, and so she saved two places at her table for the visitors. Ben Tosh was sitting at the fourth.

"So, Lou. Tell me about this new beau of yours." The big man grinned. Everyone on the rig was aware the good-looking inspector was the furthest thing from a romantic interest for the rig's safety coordinator. That was something Lou had made very clear to everyone within earshot ever since the papers arrived telling of this man's impending visit.

However, Ben felt very comfortable teasing with this woman. He had protected her the first day she arrived on the rig. He also knew that when he'd shown up, she'd been putting up quite a fight. She might have been too small to win, but she had been a wildcat backed into a corner, and those two ruffians who had thought she was easy takings would carry scars to their dying days. That night had bonded Ben and Lou, and while theirs was more of a father-daughter relationship, it also had a level of sensuality that no father-daughter pair should ever attempt.

Ben placed his weathered hand on top of Lou's youthful one, and its blackness was in sharp contrast to her creamy whiteness. His massive thumb moved back and forth in an endearing motion as he waited for her answer.

Lou pursed her lips, and the humor that hovered there was very cynical. "He's not my beau, Ben. You're a scoundrel. You do know that."

He laughed, and it was deep and solid. Others in the room turned, and seeing Ben hovering a head taller than almost anyone else, they understood and returned to their own conversations.

"I do know that, and I know something else. I see a woman sitting in front of me, and I don't see the face of an angry wildcat whose territory has been invaded." He smiled broadly at that, and he removed his hand to pick up his cup of coffee. He raised it to his mouth slowly, with a massive arm that seemed as if it might suddenly flash out of control if he didn't give it his full focus.

He winked at her. He'd gotten her attention, and he knew it.

LOU STUCK out her tongue at the old man. His eyes were bright in his dark face, and when he laughed, his lips revealed great, white teeth. She knew he was proud of how perfect they were, and that they were his own.

"Never been to the dentist except once after I got into a fight. One was loose, and I wanted to keep it."

She had heard him tell that more than once. Truth? Maybe not, but she had no reason to doubt her friend's story. And, if it wasn't exactly true? It made him feel good to say it. She still had news to reveal about her interloper,

82

though.

"Ben, he has a son. Here." Her words were terse with meaning. Even as she had been charmed by the boy, she saw the trouble he'd bring.

Ben laughed again, and he pressed his arms against his waist to rein in his humor. "I know that, Lou. We all do. This place is a sieve. Something happens, and it leaks through to everyone else even before it's through happening. Tell me something I don't know."

Lou smiled in spite of herself. She knew Ben, and she knew what he was doing. In spite of the leaks, he wanted all the information he could get about this man, and if anyone would know, it was her. After all, she had been the one to spend the afternoon with him.

Ben was right about the sieve, too. Anything she told this man would be all over the rig before she could exit the room. That was life on an oil rig, or at least this one, and Lou didn't fault anyone on board for that. That very sieve effect was one of the ways discipline was enforced. Anything anyone did was soon common knowledge, and each of the workers on board knew it.

Lou tapped the table as she waited for Chad and his son to arrive. Ben's expression had quieted, but she could still see his teeth threatening to peek through with another quick laugh. His eyes watched her in anticipation, and she laughed him off. The places in front of them were empty, and Cookie didn't like to see that. She and Ben had told Cookie their guests might be late, and he had grunted. He liked to whip up the meals and get them out as soon as the workers arrived. Someone in the dining area with no food was like a fault that he had failed to correct. Lou was getting hungry, too. She hadn't been teasing earlier when she told Chaddie she hadn't eaten.

"His boy looks older but is only thirteen." Lou's eyes glanced up to see Ben's response.

He grinned. "Done know that. Everyone does. Something I don't know. That's what I want to hear."

She chuckled. She was pretty sure he didn't know her next piece of information. "You promise you won't tell about this?"

Ben grinned and made a big X over his heart with one beefy hand. "You know me."

She reached and slapped the lined hand still on the table. "That's why I want you to promise. I *do* know you, Ben Tosh."

"You got me." He chuckled. "You do know me. Now, give. What is it?"

She narrowed her eyes. "That wasn't much of a promise. You think because I'm tiny that I've got no sense. Is that it?"

It was time for Ben to purse his lips. "You're here, aren't you, on this oil rig? If that's not proof enough you've got no sense, then I don't know what is." His mouth broke into a crescent of white that lit up his face.

Lou wasn't ready to give, though. She pressed the man across from her for what she wanted to hear. "Promise, Ben. With words, or you hear nothing."

He made a circle of his lips and whistled out a hard breath. Then his eyes looked to his hands, and he laid his fingers flat. "No holdbacks. I promise." He jerked his eyes up and let his grin escape. "Good enough?"

She laughed at him, pushing his hands off the table. "I

shouldn't have called you a scoundrel. I should have said conniving, devious, lying scoundrel."

He laughed again. "You'd have been correct on all accounts, my good friend. Now, tell me the news. It'll stay in here." He tapped the side of his head.

"For a day or two. That's all I ask. Then I think the situation will have resolved itself. His son is a *stowaway.*" She looked around to make sure no one else had heard her.

Ben looked serious for a moment, and then he fought to keep his smile tamed. "A stowaway? For real? That's rich. I should have been so brave at thirteen. I only did things I was ashamed of at thirteen." He leaned forward to rest his elbows on the table. "Now I wish to know just how this young man managed this. Thirteen is very young, still. How did no one catch him at this game?"

Before she could answer, Lou's eyes caught movement at the door, and she felt something else that Ben didn't know. At least he didn't know the whole of it. Her butterflies tickled her stomach, and she remembered squeezing past Chad to exit the helipad. There was the masculine grace he had carried in his movements, and she was very aware she was seeing it again. She also knew without a shadow of a doubt that this time she wasn't seeing Tracy in this unknown man. She was seeing Chad, and he was still very much under her skin.

She placed a hand on Ben's arm to quiet him. "It's them. Later, Ben. I'll tell you all about it." As she stood, she had to hold the table with one hand. Her knees seemed uncharacteristically weak as her free hand waved to attract Chad and his son's attention. That and the noise in the room seemed muted for some strange reason, and dang it if the only thing she could see was the matching strides of the father and the son as they walked across the floor.

She didn't realize she was grinning stupidly until she felt a hand on her arm. Surprised, she looked down to see Ben pulling her into her seat.

"Down, girl, down. Do you want the whole rig to know you're in love? Or should we just stand right here on the tabletop and belt it out in song? I think I remember a musical that has a love ballad for a theme."

Lou dropped into her seat, her connection with the approaching men bruised. She looked at Ben, scowling, her eyes locked on him. She made sure her voice sounded sharp and exasperated. "How dare you say I'm in love! I don't even know this man. I've barely even met him." She paused, speaking more slowly. "Sympathy for a man who doesn't understand his son, maybe. I'll admit that. The son has charmed me, for sure. Love? Ben, grow up. Love in my life died five years ago."

Her need for it hadn't, though, even if she did keep it buried beneath the brusqueness she brandished about the rig.

Ben knew all about Tracy. He and Lou had met off-shore on leave one day early in Lou's employment on the rig, and they had made the rounds. Ben drank, and Lou drove. He had also sung quite a few musical theme songs, and quite well. Later that evening, sitting together on the Galveston seawall, she'd bled her heart to him, her anguish over a lost love she had been married to for only a year. She also told him she'd never love another man. She'd meant it, too. Now he was accusing her of being in love with a man she didn't even know.

That got under her skin.

She put a pleasant but distant expression on her face as their dining companions walked up to the table. She heard Ben chuckle, but she refused to turn to look at him.

"Mr. Reinhardt, Chad, this is my friend, Ben. Chaddie, Ben. He looks mean and ugly, but don't judge him by that. His heart is lead. Oh," she looked at Ben, "did I really say that out loud? I meant his heart is gold." She smiled as Chad and his son looked at each other before pulling out their chairs.

Ben took over with a chuckle. "Lou's mad at me. Pardon her introduction. I just pointed out a certain characteristic she feels she has well hidden. She doesn't want to admit to it." Then Ben changed directions with his words, looking directly at Chaddie. "Young man, you are thirteen, I believe."

Chaddie looked at his father and then back to Ben. Hearing only innocence in the question, a grin broke out on his face. "Yes, sir. Thirteen and a half."

Ben roared with mirth. "That half's important, too."

"You bet it is, sir," Chaddie agreed. "What do you do here?"

The old man turned to Lou. "I like this boy, Lou. He's to the point. When he's interested in something, he just asks, unlike some people sitting here at this table." He looked back to Chaddie. "I'm a motorman."

Chaddie dropped his eyes then looked to his father. He snickered, continuing to look down until he got it under control. Looking back at Ben, he smiled, "My dad says I'm a motormouth. Is that like a motorman?"

Ben slapped the table, causing the condiments to jump.

"Lou, I can see why you have love in your eyes. This boy is the freshest breath of air that's ever stepped aboard this rig. You say he's staying the full month?"

Lou gave Ben a dark look. No such thing had come out of her mouth. She looked to Chad and back to Ben. Then she saw the hopeful expression on Chaddie's face.

"Ben," Lou started, "you know I said nothing of the sort. Chad? Dad? Can I have a little help here?"

She felt her control of the situation slipping away, and she knew one thing for sure. There was no way that boy could be allowed to stay the full month. It simply couldn't be allowed.

CHAD WAS preoccupied with his own inner turmoil, and he had no quick answer for Louinda's question. He had heard Ben's statement, and he wondered if it was an intentional slip of the tongue. *"I can see why you have love in your eyes."* For Chaddie? Chad hadn't seen that. Certainly it wasn't for him . . . although . . . .

He couldn't allow himself to finish that thought. Her coconut hair was too sharp in his memory. How could he forget something that reached into the deepest recesses of his memories like the smell of her hair had? However, this woman's manner had been continually sharp, and her message had come across very clearly. She didn't like him much, even if she was occasionally polite to him. They were only dining at the same table because she had promised his son. Love in her eyes? Dear God, no!

Chaddie broke the growing silence. "Dad, do you think I really can? It won't bother me to sleep on the floor. There's enough space under the desk in our, um, your room. Sorry. It's your room, but the floor will be fine for me." He turned his eyes to Lou, and he pleaded with her. "If you've got blankets, that's all I need. My bag will do for a pillow."

This time the boy's eyes turned to the big man Louinda had introduced as Ben. "Please, Ben. Tell them. I won't be any trouble. I'm not really all that much of a motormouth. My dad just says that. I can be quiet if I have to. Do you have an extra bed in your room? If you do, I could maybe even stay there."

Ben held one hand on his stomach to keep his laughter under control, and the other was in the air to signal this boy to slow down. "Boy! Your dad knows you well, and no, I do not have an extra bed in my room. All six are filled. However, I do know where the other mattress is that we took out of the room Lou assigned to your dad. It could go under that table. What do you think, Lou? Can the boy double up with his dad?"

ABOUT THAT time, plates of food began arriving. Lou looked at hers with a sigh of relief. Ben wasn't helping, and now Chaddie had his hopes up. She needed some time to think. Certainly this boy could double up with his father—that was if he were staying the whole month. However, she doubted that would happen. He wasn't sup-posed to be here, and calls would be made tomorrow. She would see to that.

She decided to put the problem off for now.

"Ben, the dinner is here. Chinese. Chaddie already has a place to sleep tonight. We've taken care of that. The rest we can worry about tomorrow." She turned to the boy.

"Can we do that, Chaddie, worry about it tomorrow?"

A look flashed across the boy's face, and she knew her "solution" wasn't quite what he had hoped. To him it must have seemed that things were opening up, and now he was being shot down again. By her reckoning, one day was better than nothing, though. To hope for longer was a pipe dream, especially since she was the one who called the shots.

CHADDIE SHOVELED three bites into his mouth, his eyes on the others as they took careful bites of food. He put his fork down and pointedly asked the big man, "What does a motorman do?"

Ben chuckled as he finished what he was chewing. Swallowing, he started with an explanation that wasn't really an explanation at all. "Mostly, jobs on a rig are exactly like they sound. Pumpman. Mud logger. Shaker-man. What do you think those jobs entail?" He put his fork down and sat back in his chair to wait for the boy's answer.

Chaddie thought for a moment, and then he said, "If the jobs are what they sound like, then a pumpman must pump something. Oil, I guess. Right?"

"Right you are," Ben replied. "The others. What do they do?"

"Well, the mud logger probably writes down information about what the sea floor is like. I guess mud comes up in the pipe, and he would figure out if it's good mud." Chaddie grinned and ducked his head at what seemed to him a sloppy answer.

"Why do you say mud comes up through the pipe?" Ben's eyes twinkled.

Chaddie seemed surprised at the question. "Of course, mud must come up. That's what the seafloor is. The rig is drilling into mud. Mud's going to come up at first."

Ben reached and patted him on the shoulder. "That's close as a second skin. I want you on my watch, boy. I know men who've had schooling to do this, and they don't know that. Now, about the last one. Shakerman. Can you tell me what he does?"

Chaddie took a deep breath. Two out of three was pretty good for guessing, and he didn't want to fail on this one. "A shakerman must shake up the mud that comes out of the ground."

"And why would he do that?" Ben looked intently at the boy as if the answer were really important.

Chaddie was pretty sure he knew this one. "The mud can't go in your car. It has to be shaken to get out the oil, maybe."

"Close enough!" Ben beamed. "Now's the real test. Tell me, boy. What do I do?"

"Um, well, you're the motorman. That means you keep all the motors on the rig running."

Ben turned and looked at the other two sitting at the table with them. Then he flashed his brilliant grin. "I'm signing this boy up. One full month. Room and board provided. Lou, don't you tell me no. I'll find that mattress, and this boy'll have a bed tomorrow."

LOUINDA SIGHED and spoke quietly to the big man, "Ben, it's not quite that simple." She noticed that the boy's father had closed his eyes, and she heard him give a pronounced sigh, one much louder than hers. Still, Chaddie's eyes sparkled.

Ben tapped the table, and then he picked up his fork. Before he took a bite, he looked at Lou. "Sometimes it *is* just that simple, Lou. You just don't want to see that. Let the boy stay."

She looked at Chaddie to see him break out into a brilliant smile. It wasn't quite as overpowering as the big man's at her side, but it was close. It was really, really close.

Chapter 5

"DAD, IT WAS cold when we left the mess hall. From that outside door? It was open still. Did you notice? The wind was really strong, too. I bet the waves'll be big tomorrow. I'm glad they have central heat and air. See that vent in the wall? That's how I know. I saw the air conditioning units when we landed, too. We were right on top of them. If they have air, they must have heat, because I didn't bring a real coat." Chaddie sat on the bed wearing his flannel sleeping pants and grinning. He leaned over to pull the covers aside, and he threw his long legs underneath. He looked at his father sitting in a chair and leaning over the makeshift table, writing something in a notebook. "Dad? Is anything wrong?"

Before his father answered, the boy knew he'd asked a

stupid question. In his father's eyes, everything was wrong. This woman that Chaddie was really starting to like was his father's enemy. Chaddie shouldn't be here, hadn't been asked to come, and had come anyway without telling anyone where he was going. His father didn't even have his own bed tonight. Before his father even turned to look at him, Chaddie wished he could take the question back.

THE QUESTION Chaddie asked floated between them. Chad pressed his lips together and leaned back against the table, crossing his arms over his chest. He took his time before responding, afraid to once again say the wrong thing to his son. Today he had watched this boy he hadn't wanted to bring with him. He'd seen him among the other people on the rig, and he'd been aware his son had reacted favorably to each one of them. In addition, Chad was aware, brutally aware, in fact, of how his son had reacted each time he'd interacted with his father. The difference had been a gulf wider than the one the rig sat in.

Sure, Chad was irritated that his son was here. He was even more irritated that the boy had deceived the adults who were responsible for him in order to get here. Chad also remembered the words his boy had spoken, and they had burned into him throughout the day. *"I just wanted to be with you, Dad."* Now, here his son was, cheerful and full of conversation, and Chad didn't know how to talk to him. He had pushed him away for three years, and now he didn't know how to find him again.

He was lost in all of this, this parenting through his hurt and anger. He could see his boy across from him lying on the bed. Chaddie's face was so much like his own he could

94

almost be looking in a mirror. The boy even had the same smile that was in that picture he loved so much. All it took was a glance to see that.

Then, there was this woman. Was he mistaken, or had she eased up on him? Then, Chaddie had said something to him earlier. *"It's okay, Dad. I like her, too."* What did *that* mean? Like her, *too?* In any case, Chad did have to work with her for another month—minus one day, thank goodness. Could he actually *enjoy* her company during that time? She was certainly beautiful, and she *had* charmed his son. When the boy had been upset, she had spoken words of magic, and his son had danced for her. Dear God, Chad wished he could do that with the boy.

If his son did stay for the month, and Chad didn't see how that was possible, but if he did, then perhaps Louinda could teach Chad how to relate to this thirteen-year-old mystery looking at him. That would certainly be one bene-fit of having the boy here.

Of course, that would also mean Chad would have to talk to her, have discussions with her, possibly over meals. He might have to request that she be released from her menial duties to assist him—and Chaddie, of course. Perhaps she could come into his room to work with his son, and he could be here at the same time, sitting at the table working on his reports.

It wouldn't be like there'd be anything romantic going on, would it? It would all be aboveboard and proper. There would be a chaperone, Chaddie, and if their hands should touch, then so be it. They might reach for the same pencil, and they would laugh. Then his arm would brush against hers, and she would smile. He'd place his hand on her shoulder to apologize, and he would allow it to rest there just a little longer than necessary. The next time he reached for a pencil, he would be especially careful in his actions, and in doing so, his shoulder would come to rest against hers. She would pretend not to notice, and when his breathing increased in speed, she would again pretend not to notice.

Chad wasn't sure how she'd fail to notice when he took her face in his hands and placed his lips on hers. Surely she would notice that and say something. Perhaps not. After all, his son would be in the same room, and the boy must be kept in the dark. She would be aware that he was their chaperone.

"Dad! Can you hear me?" Chaddie was off the bed, and he grabbed one of his father's shoulders and shook him gently.

Chad blinked and coughed. Licking his lips, he turned to the table to keep his face aimed at the wall, and not his son's direction. He didn't need Chaddie in front of him. He needed time to regain his composure.

He chuckled roughly, doing his best to focus on anything other than this Louinda woman, and he called over his shoulder to the boy, "Chaddie, did you really change the bus tickets?" He heard the boy draw in a sudden, sharp breath. "Did you, Son?"

"Yes, sir. But Dad—"

"No buts, Son. Are you supposed to be at your great-grandfather's house for the month?" There was a long sigh this time, and Chad heard the bed creak, telling him his son had sat down.

"Yes, Dad. I'm supposed to be at Gramps' for the

whole month of August. Mom said you couldn't bring me out here. Even when she told you I was staying with you no matter, she didn't think I'd be allowed. She called Gramps a week ago. She just wouldn't tell you."

"You're here, though, right?"

There was a pause, and then anxiously, Chaddie let himself go. "I'm sorry, Dad. I shouldn't have made all these plans on my own. Gramps will be angry, and Mom will, too, eventually. She won't know until she comes back from Hawaii, but she'll sure be mad then. You're in trouble, and Lou can't find me a place to sleep. The only one who wants me here is Ben, and he doesn't have room for me."

That got Chad's attention. He had been thoroughly skewered earlier in the day by the statement his son had made, and this more than drove it home. He turned and looked directly at his mirror image sitting on the bed, and his words were direct and clear.

"Son, did you really do all this just to spend time with me?" When Chaddie looked at him with red eyes, Chad pressed him, "Come on, Chaddie. Did you really do all this for the reason you said? Or was it something else?"

Chaddie dropped his eyes to the bed and began drawing circles in the bedding just next to his leg. He sniffled and reached the back of one hand to press it against his nose. Then his eyes flicked to his father's and back to the bed, his hesitation obvious. The grin at the corner of his mouth was equally clear. "Well, Dad. It was like this." He cleared his throat and paused before continuing. "Mom had this series of blind dates planned out for me for the whole month of August, and even though I told her I was too young to get married, er, date, there I was." He looked up, and his father could see a grin bleeding across his face. "You see, she wants to spend all her time with Chip, and Gramps wants to golf all the time. Everyone wants me married by Christmas, so I'll be out of the house. You were my last chance at happiness, Dad. It was you or nothing."

That made Chad chuckle. "So, I'm your last chance at happiness, am I? Do you think we could convince your great-grandfather of that? He comes on pretty strong, sometimes. We do have to call him, you know. You can't just disappear for the whole month of August."

Chaddie beamed, his relief obvious that he might not be sent away. "I'm willing to try, Dad, that is if you're really willing to let me stay. Please?" The hope in the boy's eyes was unmistakable, and his father was glad he'd finally let down his guard. He'd have to work on this parenting thing with this boy-man who had taken over his bed, but he intended to give it a shot. After three tedious, lonely years, he'd finally reconnected with his son for this one isolated moment, and he couldn't fall down on the job again.

"Absolutely, Son. If we can pull it off, you can be mine for the whole month. Mind you, I'll put you to work. You won't be playing, you know."

For an answer, his son pumped an arm in the air and yelled a very strong response, "Yes!" He stood on the bed and began to do a happy dance, chanting, "I'm so happy," over and over.

At a knock on the door, Chaddie dropped to the bed and pulled the bedcovers up to his waist, and his father called out, "Come in."

LOUINDA OPENED the door a bit and asked, "All decent?" When there was no answer, she swung the door wide.

"No!" Chaddie yelled out belatedly, laughing. When Lou jerked back, he called, "You fell for it. I'm in bed and covered up. It's safe."

She made a face at him and stepped to the bed to slap him on the leg. "Shame on you. I thought you were thirteen. Now the truth comes out. Your father brought a twelve-year-old with him."

"Sixteen!" Chaddie's voice was adamant. "Everyone says I look sixteen!"

Lou laughed. "All right. Sixteen. However, I know the truth. You better be good, or I'll let your little secret out."

She loved it when the boy smiled like that. She'd seen him shine repeatedly ever since stepping on her rig, and each time it melted her heart. Then she turned to his father, and her good humor fell away. Not only was she attracted to this man, but she hadn't connected with him. She could afford to tease with the boy. If he rejected her, there was no loss. She might have her feelings hurt, but emotionally, she would be unaffected. This man, though, was a different story. His responses could easily become critical to her, and that was something she'd have difficulty with.

"Is it my bedtime?" Chad drummed his fingers on the desktop, but he had a smile on his face.

She chuckled. "If you say so. You don't have to go to bed, if you don't want. However, I would like to show you where my cabin is, if you don't mind. That way *I* can go to bed. I was up early, and this has been a very tiring day for me. Also, the wind's picked up, and anytime the wind blows out here, it always makes me sleepy. Ready?"

She looked to Chaddie to see him give her a thumbs-up sign. She smiled at that, although she wasn't sure exactly what it was for. Surely he didn't mean to suggest anything that might relate to what he said earlier. *"He thinks he doesn't need a wife. I'm working on that, though."* There was no way this boy was playing match-maker between two people who had just met. She did wink at him to bolster the budding camaraderie the day had seemed to offer them.

She turned back to his father. "Ready?" Chad reached for his safety gear, and she reminded him, "We'll be inside for this part of the tour. Have your seatback tray in the upright position and your seatbelt fastened. This will be a rough ride." She noticed his son laughed, but Chad just licked his lips nervously. Surely he didn't take her seriously. That would be too much. "You probably should carry your gear. In case of an emergency, you understand. You, too, Chaddie, should listen to what I'm about to say. If there's a real alarm, make sure you put on your gear before stepping from this room. Safety comes first, and you're never safe without that gear. All of it. Come, Dad. Let's get you tucked in."

She stepped from the door, and from his snort of amusement, she knew he was following. At her room, she swung the door wide, and she indicated for him to step through.

"After you, ma'am." He motioned to her with one hand.

"No, I'm not coming in. Make yourself at home." She

stepped back from the doorway. "I have my things already, and I don't want you to feel you're intruding. You'll notice it's not pink, and there are no frills." She chuckled at that.

He paused before entering. "I appreciate this, you know." He took a deep breath, then turned to look directly at her. "I'm not as hard as I seem. Really. Chaddie's mother and I, well, the divorce was difficult." He dropped his eyes, looked into the room, and cleared his throat. "Can we be friends? Or, friendly, at least? For Chaddie's sake?"

Louinda took a deep breath. Friendly? At this moment, she would readily agree to more than friendly. However, she couldn't let this man know that. Standing for a moment, she drew several deep breaths before she replied.

"This is my home. This rig. I *live* here. Can you keep that in mind?" She looked away, immediately regretting her abrasive response. Despite her unwelcome attraction to this man, she strongly felt the need to fight to defend this rig. She couldn't go both ways. She so wanted to say polite words, and she couldn't. She just couldn't.

He touched her arm in reply. "You *work* on this rig, Lou. You *work* here. There are other rigs."

That touch was electric to her, and it seared her inside. She had to get away, and she had to do it immediately. She stepped from him, breaking the connection, and without looking back, she called, "Live, Mr. Dickson. Live. Please remember *that*."

Then she was gone, and Chad was left standing in the door.

TURNING INTO the room, Chad stepped inside, the open door forgotten, and in that movement, he was in her world.

101

The room was much the same as the one his son occupied, except smaller, but in another sense, it wasn't the same.

As he was pulled to the bathroom, he was intensely aware of what had drawn him in, what wasn't the same. It was the smell of coconut. The aroma was soft and pleasant, and it permeated the space. It also permeated his very being, and he could feel her brush against his arm, and his lips were pressed against hers. His emotions welled up inside of him, and he was glad he was alone, that his son was in another room, and that this woman was not at his side. He was entirely too entranced by her just now. She would do well to stay far from him.

Then, with a sharp rapping at the open door, she stood in the corridor once again. He turned at the sound of her voice, and her words were overly bright in their presentation.

"I'm sorry, Chad. I forgot my alarm clock. I regret leaving you without one, but I must be up early. I won't bother you again. I'm shutting the door this time." She stepped inside, made her way past the bed, unplugged the small device, and then she was gone.

Chad sagged against the bathroom doorframe. When she'd reappeared, there had been a sudden, raging hope. Now it was drained away, and he could barely stand.

Stepping to the tub, he turned the shower on and let his clothes drop from him. Climbing inside and pulling the curtain, he let the water beat against his skin. He shook his head to clear his mind of her, and he couldn't do it. Taking a deep breath, he knew why. Her smell permeated this space. It was in the shower curtain, the lotions, and the soap. He looked around and realized his own toiletry things were in his case back in the other room with Chaddie. He only had access to hers.

Each item he opened brought him misery. The soap coated his skin with the essence of this woman. As he forced the shampoo against his scalp, in that overwhelming aroma of coconut, he felt the woman whom he had met only twelve hours before. He tried to tell himself it was simply the memory of that villa on the Baja Peninsula that taunted his body, but deep inside, he knew otherwise. When he'd brushed by her earlier in the day, the smell of her hair had twisted him with an emotion he'd accepted as no more than a brief and isolated connection to a time in his past. Now, though, it wasn't that villa. It was Lou who twisted his emotions.

Realizing the hazards this situation could bring to his assignment on this oil rig, he did his best to rinse the remnants of the coconut away. However, as he ran one of her towels over his body, he knew his efforts were well intentioned at best. She was still with him, or at least the smell of her, and that seemed much the same. Falling into the bed, he made a desperate bid for sleep to push this woman from his mind. Yet, even as he pressed his face into the pillow, he felt her presence in its softness. How there could be a hint of coconut even in the fabric of the bed itself, he didn't know. He did know, however, that it would be a very long night.

It was as the morning light began to filter in through the small window that he realized something. The bedding around him was damp with sweat. He'd kicked his blanket to the floor, and still, he was too warm. Throwing the damp bedding back, he could also tell the room was colder than he would have expected on the Gulf of Mexico. Stumbling to the window, he looked outside through bleary eyes. At first he thought he simply wasn't awake. Then, he realized his eyes were fine. It was spray from the sea lashing the side of the oil platform and coating the glass. The weather blurred the scene outside. He was aware of a distinct vibration underneath his feet each time a new spray of seawater flung itself against the wall.

"I thought the storm was headed away from us," he muttered, still groggy from his restless night. "The wind must be horrendous out there." He also remembered the reports that had sent him here in the first place. In addition, there were his own, early observations. This place was not in the best of repair. That worried him. He wanted to live through whatever weather might blow through.

One more realization crossed his mind, and it jerked him awake. How was his son doing in this weather? As a small boy, strong storms had always frightened him. He had no idea where his father was on this rig. He would feel all alone. He had to check on him.

Throwing himself to the door, he yanked it open to see no one about, and in that instant of awareness, he remembered all the emergency measures Lou had pressed on him the previous day. Muster points. *Evacuated!* He knew it. They were gone!

Then, reality raising its errant head through his haze, he glanced down at himself. He couldn't go out like this, wearing just what he'd dropped into bed with. His clothes. Safety gear. He must locate all of it before going to find his son. He turned as he attempted to rub the remaining sleep from his eyes. However, the things he needed were nowhere to be seen.

He knew he must be disoriented from lack of sleep not to be able to find something so ordinary as clothes. After a few minutes of searching, he realized they weren't in any of the drawers. These things were all Lou's. His must be elsewhere. He grabbed the blanket he'd kicked aside during the night and breathed relief to see them underneath. He bent over, grasping at them.

Pulling them on, he tied his shoes and reached for the rest of the safety gear. Dashing out the door, frantic that he was surely the only one left by now, he headed first to the room Chaddie was in. Grabbing the door handle and throwing the door wide, he was totally surprised to see his son still bare-chested and in his sleeping pants. He was sitting at the makeshift workspace. There was breakfast on a plate just in front of him, and steam was rising from a mound of scrambled eggs.

Even more disconcerting was the woman sitting next to him. She was the vision that had haunted him during the night, soaking his bedding, rather, *her* bedding, with his sweat, and who had left his eyes bleary with sleep.

"Good morning, Dad," Chaddie called cheerfully. "You must have smelled my eggs. Since Lou slept next to the galley, she was up with Cookie, and she brought me breakfast in bed. I got up anyway, though. You can share, if you want some. I won't want it all."

His adrenalin still racing, Chad sank to the floor and ran his hand over his head, dropping his gear beside him. He had thought his son might *need* him, might be frightened. Now he realized he had indeed missed three years of his life. At ten, any storm would have sent the boy into his

105

parents' bed for comfort. Well, maybe not at ten. At eight, for sure. At thirteen, Chad guessed his son was past that. Instead, he was sitting in his room, dining on a breakfast brought to him by the very woman Chad couldn't seem to get out of his mind.

It didn't seem fair.

LOU WAS pleased that Chaddie's father had come to check on him. However, his shirt was buttoned wrong, and he had forgotten his coveralls, altogether. That wasn't an issue since he'd stayed inside to get there, and he *had* remembered to carry his helmet just in case an alarm was sounded. His head would be protected, and that was good. His crotch might not. He had forgotten to close his barn door, and she found that funny. She also enjoyed the disarming disarray of his hair. The man was almost endearing in his disheveled state, and this time, it had nothing in the least to do with Tracy.

She turned her eyes to the boy munching on his eggs and toast, and she smiled. She had to correct herself. This man on the floor she was suddenly refusing to look at was not *almost* endearing. He was completely, totally, and most absolutely endearing, and in that particular moment, she found him very attractive. However, his son was sitting next to her. That meant she had to consider more mundane activities.

"Chaddie, tell your father what we're planning to do this morning." She let her eyes jump to the man on the floor and back to his son. She found this very amusing, seeing this man in a shambles, but his son and she did already have plans. The boy's father could tag along if he wanted. As far as she was concerned, he was certainly welcome, very certainly welcome. Placing her hand on the boy's arm, she suggested, "He might want to go with us—after his barn door is closed, of course." She turned her face to the wall and put her hand over her mouth to cover her smile. She heard exactly the response she wanted from Chaddie.

"Barn door? Dad, do you know what she's talking about?" The boy touched her on the shoulder to get her to look at him. "Lou, there aren't any barns out here, are there?" Then he laughed. "Oh, I get it. Dad? We're heading to visit the desalinator. Dad, did you know this place has a real machine to make fresh water from the sea? I thought maybe they had to bring it all out in plastic bottles or something. Save a bottle, save the sea, right, Lou?" His excitement from his arrival the day before was back in full force.

A wry tone sprinkled his father's words as he spoke. "Chaddie, Son, the desalinator isn't the barn door your friend is talking about. It's a little more personal, and I forgot to close mine. That's all."

Louinda turned just to where she could watch Chad as he corrected his son's misunderstanding. Her eyes caught him shifting his position on the floor, reaching his hands to his crotch as he adjusted the fabric there. Then she caught Chaddie's look as he turned to his father and back to her. He grinned, quickly catching onto what was going on.

"I get it, Dad. Your pants. You forgot to zip them." Then the boy snickered, catching Louinda's eyes. "That was funny. Barn door. I'll have to remember that so I can say it to my friends some time." Then, with his thirteen-year-old attention span, he shifted gears in mid-thought. "I'm about finished with my food. Can we go now?"

She stood and patted his bare shoulder. "Shirt, Chaddie. Pants, too. We'll be outside, and the wind is fierce this morning. Wear your safety equipment, and I'll bring rain gear." She stepped to stand over his father, and she chuckled. Calling back to the man's son, she knew Chad would read her loud and clear. "And Chaddie, be sure to close your barn door before I get here. Your cows might get out."

Chad looked up to catch her eyes as she stepped over him, and she was certain there was no irritation in his expression. In fact, if she weren't mistaken, there was a glint of amusement present, and perhaps even a wink. Seeing that gave a certain perkiness to her walk as she stepped down the corridor, and she didn't dread spending the day with this man and his son any longer.

Chapter 6

LOU KNOCKED three times on the door and called out, "Chaddie? Are you ready? Are all the barn doors closed?"

"Just about. Let me get my shirt. Come on in." She pushed the door open, and in the mirror, she saw him slip a long-sleeve knit pullover over his head and force his arms into the sleeves. She couldn't help but notice how similar this boy was to his father. In her imagination, she added three inches to his waist and a little roughage to his chest, and she pictured what his father would look like if he were the one getting dressed.

Quickly turning, she knew that wasn't a line of thought she ought to be pursuing. Yet, even in that reprimand, she knew it was something she *wanted* to pursue. This thirteen-year-old was infectious, and his father, well, his father was perhaps not infectious. Masculine? Perhaps. No, make that definitely. Alluring? Certainly. Endearing? She had seen that as he sat on the floor that morning, his clothing in disarray.

However, she realized that even in her attraction to this man, and yes, she would have to admit, her attraction to his son, also, there was another layer. This man was not here for a romantic interlude. He was here to do a job, and that job was one that was in direct opposition to hers.

As she waited for Chaddie to get dressed, she glanced out through the small window. The waves were gathering, and the spray was repeatedly blowing off the crests in sheets. It wasn't really *bad,* not yet. Not especially, anyway. The supply ships could still come and go, and the helicopters would have no problem landing. None were scheduled for today, but they could manage this weather just fine, if the occasion arose. One would have to if this boy were to be sent home today.

Yet, Lou had enjoyed her small jaunt back into the intensity of life over the past 24 hours. That man and his son had pulled her there, jarring her unwillingly back into existence for a short time, and she had found it enjoyable, even if it must end when the boy returned home. Feelings and sensations had surged through her, ones that she hadn't allowed herself to feel for five years. This man had done that to her, this boy's father who had left his zipper undone and let his eye wink at her. She smiled at the memory, still certain she had seen that wink.

In that moment, she decided. For the boy, she could give this man twenty-four hours. This boy might, no, *would* be going home today. The father would stay, and he would be allowed to prove himself. Reaching to touch the glass that separated her from the force of the wind that was sending spray against the rig, she knew that Ben would push for Chaddie to be allowed the *might*. It wasn't Ben's decision, though.

Even so, she understood just how this boy had charmed her; and his manipulation of his travel arrangements just to spend time with his father had hooked her heart. She had fallen in love with Chad's son, had allowed her heart to become captivated by him, and she would give his father the benefit of the doubt while his son was here. She would do that for Chaddie. After he was gone, then she would deal with the real purpose for Chad Dickson's visit. There would be plenty of time for that once the boy was headed back to Fort Worth or Dallas or Boulder.

That settled in her mind, she stepped from the window to see the tall, blond, green-eyed thirteen-year-old stepping from the bathroom, his hands tucking his shirt deep into his jeans. He grinned at her, and his face lit up. His eyes sparkled, or that's how a poet might write it, and the description would be accurate. Lou accepted that she *was* in love with this boy, even if she was a bit dishonest with herself, as she used him for an excuse to not push his father away.

Still, her twenty-four-hour truce was all for the best. Chaddie needed his father's attention—she could see that—and Chad would have a chance to reconnect with his son; and, as for her . . . well . . . every heart deserves a respite from sorrow, especially sorrow that's surrounded a person for five full years, even if that respite is only for twenty-four hours.

"I'm ready," Chaddie called, breaking into Lou's reverie. She looked up to see his coveralls on over his clothing, and his boots on his feet. His helmet was in his hand, and she could see his safety glasses resting inside.

"You said you'd have rain gear," Chaddie questioned. "Is it really raining? I watched the sky this morning, and it looked more like spray carried by the wind instead of rain." He grinned.

Although he was just a boy, it was clear he really wanted her to like him. That was because he was thirteen. At sixteen or seventeen, he'd be preoccupied with girls. At thirteen? He needed adult approval. He didn't even know how charming he was. His behavior was as natural to him as breathing. What he did worked, though, the charming part. It was working now, even if he only knew the smiles he achieved, and not the charm he used to bring them about.

"You're very right, Chaddie." She laughed, taking his arm. She could certainly feel the charm, even if the boy was unaware of how he used it. "We have clouds outside, a little wind coming through the rig, and a little sea spray against the windows. We can still get very wet. Your rain gear is just outside the door. I brought some for your dad, also. I suppose he's in my room getting ready. Did he say if that's where he went when he left here?"

Chaddie giggled, and he immediately stopped. His eyes twinkled again, as he asked a pointed question. "Your room. Is it really pink?"

She *was* amused at this boy. She liked his sense of humor. "You'll see. Just wait. Are you ready to head down and see if your dad's ready? The desalination station awaits!" She put a very melodramatic lilt to her final words, one hand twisting in the air, and that tickled the boy to death.

"I'm ready," he replied, leading her into the hall. "Which direction?" He glanced both ways. "I guess anyone staying here all the time would know where to go. I've just been here one night, and I haven't visited many other places on board, much less any of the other sleeping quarters. I'm lost."

She pointed. "That way, Squire Dickson. Your father awaits, and the answer to whether he slept in pink will be revealed upon our arrival." They laughed together at her dramatic rendition.

"That was funny. I know Shakespeare. I was in one of his plays at my junior high." He had his hands tucked in his pockets, and he whistled several notes before abruptly stopping and laughing at himself. He cleared his throat. "What if Dad's not ready? He looked like he'd just gotten up when he was here earlier. He might have gone back to bed."

"Directions, my boy. We'll give him directions to the desalinator, and he can meet us wherever we are. Come on. You can knock on my door and talk to him. I think he's listened to all of me he wants for the morning, at least until he gets his first cup of coffee."

CHADDIE FOLLOWED Lou through the unfamiliar rig. She stopped at a closed door that looked very much the same as the one they'd just stepped out of a few moments before. The number on it was different than the one they'd left, but the surface was the same color, and the knob was identical. The faint sound of water could be heard running on the other side. Lou pointed and pantomimed that Chaddie should knock.

When he did, he heard the water shut off, and his father called out a muffled, "Yes?"

Chaddie looked at Lou and grinned. Then he leaned in close to the door and replied, "It's me, Chaddie. Lou's here, too. Can we come in?"

He heard his father clear his throat.

"Chaddie, I think just you should. I'm in the bathroom shaving."

Lou smiled and looked away. She turned the doorknob to swing the door into the room and pushed on Chaddie's back. "Go on in. I'll wait here."

He leaned in and looked to see the bathroom door open. His father was standing wearing only his shorts. He had shaving cream spread over his jaw, and he peered in the mirror as he scraped it away. Chaddie stepped through and closed the door after him.

"Hey, Dad, the room's not pink." He was disappointed to find it was just like the one he'd slept in, except smaller.

His father chuckled as he turned his eyes to his son. "Pink is as pink does. This is definitely a woman's space, Son. Trust me."

"Dad?" Chaddie set his helmet on the bed and leaned his shoulder against the doorframe to watch the razor as it scraped his father's skin. "You never shave that way. You know, with soap. Where's your electric?"

CHAD REALIZED some of what he'd lost by pushing his son away. He was determined to correct that, and part of it was talking to this boy who looked so much like him.

"I always shaved this way before you came along. I sometimes get nicks shaving with a hand razor, and your mother never liked that. Coming here, I wasn't sure how the bathrooms would be outfitted, not on this old rig, and this only requires water and soap. I thought it was a safe bet to assume I'd at least find that out here." He pulled the skin on his neck taut and ran the razor up past his Adam's apple. "See? No nicks, either. I've learned a bit in fifteen years."

Chaddie looked back to the door where Lou waited. "We're headed to see the desalinator. Do you want us to wait on you? Lou said if you wanted, she could tell you where to go, and we could meet you there."

Chad pinched his nose and scraped at his upper lip. When he finished, he motioned with his hand. "You two go on. Leave me directions. I'll still be a few more minutes at this."

Chaddie opened the door to lean out to Louinda. "Dad's not dressed." He glanced back inside to see his father still standing in front of the mirror. Looking out the door again, he whispered, "He's shaving. He doesn't even have a shirt on. You probably shouldn't come in, even though this is your room. Where should he meet us? I'm good at giving directions."

LOU FELT her face warm. This boy's father probably wouldn't appreciate the amount of descriptive detail she was receiving, but that was his son's fault, not hers.

"Tell him to go to the main offices. Look for a door with my name on it. We'll wait for him there." She also knew he would find out that she was good at something besides just mopping the floors. Anyone could do that, and when things were slow, many of the job assignments allowed the rig's employees to be reassigned to whatever work needed doing. However, she was the only one on the platform who handled rig safety and training. Unlike most others aboard, she never mopped the floors. She thought Chaddie's father might be surprised to learn that, and she wanted to see his reaction when he did.

THE DOOR to Lou's small office flew open, and underneath Chad's very wet hair, a frown creased his forehead. Then, he closed the door, unzipped his wet coveralls, and pulled his safety glasses from his face. Glaring, he roughly dropped the glasses into the helmet he still held in his hand. Across from him sat the two people he was most irritated with, and they seemed to be enjoying each other's company immensely.

"You could have told me, Louinda." He let out a deep snort of frustration.

She smiled with a placating grin. "Lou, please, and told you what, Chad? Were your son's directions confusing? You made it here, didn't you?" She looked at the boy and poked his arm. "Is he mad at you or me, Chaddie? You know him better than I do. You tell me."

Chad barked, "Stop it. Rig Safety and Training Coordinator? That's right at the top of rig management. You let me make a fool of myself, talking like you were a roustabout." He glanced at a small shelf and roughly placed his gear there.

"Like a roustabout? No, no," Lou corrected, turning to

116

Chaddie with a wink. "You were very clear that I was, indeed, a roughneck. At least that's the way I took it. That's a step above a roustabout. I felt very honored that you didn't place me at the bottom. I've been there before, and I've worked very hard to improve my situation."

Chaddie just grinned. "Dad, it's okay. I didn't know, either. I found out the same way you did."

His father glared at his son. "Are you teaming up with her? You didn't say stupid things to embarrass yourself yesterday. You were smart and charming. Look at the two of you, now. It's obvious she loves you, Chaddie, and I can't say anything around this woman without putting my foot in my mouth." He put his hands to his head to run them through his hair, and he pulled them away in disgust. "I'm soaked. That short walk outside, and I'm soaked. God, how did my *hair* get wet? I had that stupid *helmet* on!"

Chaddie stood to touch his father's hair to see just how wet it really was. His hands came away dripping. "Dad, we left you rain gear at your room." The boy looked at Lou for confirmation.

"Right outside the door, Chad. Surely it wasn't gone?"

He closed his eyes and leaned his head against the door. "I looked inside the room. I couldn't find it, and I thought I could stay fairly dry if I hurried. I'm a dunce. I never looked down as I stepped outside." He banged his head against the door once just for emphasis.

Chaddie quipped, "That's okay, Dad. I like you when you're a dunce."

Chad opened his eyes to see a grin on his son's face.

Lou's reply was quieter, but both of the males in the

room heard every word. "Especially when you're such a charming dunce." She may not have intended for her words to be heard, but then she did voice them. They weren't quite whispered, either, Chad noticed.

In spite of his frustration, Chad was very glad to hear that suggested compliment. Somehow, those words went well with a very recent and sleepless night spent in coconut memories immersed in the presence of a beautiful woman, or at least surrounded by her things. Her words put him in a better humor, too, and with an uncharacteristic move, at least uncharacteristic for Chad during the past three years, he threw her words back at her.

"Did I hear the word charming?" He cleared his throat before glancing way. Then he ran his fingers through his hair again and looked her direction.

She leaned her head back and laughed aloud. "You heard dunce. If the word charming was next to it, then pardon me for any inaccuracies. I must have been speaking of the good Chaddie. He *has* charmed me." She reached with her hand and grabbed the boy's chin, then she let him go to look at his father. "You? I'm still waiting."

Chad began to struggle out of his wet coveralls. "My ex once called me charming. Then she dumped me like a hot potato. I don't know that charming is entirely a compliment." He grinned and looked at his son. "Sorry, Chaddie. Nothing against you, Son. That's just the way it is. Get ready for when you start to attract girlfriends. If they say charming, run!"

Lou stood and crossed her arms, giving Chad a look of mock hurt. "I am offended, good sir. Shall we take this outside? I will defend this young man's honor before God and man." She lifted her chin and looked down her nose at him.

Chaddie grinned. "Careful, Dad. She knows Shakespeare. You're not going to win."

Chad sat and struggled to get his boots off. He popped one loose in his hand and tossed it aside. He smiled as the other came off, also. Then he stood to finish removing the wet coveralls, leaving him in just his pants and shirt. He held the wet clothing out in front of him.

"I'm not going back out to fight for your honor wearing this. I'll bow to your advice, Son." He paused as water dripped from the hem. "These are soaked. What did your grandmother used to say to you? *Sugar melts, so I need an umbrella. Salt is sour, so you just be a tough fella.* Something like that, anyway. I'm glad I'm not sugar today. I would have melted away to nothing."

Lou smiled at his story, but she sighed at the coveralls he held. "You'll have to have those back on when you go outside, you know. Do you intend to wait for them to dry in here?"

CHAD'S EYES focused on hers, and to Lou, it was cruel to see that he had that exact same look as his son, that same charming appearance that had stolen her heart just the day before. It didn't matter that this man's eyes were blue instead of green, because in that moment, she could feel herself falling into them. She wanted to stop herself . . . no, she admitted, she didn't want to stop herself, and didn't need to, either, because she had the rest of her twenty-four hours. She could crawl out then. If she could. Right now, all she wanted to feel was the sense of vibrancy this blond-haired father had brought back into her world, even if it was only to be for his allotted day.

The words he was speaking finally registered. He had begun talking to her, and as her thoughts had wandered, she apparently missed part of it.

"Can I let the coveralls dry? Just a bit? The water was beginning to soak through to my clothes underneath. I'd be mortified to get any wetter. I can't afford to take anything else off. So, Lou? Are you listening?"

She glanced down and paused before answering. She had to get this under control. He had been shaving without his shirt. Now, here was the opportunity to get him to take off another layer of his clothing in her office. She even had a chaperone to keep matters nice and aboveboard. No one could possibly find fault in allowing this man to dry out thoroughly before venturing back into the weather. She smiled without looking up, and spoke as if she were very serious.

"Um, Chad, I think I need you to put your coveralls back on and step outside. Stand on the pipe deck a few minutes. Then you may come back in."

Chaddie grinned as his father's eyebrows jumped in astonishment.

"You're serious?" Chad stared at her. "Stand outside in these and get completely soaked?" He reached one hand to squeeze them and water dripped to the floor. "I'd be wet through and through."

Lou tapped her chin for a moment as she glanced at Chad with a glint of mischievousness in her eyes. "Except your pants. Don't let them get too damp. After all, you have to wear something while your other things dry."

As the boy at her side tucked in to a ball and cackled with laughter, she looked away. She felt her face flush with heat, and she was appalled at what she'd suggested. It wasn't like her to hint that a man take his clothes off in front of her.

Then she began to chuckle. He'd suggested it first, so it wasn't really her idea, was it? Somehow that made it truly funny to her, and she turned to the man still standing at the door holding his wet coveralls in front of him. She took mercy on him and reached to take the wet item out of his hand.

"Here. They can hang on the hook above the heating vent. They'll dry faster there." She looked to the boy next to her and pointed. "I have a checkerboard in the drawer right where Chaddie is sitting. We can play a game, or several if we have time, while your coveralls dry. We can't have you shirtless, after all." Looking at Chaddie, she grinned. "What would my co-workers think?"

Chad's face was red, although he looked relieved. "Absolutely not shirtless. Thanks. I'd love a game of checkers while my coveralls dry Two if it takes that long. Let me get the game for you."

When Chad leaned to open the drawer, his son grabbed his shoulder and whispered into his ear, "She likes you, Dad." When he turned his head to glare at his son, Lou caught his eyes. She had heard the boy's words, and she felt her neck grow warm.

Today might turn out to be more awkward that she'd bargained for, either that or the best day of her life. She wasn't sure which she hoped for now.

Chapter 7

LOUINDA SMILED at the boy in front of her. Chaddie danced along the outside catwalks, his excitement mirroring the beat of the waves beneath his feet. It had taken a dozen games of checkers for his father's coveralls to dry, and the three in the office had traded partners with abandon, trying to see who could outfox the others in the most devious way possible. Finally, at one especially vengeful series of jumps, Chad had leaped from his chair, claiming with an uproarious laugh that there was duplicity in the air. His son was for sure in cahoots with the woman across the room, and with those words, he had grabbed the boy from behind, and in a bear hug, he let his fingers dance over his son's rib cage until Chaddie broke down in a fit of laughter and admitted that yes, Lou had been giving him signals when Chad hadn't been watching.

Now outside, there were men working, even in the stiff weather that assaulted the rig. Despite the wind, it was dry high up on the drilling deck. The spray that thrashed the lower decks didn't reach quite that far.

"The desalinator was cool, but this is cooler." Chaddie's boyish enthusiasm bubbled forth in his words. "When do they shut all this down?" His arm swept over his head as he turned in a circle to indicate the entire facility.

Lou glanced to follow the sweep of his arms. "What do you mean, shut it down? Everything?" She watched the boy as he turned to take in the drilling operation currently in progress, the massive collars being snapped around the piping being driven deep into the seafloor. Even through their earplugs, the clanking of the metal and the deep-throated burr of the cranes were clearly evident.

He twisted around to face her, his interest shifting to several birds he saw coming in close to the platform. "Birds! Out here! I thought we were too far from shore for birds. This is so cool!" He looked back at the drilling crew in operation. "Well, when do they? The weather already feels bad out here. It's really windy. Can't you feel it?"

Lou caught up with him and leaned against the rail, looking out to sea. "You haven't seen bad. I hope you don't, either. Operations will continue except when we see an actual hurricane. This isn't even tropical storm strength, yet. We won't be shutting down operations anytime soon." She turned to lean back against the rail, resting her elbows on the top bar for support. Glancing at his father, she nodded with her head and said, leaning in, "Do you think your dad is frightened being out here?" Her eyes turned to Chaddie to find his face sparkling.

"Maybe. I don't really know, but if you say it's safe, then I'm fine with staying." He grinned like he knew this was no more than a joke played on his father. "The birds like it, though. Do you think that helicopter out there will really try to land here if it gets close enough?"

She frowned. There was no helicopter scheduled to land today. She also knew she hadn't scheduled transport for Chaddie to return to the mainland, and there was no other reason for anyone to be flying in today. Two full weeks of supplies were delivered when Lou arrived just two days ago.

"Helicopter?" Lou glanced at the helipad to make sure there was no activity that she was unaware of. "Did you actually see one somewhere?"

He pointed out to the sea. "There. Can you hear it yet?" He put his hand on his helmet to pull the brim down and block the sun. "I can."

Lou was used to the deep *whup, whup* of a big copter, and that was why she'd missed this one. When she looked, she could just catch a small speck of something out there, and when she listened closely, she could make out a high-pitched mosquito buzz coming from over the water. What would a tiny chopper be doing this far from shore?

Then it dawned on her. Big freighters often carried small helicopters for short haul flights. That was what this one sounded like. It was growing closer, too. She turned and noticed Chad had walked up beside her.

He leaned his hip against the rail and crossed his arms. Grinning, he asked, "What have the two of you been cooking up?"

His son pointed, and his voice held the excitement of someone getting to experience yet another new event out on an oil rig, an unexpected adventure that was tailor-made for his enjoyment. "Somebody's coming. Maybe, anyway. What do you think, Lou?"

"Maybe, Chaddie. That's a very small helicopter, though. There'd be no way for it to fly all the way in from shore."

Chad frowned. "Could it be based on another rig?"

Lou thought about that for a minute. "Maybe. Do you see a ship anywhere? That'd be my bet. Mostly small copters are ship based, just for doing short hops."

"Like that?" Chaddie pointed off to another speck they could see when the waves were just in the right position. It was red and long, and definitely a large container ship. "Could it have come from there?"

"Possibly. Follow me. We'll find out." She headed back the direction they had come.

"Where are we going? The helipad's right there." Chaddie jumped ahead to Lou's side, as he pointed to the top of the accommodations block. "Lou?"

"The radio operator will know. If she doesn't, well, then she can earn her pay by finding out."

"How?" Chaddie was hopping along backwards again, and Lou grabbed his arm to turn him around.

"Forward, boy. Remember what we talked about before. Stairs, falling, and going overboard. Only move ahead if you can see where you're going."

He turned to walk beside her, glancing at his father bringing up the rear. "How can she earn her pay? What do you mean?"

She adjusted her grip on his arm to guide him around a corner and head down a set of steps. "Helicopters can't just land here. They must radio in, get permission, and all sorts of things like that. If, and I mean if that helicopter is headed this way, he will have either radioed in, or he must be contacted to declare his intentions."

As they passed her office door, they came to one that said *Radio Operator*. Chaddie put his hand on her arm. "Why can't he just land?"

Opening the door, she leaned to him and whispered, "This is an oil platform, Chaddie. Boom. Blow up. There are bad people out there, you know. We call them terrorists."

Chaddie looked to his father, just then arriving, with wide eyes of understanding.

"Terrorists?" Chad questioned his son with a frown on his face. "Surely those aren't terrorists coming here."

His son looked panicked for a moment. "Maybe, Dad. We don't know." Then he poked him with his elbow and grinned. "Lou's going to find out."

After a few whispered words to the radio operator, she turned to her two escorts. "Yolanda says they've already radioed in. It seems we have an emergency on hand. Do either of you know a Wally Saunders? It seems there's been a kidnapping, and Wally Saunders is here to save the day." She looked directly at Chaddie as if her answer might be found there.

His face melted behind his safety glasses. Reaching to pull them off, he turned devastated eyes to his father. "It's Gramps." Turning to Lou, he asked hesitantly, "He's not sending that for me, is he?"

Chad stepped up, interrupting, "I'm sorry, Lou. I hope this doesn't present a problem for the rig. Wally is a rather forceful character. When he wants something done, everyone usually jumps out of the way." He caught his son's eyes. "It'll be fine, Chaddie. Don't worry about Gramps."

Lou cleared her throat. "Um, he's not just sending this copter for his grandson. Wally, Gramps, rather, is on that helicopter." Chaddie went pale. Chad coughed and looked the other way. "What?" Lou frowned. "Come on. Own up to whatever you two aren't saying, because I don't like the looks of this."

Chad turned to her hesitantly. "I want to apologize for Wally ahead of time. I was being generous when I described him as forceful. Try exasperating on for size. Very exasperating."

His son was almost in tears. "Dad, do I have to go?"

Chad put one arm around him and squeezed before letting him go. "He's not here, yet. Let's get him off the helicopter and see just what he wants. We don't even know that. Maybe he needs something else."

Chaddie's voice broke. "Yeah, like maybe he hit a golf ball all the way out here. He needs me to retrieve it."

Mystified, Lou interrupted, "Golf balls?"

Turning to explain, Chad clarified his son's remark. "Chaddie's great-grandfather—on his mother's side—is nearly eighty, and he still golfs every day. When his great-grandson visits, the old man loves it, because he doesn't have to pay a caddie."

That really didn't explain much. "Great-grandson? I heard you call him Gramps."

Sniffling, Chaddie tried to put it in plain words. "He's my mom's grandfather. Mom calls him Gramps, and that's just what I picked up. I don't want to golf every day for a month. I want to stay here. This is way cooler." He turned away and pushed outside. When the other two followed, he kept his back facing them, refusing to look their direction.

Lou had seen the red eyes, though, and she put her arm around him. "Golf is cool, too, Chaddie. If you do have to go, you can have fun with your great-grandfather." Then she reached to his safety glasses. "Put those on, please."

"Sure." His tone didn't agree with his word, though. He continued sourly, "At eight it was fun. Then, fifteen visits later, it wasn't fun any longer. When I'm with Gramps, all I do is chase balls. I want to be here with you two. At least this is interesting."

They looked up at the increasing rotor noise of the approaching copter. The machine was very small, unlike the one Chad and Chaddie had flown in the day before. It was more of a flying frame with a motor rather than an actual helicopter. They could see Wally inside the bubble of the cockpit, and his head of white hair framed a face masked by sunglasses. He didn't look very happy. He also seemed to be ferrying something black under his feet.

Lou turned to head towards the helipad. To judge by the expression on their new visitor's face, this might not go very well for Chaddie." To the two with her, she called brightly, "Let's go meet this great-grandfather. Surely it can't be the end of the world."

Both Chad and Chaddie closed their eyes, preparing themselves. Lou noticed they did it at the same time, and that warmed her heart. This father and son were more alike than they knew, and if that were true in every way, then the charm that burst from this boy was certainly there in the man. She had seen it starting to peek through. Surely there would be a way to work around the conflict of their jobs. Hadn't she always heard that love would find a way? She had the rest of her twenty-four hours to see if that was true.

She also allowed that if twenty-four hours weren't enough time, it might be possible to fudge the deadline to thirty or even thirty-six hours. Longer? She would have to get there and see. For now, she had a great-grandfather to meet.

CHAD OPENED his eyes first, and he stepped to his son. Now they had a common enemy, and the changes that Chaddie had worked to bring about over the past day snapped more clearly into focus for his father. What the boy had really done was get his father to let down his guard, and when that happened, two people had grabbed onto his heart.

One was the boy he had shoved away for three years. Chad found he had missed the boy that he raised for the first ten years of his life, and he wanted the good times they'd shared back again.

The second was the woman at their side. Chad now understood something else he had somehow missed. All women were not Diana, and he liked women very much. He felt especially drawn to this one, and the fact that she and his son had so obviously hit it off only sweetened the pie.

However, he first had his son's great-grandfather to meet.

CHADDIE FELT his father's hand on his shoulder. He turned and caught the same expression on his father's face that he knew must be on his own. All he wanted was time with his dad. That's why he'd snuck away. He remembered how much fun they'd enjoyed when he was younger. When his parents divorced, it felt like his father divorced him, also. Coming here had given him back his father; at least that's the way it felt to him.

Plus, there was a bonus. Lou. His father liked her; she was pretty, too. Chaddie liked that.

Now, he had his grandfather to meet, and it wouldn't be pretty. He was equally parts frightened of what Gramps might do and who his heavy-fisted grandfather might aim his punches at. He knew his father would likely take the brunt of it, and he didn't want to lose what the past day had given them back.

One other thing bothered him, too. Lou. Chaddie might be only thirteen, but he thought big in many ways. He wanted to protect his new friend, and he hoped she stayed out of the line of fire. He liked her, and his great-grandfather had the knack of running over people. Chaddie might be still be a kid, but he wasn't stupid. He knew Gramps; he just hoped Lou listened to his father and remained clear of the damage zone.

Then they reached the top of the steps to the helipad. At least they were far enough above the ocean to be free of any possibility of windblown spray. It was even higher than the drilling deck. The three of them, one in a white helmet and two in green, held on as the rotor wash buffeted them. Still, even as high as they were, small pricks of water hit their exposed skin, driven by the small helicopter's rapidly spinning blades. Chaddie loosened his safety goggles on one side, wiping his cheek with the back of one hand. He was glad for the rotor wash. He wouldn't want to admit to tears.

The person that stepped off the helicopter was stocky and wound like a spring. A big black Rottweiler jumped off after him, her legs shaking as if she were afraid of the beating blades just overhead, the big man at her side, or maybe even of the rig, itself. As soon as she was clear, the small craft was back in the air. The man whipped off his sunglasses and stomped up to the trio greeting him. Anger was in his every movement.

"My God! What I've had to put up with! You, Chad! You're supposed to be this boy's father. I should rip your balls off!" Lou grimaced and looked away, cringing when the old man continued to berate Chad. "How dare you bring this boy out into this danger! Strike a match, and you could blow yourselves up."

The white-haired old man reached to the big dog at his side and rubbed her under the neck, giving her rough reassurance. "Easy, girl. You're on firm ground again." As quickly, though, when the animal reached to lick him, he pushed her away with a snort. Then he stood ramrod straight and attacked Chad once more.

"Chip is a better parent to this boy than you ever were. Thank God my granddaughter had the sense to divorce you and marry him. And you!" He turned to look at his great-grandson. "You lying little weasel. I've babysat you and changed your diapers. I've already given my caddie the whole month off, and what am I supposed to do? Call him up and tell him my great-grandson snuck off to the Gulf to live on an oil derrick for a month? Good God, boy!" He reached and slapped Chaddie's shoulder with the flat of his hand, and Chaddie stumbled. "Think! Now take your sissy dog. She's peed herself three times already." He threw the boy a leash and pushed the dog that direction.

Next he focused on Lou, and Chaddie cringed. "Who are you, woman? This man's girlfriend? Lover is more likely from what my granddaughter says to me. There had to have been some reason for my beautiful granddaughter to divorce this man. Are you her?"

Chaddie shrank inside. What he'd run from had come and found him. How could his summer get any worse? He knew it could, though. He could be forced to go home with his gramps, and then he'd catch it all over again, every ugly word.

He tried hard to keep the tears from coming, and he didn't know if he could.

LOU GLANCED at Chad's face and the mortification written all over him. She understood now why they had cautioned her, but she didn't quite know how to take what this old man was spouting. Could it be true about Chad, that he'd been sleeping around on his wife, and that was the reason for the divorce? She had no background to prove the accusation one way or the other. However, "Gramps" had asked her a direct question that was very simple, and as a senior member of the rig's personnel, she at least owed him her name in reply.

"Louinda Reinhardt, Rig Safety and Training Coordinator." She stood tall and looked him in the eyes. No matter how angry he was at his great-grandson—as well as the boy's father—she had done nothing wrong. She worked here, and he was the intruder.

She watched his face harden and wondered just what she had done that could make him any angrier than he already was.

"REINHARDT, YOU say." His eyes narrowed as he looked at the hair flowing from under her helmet. He had known a Reinhardt. It was many years ago, but he hadn't forgotten. High school had been one of the best times of his life, and he'd had the prettiest girl in school as his own. He'd also been the captain of the football team, but even so, it hadn't been enough to convince her to put out for him. When his girl hadn't been willing, he'd found those who would. All he'd had to do was whisper sweet promises of love in their ears, and their skirts had come right off.

There had been plenty, too, and many of them more than once. Finally, it had been the night of the senior prom when his good times had caught up with him. He'd been voted king, and he'd made his way onto the platform and stood there so proud of himself. Hell, he'd deserved it, and he'd smirked at the fools standing and watching, especially those who had run against him. Then, the name of his queen was drawn. He wanted to announce it himself, and so he asked for the slip of paper. There was the name he expected, Linda Reinhardt. He'd known it would be. He'd bought enough votes with his daddy's money that he hadn't doubted. He kissed the paper and spoke into the microphone. His words came back to haunt him, though.

"The girl I love gets to be my queen. Come on down, baby!"

He'd looked right at her, and she'd smiled back at him. However, before she could start his way, thirteen other girls had run onto the stage, ecstatic and crying with excitement. One had even jumped up on him, wrapping her arms and legs around him, and planting a kiss on his lips.

It was the fight that started among the girls that drove Linda away. The girls on the stage yelled more truth to each other than he ever dreamed would come out, and the microphone picked up every word. The last he saw of Linda was as she turned and headed to the door.

"Reinhardt," Wally repeated. "Not the Oklahoma City Reinhardts, I wonder?"

"Yes, sir, and I'm proud of it. My daddy and my granny, too." She stood even straighter.

Wally saw something else. He saw an old high school flame who had never put out for him, and who had made a fool of him by walking out on him in front of all his friends. He'd never forgiven her for that. In this woman's speech, with the timbre of her voice and the inflection of her words, he could hear his Linda as she lectured him.

"Go take a cold shower, Wally, but take me home first. What's under my dress is none of your business."

She'd told him that enough times that he still repeated it for laughs to his old golfing buddies. He still had the timbre and tone down even after all these years. He knew that voice, and this woman's was the same.

He also knew he *had* taken her home, but he never took

that cold shower. He called Junie or Mary or Betty. He was captain of the football team. He'd gotten all the sweaty action he'd wanted.

He studied her face. From what he could see, the resemblance was remarkable. *Damn, woman,* he thought. *Take off those glasses and let's see.* Her body he could make out as the winds whipped her clothes against her. His old man's glands were stirred as he saw the signs that told him this was Linda all over again. With that possibility, he felt eighteen flowing in his veins once more.

"Not the Bethel Baptist Reinhardts?" His voice ground out the words, and he didn't care how harsh they sounded. This was an opportunity to be grasped by the horns, because it might never come again.

LOU HEARD the change in his tone, and she put a new edge into her words. "Yes, sir. My father ministers there. Senior pastor. All my family attends, from my Granny Reinhardt to my younger brother." She had no idea what she'd done to stir this man up. However, she didn't have to bow before him, even if he was Chaddie's great-grandfather. She wouldn't, either. She had her grandmother's iron backbone, and if she were forced, she could be cruel in order to show it.

The old man guffawed. "Granny Reinhardt. She goes by Linda, I bet. The old woman must be nearly eighty by now. Have I got her right?"

Chad interrupted, "Gramps, your argument isn't with Lou. Leave her alone, please." He put his arm around his son. "If you came here to deal with us, then aim your barbs the correct direction."

JUST SAYING that unnerved Chad. There was no telling what the old man would do. Because he had money, he expected others to cater to him, and he ran right over them when the mood struck. He had certainly blindsided Chad by his comment about being Lou's lover. The unexpected jab had stung, although Chad knew it shouldn't have, not as deeply as it did, anyway.

Wally turned on Chad, and he snapped, "You need to keep that teenager of yours in line, young man. I spent the night on a filthy freighter to get out here. That dog! My God, there wasn't one kennel that would take the animal on such short notice. Do you have any idea how hard it was to arrange passage on a boat that would take that dog *and* had a copter to offload me to this rig?" He stomped his foot to make the dog jump, and she wrapped herself around Chad's legs.

"I'm sorry—" Chaddie's voice broke.

"Armenian!" The word blasted from the old man, running over his great-grandson's apology. "Everyone on that ship spoke Armenian. I had to have one of the sailors translate for me. I'm taking Chaddie home with me, and you're lucky, boy, if I don't press charges for kidnapping. You don't have custody, and you can't nab this boy anytime you want, even if you did have balls enough for one night to father him."

"Gramps," Chaddie interrupted. "I came on my own. Dad didn't have anything to do with it."

His great-grandfather skewered the boy with his gaze. "Chaddie, get your head on right. You telling me you hired passage on a freighter and got them to fly you over on their own private copter? How'd you get the money for that?"

CHADDIE LAUGHED nervously and looked to his father for help. How could Gramps think that? Chaddie didn't even know that was possible—well, he hadn't known that, not before now.

"I took the bus to Dad's house and came down with him. We rode out together in a Rampart helicopter from Galveston." He reached down to wrap his arms around his dog. "It's okay, Stinky. You won't fall." Glancing to his great-grandfather, he spoke up for the frightened animal, "She's scared, Gramps."

"My point, exactly, boy. You should be, too. You were brought here, obviously, and against your will." He pointed to the boy's father while keeping his eyes on his great-grandson. "You may have lied to get this man that you call your father to bring you here, but he knew better. You wanted to do the right thing, even if you did have a slip in judgement. You're in danger as long as you're on this derrick, too." He turned to Louinda, "How soon can I get this boy off this oil derrick?"

"WALLY," LOU began, but she quickly switched to his surname. Unwarranted familiarity with this man wouldn't serve her well during his visit. "Mr. Saunders, a derrick can only be found on land. I know. I worked them for years after my husband died."

Wally blew his cheeks out in disdain. His narrowed eyes only made her angrier.

She continued, "You're standing on an oil platform, an oil rig, if you will. We're nowhere near land. As you can

137

see, we don't maintain a helicopter on this rig. If you had difficulty getting to us, then you can imagine the difficulty we will have in getting you transportation back ashore. Maybe tomorrow. It might be the next. You can see the weather. It may be in two weeks. I have one other thing to tell you, Mr. Saunders. I have no place for you to spend the night."

He laughed at that. "I'll room with Chaddie. He'll take me. Also, it had better not be two weeks. I want off before this tropical storm hits. I caught that damned-fool idiot on the weather station with his Forecast on the Fives. The storm's coming right this way. This is a sad wreck of an oil derrick. I've lived in Oklahoma for more years than most, and even I can see that. It might just go down before it's over."

Lou glanced at Chaddie. She knew the storm system that was coming, even if she'd shaded her earlier response to the boy. She didn't know it had become tropical. It wasn't yet, at least not here. However, it wasn't fair to scare the boy unnecessarily, especially when he was supposed to have headed out today.

She groaned. She'd never called about that. Now she wouldn't, for sure. After what she'd just said to Chaddie's great-grandfather, she wouldn't call for a helicopter even if it meant she had to take an official reprimand for it. This man had insulted her, had insulted Chad, and had even insulted his own great-grandson. He needed to be put in his place.

Chaddie looked at her, and his face was frozen in disbelief. "It'll get worse? The weather out here? We won't blow down, will we, like Gramps said? You told me this wasn't a real storm, yet." It was clear his "Gramps" had sapped this boy's boundless enthusiasm for anything that had to do with being on an oil rig. He was deflated against the old man's roughness.

She reassured him. "Chaddie, I'll let you know when to worry. Otherwise, just stick with your father, and you'll be okay. Your dog, too, I guess." She wasn't sure about this animal on board. The situation had grown more and more bizarre by the minute. She turned to Mr. Saunders. "Rooming with your great-grandson might be a problem, sir, unless you want to share his bed. There's only one." She turned to see Chaddie's arms waving in a frantic attempt to interrupt her before she went any further. "What, Chaddie?"

His eyes jumped from his father's face to Lou's in a desperate bid for support. "I've already got a roommate. Right, Dad? I'm staying with you. Remember that mattress on the floor? That one's mine. Ben promised. You've got the bed, Dad, and I'm staying on the floor under the work table in the corner."

THE BOY'S face worked his question, pleading for his father to agree with his version of the situation, and Chad couldn't turn him down at this point. Not with Wally berating the boy to the point of abuse. Chaddie was correct, anyway, even if his timetable was off by a few hours. Ben *had* promised to deliver the mattress today.

However, that still didn't give the old man a place to spend the night. Wally couldn't possibly be allowed to sleep in Lou's room, not after Chad had spent the night in there tossing over his dreams of her and her coconut hair.

He didn't know how to resolve this, or if he even could. However, he had to try. The old man's vicious attack on Chaddie made one thing for sure. He and his son would be rooming together tonight, and if that left old Wally out in the cold, then he could sleep there and enjoy it.

Chad turned to Wally, and he watched the old man narrow his eyes as he spoke. "My son's right, Wally. When Chaddie showed up with me, Lou didn't have a bed for him, and we've had to put a mattress on the floor in my room." He didn't mention that he'd slept in Lou's bed last night. It was irrelevant and didn't change the *intent* of the truth. The previous night had simply been an emergency solution—one that was also very temporary—to an escalating emotional blowup. "Our room is very small, too. Lou's is even smaller. I have no idea what you're going to do." Chad glanced at his son and could see the obvious relief on his face.

As his son relaxed, Chad remembered what Lou had said. She was widowed. That explained a lot. It also meant she wasn't married. He felt a smile and fought to keep it from his face.

As Chad glanced back to Wally, the man turned, and disgust was written all over him.

WALLY FUMED. The small helicopter was gone from sight, Chaddie's sissy dog was at the boy's side, and the wind whistled through the thousands of openings in the oil rig, keening in the stronger gusts, and moaning when it settled back down. Then Chad's words came back to him. How did he know the size of this woman's room, this broad, this descendant of that hussy Wally had lusted after so many years ago?

Linda, damn her soul. She had made a fool of him, and he'd never gotten over that. Even after he took over his father's business and moved the management division to Dallas, there were nights when memories of that prom had come back to haunt him. It wasn't pretty. He remembered standing there as king, and in sweaty dreams, the mortification he had felt ran rampant over his emotions just as strongly as it had the night she'd walked out on him. She'd been *his*. She didn't have the *right* to just walk out.

For years he'd taken it out on the business, bolstering his ego by flinging money carelessly into new products and procedures, only slowing down once he'd run the business to tatters. However, he'd been smart to skim enough profits from the company's receipts to bail out with all the money he'd ever need. When he sold, the new owners were taken for a spin, the business tanking and declaring bankruptcy just a few years afterwards. He hadn't cared. Wally's bank accounts had survived just fine, and that was all that mattered.

Now, this woman, so much the same in her looks and even her speech, was doing it again, refusing to let him do what he'd come to do, and in the process, making a fool of him. Wally resolved one thing. He would humiliate this broad in retribution for what had occurred all those years ago. It might not be the same as making Linda pay, but it was the closest he was likely to ever get.

He turned to her, jabbing at her with his words, "Let's get this done. I need either transportation off his hellhole today or accommodations for tonight." His glare pierced Chaddie as he said his next words. "If my great-*grandson* has no space for me, then I'll take what you've got. Damn, it's awful out here. I'm getting inside." The old man turned to the steps, and without waiting, he began to stomp down them.

Louinda looked apologetically to the men at her side, and she shrugged. "I've got to go after him. Sorry." She paused for a moment before heading down the steps, and she turned back to Chad. She mouthed, "Lover?"

She took a deep breath, and her eyes narrowed, but there was no time to waste. She darted down one careful step after another to rein in the brutal man who had shown up to take Chad's son away.

CHAD TURNED at a touch on his arm.

"Dad? You won't let him, will you? Take me? I want to stay."

The boy's red-rimmed eyes looked like they were about to become fountains in his face, and he threw his arms around him and pulled him tight.

"No, Son," he said to him. "I'll fight to keep you here with me. I feel like I've just found you again, and if Gramps thinks he can break us apart, he needs to rethink his plans."

Chad was gratified to feel his son's arms wrap around him, too. This had been a long time coming, and while it was something he hadn't even known he was missing, now that he'd found it again, he wasn't about to let it go—or let a self-centered old egomaniac try to steal it away.

Chapter 8

WALLY LOOKED disparagingly at the equipment Lou pulled from the shelves. There were a green helmet, coveralls, and steel-toed boots. They were all stacked neatly on the counter, and he watched as she placed a pair of safety glasses inside the upturned helmet.

"I'm only here until a helicopter comes to retrieve me. The boy, too. I assure you I won't need these things."

She looked hard at the lined old face, and she remembered his tornado of words from the helipad with antagonism. She also remembered the word he'd used to describe her. It had been unthinking and cruel. *Lover.* She might have let herself be attracted to Chad, but she didn't really know him. Lovers? Not likely. Not yet, anyway. Besides, the man's thirteen-year-old son was here, and that was the only reason she'd initially given his father more than the cursory time of day. The ice had barely broken between them, and it could just as easily form again.

"Oh, and I have something you'll be interested to hear."

Lou looked up to see a smirk on Wally's face. She waited with disinterest for his comment.

"I slept with your grandmother, you know."

WALLY HAD desperately wanted to. Telling the truth wouldn't serve his purpose, though. He wanted to hurt this woman in the same way Linda had hurt him.

Lou's eyes riveted his, and she was very abrupt with her words, spitting them at him hard and fast. "So, I guess that means you're really my grandfather, and I should hug you in gratitude?"

He laughed. This woman *was* her grandmother, even in the tone of her response. He'd heard Linda say similar things in that exact voice. Then there were her looks. She was every bit his Linda from all those years ago. In more ways than he could count, she was his Linda. With her safety gear removed, he'd seen that even more strongly than he had outside. It was in her movements and the color of her hair, and in the way she pressed her lips together when he jabbed her with his verbal barbs. His old man's body felt a surge of physical response that took him back once again, and he was in high school all over again.

"I'd take that hug from you, granddaughter, if you wanted to give it. I might take a little more, too. How about some of what that man out there's been getting? *Lou's room is even smaller. Did you think I didn't catch that?*

144

How would he know? I suspect that boy's father has spent a few nights in there with you. You're probably the reason for his divorce from my granddaughter." Wally chuckled, and it was coarse and mean. "Chaddie's mother told me of all the nights he came home with the smell of other women on him. I guess you could have been one of them, too. Oklahoma City's not too far from Fort Worth. I've made that drive a few times from Dallas just for a little nookie."

Wally smirked at her. Irritating this woman and getting under her skin was turning out to be very satisfying. If he had the time, he'd like to try more. Young women were especially interesting, fresh flesh for an engaging evening. He'd have to decide if he could manage that in the few hours he had before he intended to be off this derrick. It was a challenge he was certainly up to, if he could work it in.

In addition, he gloated over something else. He'd seen this woman tense up when he lied to her about Chad's alleged indiscretions. The divorce? That had been his granddaughter, no different than when she was a teenager, coming home with the smell of all her boyfriends on her. This time, he'd suspected Chip even before Chad had run. Then the woman's quick remarriage sealed the old man's assumptions airtight.

It had served Chad right, though. If the weakling wasn't man enough to hold on to a beautiful woman like his granddaughter, then he deserved to be cuckolded. Chip had been the man to do it, and Wally had been glad to help him out, financially as well as by funding the best lawyer in the state to handle the divorce proceedings. If pressed, he'd lie about all that, though. He'd become very polished at doing so back in high school while bedding the cheer-leading squad at the same time he was attempting to get under Linda's skirt.

He was still good at it, too.

LOU glared at the old man. She tried to slough off what he'd said. She really did. Chad had begun to open up to her, and she'd seen charm there, the same charm that his son possessed in abundance. Still, she didn't intend to tolerate being made into a woman of loose morals in the process.

It was also very clear why Chaddie wanted to spend the month with his father instead of his great-grandfather. Chad was only partially correct in his assessment of this man. He wasn't just exasperating; he was mean and spiteful. For that alone, she would stand up for the boy's father in front of him.

"Sir, your great-grandson's father has been very cir-cumspect with me during his time here. There's nothing untoward going on, no matter what you might try to sug-gest." Her words carried a bite that she hoped would set the old man on his ear. Still, while she would like to say he'd never been in her room, she couldn't. After all, he'd spent the previous night there. She just hadn't been in there with him.

She knew men like Wally, though. He would believe only what he wanted to believe.

He sneered. "He would be proper, wouldn't he? After all, his son's here to see everything. It wouldn't do for the boy to go home to my granddaughter telling how his father's been sneaking out at night and bedding loose women on the oil derrick, while Chaddie's supposedly asleep in the room they share. The boy's father may be firing on two cylinders where his wick's concerned, but he's not stupid. Not in this, apparently."

"Don't be disgusting." She glanced at the door, wishing she wasn't alone with this man. This could get ugly.

He winked at her suggestively. "Shore leave might be different, huh? You do call it shore leave, I suppose. Or, maybe a better word would be rendezvous. Yes, that might work. Sexual rendezvous. I bet there are times you don't mind traveling all the way to Fort Worth for your jollies. Or maybe some visits, he comes to Galveston. You two hole up for a week or two, and the world goes away in non-marital bliss. That's how I'd do it, I can tell you that."

He snorted in laughter as he flicked the thumbnail on one hand against another finger. He frowned as if he found a rough spot he thought he'd already smoothed out. He said, casually, as if to himself, "That would explain all those weekends the man refused to take the boy, spouting drivel about working." His eyes jumped to catch hers. "I see the picture clear as day. He's been working you, sure, and the only tool he needed was the one God gave him. You're just another in a long line, honey."

Lou had heard enough. She'd heard plenty several comments back, but learning to let barbs roll off her back was rig policy. This was a closed society, and small hurts could easily turn into injuries—and even death, if left to fester. However, there were times to draw the line.

"*Honey,*" she started in an acid tone that brooked no nonsense. "You've overstepped your bounds. You need to take a cold shower before you go any further. What goes on in my private time is none of your business." She was angry now and didn't intend to reveal anything to him, even in denial. He'd insulted her in every way he possibly could, from her much-loved granny to her own purported nighttime exploits, and she'd not honor that with even a barbed rebuttal.

There were other barbs she could throw, though. She had a well-deserved reputation for cutting witticisms, and if he pushed her, she would. However, for now, unable to look at this disgusting man any longer, she turned to the shelves at her back and began to straighten the items she'd moved when pulling out gear for him.

WALLY HEARD the spite in her words, and he'd be damned if he'd let it pass. It was what Linda always used to say to him, and the very expression made him boil in frustration and anger.

It also made him more determined.

He stepped to the woman, and he reached a hand around her. In a quick motion, he cupped his fingers and pulled her to him. He wanted her to feel him against her and know that he wanted her. It was like being a kid again. He hadn't had his hands on a woman this young, especially one with this much spunk, in a decade or more. His nerve endings danced with anticipation.

Louinda whipped around, and in one swift motion, her hand met the side of his face, biting into his flesh. Her words hissed from her as she blasted her rage. "You old reprobate! Your grandson ran as far from you as he could get, and I can certainly see why. You keep that *thing* between your legs away from me, and as far as my grandmother? If she ever slept with you, then at least she had the good sense not to marry you afterwards. And if I'm in any way related to you, then with God as my witness, I renounce you and curse the day you impregnated anyone in my family line."

With fire flashing, her hand once again jumped, and a second time, all five fingers landed firmly on the old man's face in nearly the same spot.

After she flung herself out the door, Wally chuckled and put his hand to his face. She had quite a wallop, and he figured he would have a mark to show for it. Also, the boy was his great-grandson. She was wrong about that. However, if it took twenty years off him in her eyes, he'd take the boy as a grandson in a heartbeat.

He looked at the gear she'd laid out for him. He scoffed as he picked it up. It was useless, as far as he was concerned, especially if he was expected to haul it around. Now, he was hungry, and he had to find food. There must be some place on this derrick to get something to eat.

Exiting the room and heading out, he found a door labeled mess hall. He laughed. Oil derrick or not, it was a dining room, and he'd call it a damn dining room if he wanted, even if it wasn't that to anyone else on this rig.

Finding a table that was empty, he set his things down, and he remembered one thing in particular about Chad's new girlfriend. Her hair smelled like coconut, and that was what he always bought his granddaughter when she was younger. Coconut. The smell of it in a woman's hair always did this to him, every time. That and fiery attitude. Coconut and fiery women.

The combination made heat churn in his blood.

He belched, the effluent sour and hard in his throat. He took a deep breath and pressed a fist to his chest, hoping it wasn't indigestion. At nearly eighty, his doctor had told him to go easy on the strenuous activities. However, a beautiful woman wasn't strenuous. *Invigorating* was the word Wally would use. Besides, nothing *strenuous* had happened. He'd grabbed her, pulled her to him, and smelled her hair. Her anger? That was what all women did, a ploy to make a man want them more. His doctor back in Dallas could go flog himself. He was doing just fine, and today he felt like a teen again. If his chest burned a little bit, then that was a small price to pay for his youth given back to him.

He also wanted something to eat. In high school, he'd lived on Mexican, the hotter the better. Something hot and spicy would do him fine.

Finding occupied tables but no food, Wally sighed. He would have to rummage his own. Prowling, he located the galley, and one refrigerated cabinet was marked snacks. He opened it and pulled out several things, more than he'd normally eat in one sitting. If he could finagle an assignation as he hoped, he'd need the extra energy, and he planned to be ready. To be sure, he took an extra item that was wrapped in foil but smelled too good to leave behind, and he carried it with the others he had already chosen to the table where he'd set his safety gear.

Digging in, he looked to see a shadow blocking the overhead light. A gruff voice accosted him. "Looks like you crossed a woman, there." A chuckle accompanied the words.

Wally nodded then turned his attention back to his food

and growled, "Yeah, but she was pretty. That made it worth it. You work here?"

The man laughed. "Can I sit?" Before Wally could respond, he pulled out a chair and fell into it. "Name's Torch. Torch McGee."

"Torch? That a real name?" Wally was chewing, and he forced the words out between bites.

"Welder by trade."

Wally motioned to the food spread on the table, "Do they always make people get their own food? I expected a waitress."

"You're new." Torch laughed. "Nah, no waitress, not that I've ever seen. Then, I'm only on for a job out on the derrick. I'll be back to my outfit soon's I get a ride."

Wally hit the table with his free hand, startling both Torch as well as a man sitting several tables over. "By God, I knew it! This *is* a derrick after all."

Torch smiled. "Not exactly. There's a derrick up topside, because I've been welding on it. However, this is a drilling platform, an oil production platform, if I want to be accurate. This one's just not in especially good repair." He leaned over the table to tap it with his finger as he shared his next point. "You see, I rove from rig to rig—on call, as it were—and I see this one more than just about any other. I'm surprised it didn't come down back in '08. Ike, wasn't it?"

The hand hit the table again, and the food items jumped. So did Torch. "Didn't I say it? I said it to them, and they laughed at me. I don't want to be here when this storm hits." Wally narrowed his eyes and picked up the foil-wrapped package. He finally decided that it smelled like sausage, and although his doctor had made him swear off the fatty foods, he loved sausage. "Gotta get my boy off and back to Dallas."

Torch chuckled and reached a hand out. "You are, sir?"

Wally wiped his hand on his pants and reached to shake. "Wally. Wally Saunders. I go by Gramps, though. How do you get from derrick to derrick?"

"Rig to rig? Mostly by supply ship, unless there's an emergency or the weather's too bad. Then they radio in. Some of the bigger rigs keep a small copter. Others like this one have to work it out to borrow when they can. I wait for rides a lot. Like now, I'm through here, and when the next ship comes in, I've got a job out on Cracker's Barrel."

"Cracker's Barrel?" Wally snorted. "What's Cracker's Barrel?"

Torch grinned. "It's my favorite platform. It's where I got my start on these rigs—and the reason why I go by Torch." Leaning back, he continued his narration. "I was an apprentice there. I wasn't supposed to be on that rig— by myself, being just an apprentice, mind you—but there I was. They needed me, and there wasn't anyone else to do the job. I was welding away, thinking I was all the man, and then boom! I hit a gas line that wasn't exactly cleared of gas, and I got torched. Get it? That's why I have no eyebrows, either. They never grew back. The word got around, and none of the crews let me live it down." He chuckled. "I get special desserts by all the cooks, though. That's nice. Flambé this and flambé that. Baked Alaska. That one's my favorite."

"Baked Alaska, huh?" Wally was halfway through his

selection of snacks, and he could see he'd taken far more than he could eat. "Do you want any of this?"

Torch shook his head. "The rest of us just ate, so throw away what you don't want. Tell me about the handprint on your face. It's still pretty red. I'd like to know what happened, if you want to talk about it."

"It's a long story—sixty years long. You got lots of time?"

"Told ya', Gramps," Torch said. "I'm waiting for a supply ship. That's my ride to Cracker's Barrel. I've got all the time in the world."

Wally pushed his uneaten food away, and he adjusted his chair before beginning. He liked having an audience, someone who actually wanted to hear him spin his yarns. This was a real whopper, too. It had just enough truth to make it believable. In this story, Wally was the wronged suitor, and all the one-night stands, from that first conquest during his freshman year in the high school locker room, to bedding the entire cheerleading squad, were forced on him by beautiful and wanton women.

He also told of vying for the affections of a high school girl, and how he'd just found the granddaughter who was his old sweetheart made over again.

"Lou," Torch said with a snort of derisive laughter. "So, you put the moves on Lou. Be careful, Gramps. It's all over the rig. She's sweet on that new guy, Chad Dickson. She'll pull your balls off if you mess with her."

Wally chuckled. "She's made that very clear to me, although not in those words. I have no doubt she'd do it, too. However, an old man can hope." It was feeling young again that Wally remembered even more. That only came

153

with close proximity to youth, and female youth, at that. He wanted to be eighteen again, if only for a night.

He'd also seen how Linda's granddaughter had thrown up her protective wings around Chaddie's father earlier, and he'd watched Chad try to divert Wally's barbs away from her. There was something going on between those two, he was certain. If a little hanky-panky wasn't there yet, there certainly would be soon, if something didn't get in the way.

Well, for a taste of that woman's charms, Wally was certain he could be the one to get in the way. He'd have to be hard and fast, if he wanted to be successful. His first step? He had to convince Chad that this woman was what Wally wanted to make her into: something no better than all the other women Wally'd bamboozled over the years. He smiled at that, picturing Linda and all the years he'd wanted to make that woman pay.

Now was his chance, and he wouldn't let it pass him by.

THE SPEAKERS above the radio console whispered an ongoing stream of words. Yolanda had a satellite feed from Houston tied in, and with the weather outside, it was on a frequency that spouted weather full time. She wanted to hear the Forecast on the Fives. Houston was important to her, because that's where most of the people on the rig connected with the mainland. Then, there were food shipments, and of course the Coast Guard, in case of emergencies. It all centered on Houston.

It was only a vocal feed, but she could imagine the rest.

However, over the years, the erratic volume of incoming transmissions had split one speaker, and when played too loudly, it gave off an irritating buzz. There was no buzz, today, and there was also no one at the console when the Forecast on the Fives broke through the latest edition of Weather in the News. When someone tapped on her door, Yolanda stepped outside to see what they wanted. Then, the conversation veered to the newly arrived visitors. Since there were no urgent radio transmissions to send out, and none expected in, there was no reason to end the discussion prematurely, either.

The radio went on without her.

"And now we take you to the Forecast on the Fives. Expect winds to pick up today as a low pressure system off the Florida coast moves through the Gulf. Temperatures are forecast to be in the upper 80s in Galveston but closer to 95 in downtown Houston. Expect lows to fall to near 80 in the early evening hours. Tomorrow should be cooler and blustery with a 100 percent chance of rain.

"Already boaters offshore are being cautioned to swing wide of this storm. As you can see, this system is tracking to the north, but another system coming west over northern Florida could push it directly into us. Stay tuned to Weather in the News for the latest updates and developments.

"Now to Ramie Zarhaire in Galveston. Ramie, I understand businesses along the Galveston Seawall are taking this potential threat seriously. You're there now. What do you see?"

"Rich, we can already feel the wind increasing. As you can see behind me, people are packing up. It's been a perfect beach day, but no longer. The Galveston County

Office of Emergency Management, however, hopes this storm will pass them by. With Hurricane Ike still a vivid memory for many Galveston residents, it won't surprise me to see a voluntary evacuation order in effect before the day is out.

"This is Ramie Zarhaire with KHOU in Galveston."

AGAINST the big machines making up the perimeter of the exposed deck, only the shoulders and lower body of a man could be seen, but they could belong to just one person.

"Ben? Ben Tosh?" Chad hardly thought this could be anyone else. Yesterday when they'd met, he'd been very aware that this was the biggest man he thought he'd ever seen. He'd been a head taller than any other man in the mess hall, and his shoulders were twice as wide. Right now those shoulders were all Chad could see, assuring him this was who he'd been searching for.

Ben drew his arms out of the machine he was repairing and looked to see the father and son he'd met the night before. His sudden grin, however, was for the new member of the party. His eyes sparkled as he began to speak.

"Why, that dog's blacker than me. A Rottie?"

Chaddie gave a pull on the dog's leash. "Yes, sir. I call her Stinky. She's scared out here. She pees herself a lot when she's scared."

"Let her come over, boy. Unleash her." When Chaddie looked questioningly at his father, Ben belted out, "Where can she go?" He swept his arms wide. They were high on the rig and mostly safe from the sea spray, although the wind whistled by them. Ben's clothes buffeted his solid

156

frame. "This is an oil rig. There's water everywhere. Surely your dog's smart enough not to jump in the sea."

Chaddie laughed. "I don't know about that. She's peed herself three times already."

Ben knelt to clap his hands gently, calling the dog to him. "Let her go, boy. She'll come to me."

Chaddie looked at his father again, and at a nod, he unclipped the leash. Stinky looked up at him hesitantly, then she ducked her head and faced the man calling her.

"Go on, Stinky." Chaddie gave her a little shove.

With her tail between her legs, she began to move that way. Then, picking up speed, she ran directly into Ben's hands. The big dog looked back at Chaddie and began to wag her tail.

"You're good," Chaddie congratulated Ben. "She never does that with anyone."

Ben stood and laughed, and it was deep and rich. "Black and black go together." He chuckled at his joke, the sound resonant in the open air of the rig. "What can I do for you two?"

"Dad?" Chaddie looked at his father.

Chad smiled and prompted his son. "Ask him, Chaddie. You know what you need. I think you can trust Ben, and remember how much you liked him last night?"

Ben's deep voice took over. "What is it, son? You need help with something?" He ran his hand over the Rottweiler's head. "Dog-sitting, perhaps?" He grinned at that, and his white teeth flashed against his coal-black skin.

Adjusting his safety glasses, Chaddie cleared his throat. "My gramps is here. That's how Stinky got on the rig."

A laugh barked from Ben's throat. "That's a good thing, I should imagine. A grandfather and a great-looking dog like this." Just then, the Rottweiler tensed up, and a whistle of escaping gas could be heard over the sound of the wind. Stinky's legs began to quiver, and her tail dropped between her hindquarters. Ben raised his eyebrows. "That was the dog?"

Chaddie smiled. "That's how she got her name. The sound scares her when she does that. Just pat her on the head, and she'll be okay. As far as Gramps, that's not so good. I need your bed."

"My bed? Where will I sleep?" Ben's face threatened to erupt into another smile. "Does the dog get to share with me, now?" He chuckled again. "Or me with her? Is that it?"

Chaddie looked at his father for help. Chad understood perfectly. The boy's great-grandfather and the dog, then he'd lied about sharing a room with his father. Chad had gone along, but the boy knew his words had been no more than hope when he'd said them. Now Ben had to come through so it could all be true.

"The extra bed from my room. You said you know where it's stored. We need to retrieve it for Chaddie. My boy wants to sleep in my quarters with me. Right, Son?"

The boy breathed a sigh of relief and grinned. "Please, Ben? You said you could. It's really important."

Ben gave him a mock salute. "Let me close this winch up. Five minutes ought to do it."

"Can I watch?" At Ben's nod, Chaddie moved closer. "What does it do?"

"See that boom?" The big man pointed to a framework

that extended over the water. "Burnoffs happen out there. When a new well comes in, there'll be a well flow test. The gas'll be flared with a water deluge curtain to protect the rig. This motor lets us adjust the boom to allow for the wind direction."

The boy's face brightened. "Are we fixing to have one of those, a flare off? That'd be cool to watch."

Ben chuckled as he wrenched the final few bolts into place. "Not without this motor operational. If we have one while you're here, I'll be sure to let you know." Standing and holding the wrench he'd been using, he looked at Chaddie appraisingly. "You're not really from Boulder, are you?"

Chaddie frowned. "Sure I am. I live there."

Ben looked at him askance as if he knew more than the boy thought. "*Fixing to* is Texan if I ever heard it. Did I hear that your dad's from Fort Worth?"

The boy's grin was back. "Oh, sure. I grew up in Dallas. Well, sometimes in Fort Worth, too. Westover Hills, really. My gramps has a house there. We still stay in it sometimes when we come to visit from Boulder. It's going to be mine, someday." He looked at his father who was standing off to the side, with his hand on Stinky's head, looking out to sea.

Chad was preoccupied. He had other things to think about, such as Wally, and how he was going to avoid the man for the next few days. Listening to the boy's voice drone on formed little more than background noise that washed over him, the facts already known and let go of as soon as they were said.

"My dad lives there, too. Highland Park. His town-

159

house is in Westover Hills, also, but you've probably never heard of the Fort Worth Highland Park. No one has. It's not the same Highland Park where my great-aunt lives in Dallas."

Ben laughed at the boy's list of places. "Hey, there. Slow down. I'm doing good to know where Fort Worth and Dallas are. Make this easy on me. Now, let's get your father and go get you a bed. We'll have to have some plastic to wrap it with to keep it dry when we move it into the accommodations block, but we can do that. I know where to find as much as we need."

"Great! Thanks, Ben. Dad," Chaddie called to his father. "We're ready. Guess what? I get to watch if they do a well flow test. There'll be a water thing, um, del—"

Chaddie stumbled over the missing word, and Ben's deep voice gave him assistance with, "Deluge curtain."

"—water deluge curtain to keep the rig safe and everything. There'll be fire and more. Won't that be cool?" He bent down to grab Stinky around the neck, still looking at his father. "It'll be just like a bomb going off."

Chad turned, giving the boy his attention, and he raised his hand to slow the boy's enthusiasm. He smiled. "I saw them do that yesterday while the helicopter was coming in. I don't remember the water, though."

"I didn't see a fire." The boy frowned as he tried to remember anything like that.

At Chaddie's perplexed look, Chad reminded him, "You were playing your game in the helicopter."

His son's face fell. "That flash of orange light? I didn't even look up. Dad, why didn't you tell me?"

Ben laughed as he encouraged him not to be too disappointed. "That wasn't a real test, boy. That's why I was working on that winch motor back there. The boom wouldn't adjust yesterday, and the crew was working out issues for the one that's coming up. Be patient. A real one is on the way. You'll get to see it. Now, let's take that dog of yours and find you a bed. Might even get Lou to dog-sit while we do this."

Chad agreed, looking pointedly at his son. "Let's. I'm taking mine back from you tonight." He grabbed his son by the neck and squeezed. "It was hard sleeping in a strange woman's room last night."

Ben's voice rumbled, "Oh? Lou's mattress is one of the best on the rig. She brought it out herself."

Chad turned to see Ben wink at him, and he waved his son to move on ahead.

"It wasn't the bed. My back was comfortable, but my brain wasn't."

"Oh? That means?" The words seemed to be filled with laughter.

Chad knew exactly what he meant. "It was the way it smelled."

Ben's voice prodded him. "Was that a good thing or a bad thing? I always like the way Lou smells. I sorta thought her bed would smell good, too."

"That was the problem. It smelled just like her. That was what bothered my brain."

"Are you sure it was your brain that was bothered? Your thinking brain? Or was it your other brain, the one that's not in your head? That's the one most young men think with." He clasped Chad on the shoulder, and with a gentle slap, he guided him after his son.

161

Chad chuckled. He was finding he liked Ben, and he wasn't offended by his teasing. He also suspected this man was a better friend to Lou than any other person on the platform. He glanced at his son to find him grinning back, throwing his father a quick thumbs-up sign before he snapped on Stinky's collar and began to dance away.

Chad mused that maybe there was hope for father and son, after all.

Chapter 9

CHADDIE HELD the door while his father and Ben wrestled the mattress inside. Once inside, Ben pulled the plastic off and carried the spray-splattered sheeting to the shower to drip into the drain. The boy popped his earplugs out, and then pulled his helmet and glasses off.

Grinning, he turned to his father. "A bed, Dad. It's the truth, now, what we said earlier." Excitement poured from him. "We're both sharing the same room. Gramps will have to go home."

"I will, will I?" The words coming through the door were gruff, a sharp-edged cocklebur intended to bring Chaddie down to size. The old man stepped inside. "I don't see your dog. Where's the peeing bitch? Did she jump off the derrick, already?" Looking around, Wally laughed, and the sound wasn't pleasant. "So, now I see how it is. Even my great-grandson has been lying behind my back. Where'd you sleep last night, Chaddie? It doesn't seem it was in here, or I wouldn't see this mattress just being set up. What's going on between you two? Your father might lie to me, but you'd better tell me the truth, if you know what's good for you. Got me, boy?"

Faced with the rasping threat, especially from Gramps, panic filled Chaddie's face, and he turned frantically to his father.

"Just answer the question, Son." Chad nodded at him, gently prodding him to be truthful.

The boy's voice quavered. "In here, Gramps. It was just like I told you."

"Not quite, boy." Wally looked as if he were peeling an onion, determined to know just what was what, no matter the grief he stirred along the way. It was as if he seemed to enjoy making the boy uncomfortable. "You said you had a mattress on the floor. What were you doing just now? Airing it out? It's wet outside, you know." The old man chuckled meanly at that.

Chad took the time to remove his safety gear before stepping into the interrogation. "What do you actually want, Wally? Does it really matter to you where anyone slept last night? You show up here uninvited, and you have to know every detail. I don't understand that. What's in it for you?"

WALLY SNORTED. It mattered, because he wanted Louinda for his own, if he could get her. He wanted to do to her what he'd never been able to do to her grandmother.

He would, too, if he could keep this man's nose out of the picture.

However, before he got too involved, Wally had to make sure he wasn't interrupting a sexual dalliance already in progress. While he wanted her, he didn't want her at the same time as his ex-grandson-in-law. If hanky-panky was already in play, he needed to kill it—even though driving them apart before it got started would be better. And if, just if he couldn't kill what was in progress, he wanted to ruin what she did have.

He turned on Chaddie, shifting gears from the bed for the moment. "Boy, I already asked you once. Where's your dog? I didn't bring her out so people could just throw her off the side."

Chad frowned as he interrupted the cross-examination before his son could answer. "With Lou. Chaddie dropped her off a short time ago."

This was his opportunity, and Wally sneered, "So, who's going to pick up the dog? You, Chad? Stay a long time, and tell your son you were just visiting? Maybe take the time for a little recreation? What about tonight? How long will it take Chaddie to get to sleep?" He chuckled cruelly, putting his foot on the bed and leaning forward with an elbow on one knee. He used one hand for emphasis. "Here. Let me help you out. Plan your little rendezvous for one in the morning. Little Chaddie here always goes lights-out by midnight. You wouldn't know that, of course, since you've spent the past three years refusing to see him. Better yet, I'll spend the night in here, and you can head on over to Ms. Reinhardt's bed. That'll be even easier. You won't have to worry about getting back before Chaddie here wakes up. It'll be aboveboard, and we'll all know just who's bedding whom."

"Dad!" Chaddie looked at his father frantically, only to see him dumbstruck with the old man's audacity. When Chad didn't respond, his son pressed him to take action. "Dad, tell him to stop."

"Shut up, boy," Wally barked. "Your father knows better than to contradict me. He's not man enough, just like he wasn't man enough to keep your mother." Wally had already gone further than he intended. Chad had taken multiple blows below the belt, and hard, too, and in front of his son, but the old man's need for revenge against Linda—as well as his desire for Louinda—was greater than his concern for anyone in this room, even his great-grandson. His hand was on the sword, and he enjoyed the thought of driving it deep. Then he would twist it until the man bled.

Wally turned to Chaddie, leering his disdain for the boy's father, and barking in punctuated tones, "Your father knew Chip was in your mother's bed long before they divorced. Isn't that right, Chad? It was happening almost daily while you were at work, and you knew every time. You deserved it, too, everything that happened to you."

"Dad?" Chaddie's eyes were red with impending tears as he begged his father to stand up to this man and the accusations he was making. "Dad, is it true?"

CHAD FELT the energy he might have fought this with drain away in the harsh reality of Wally's words. The old man was right. He had loved Chaddie's mother, at least at the beginning. Then, she had changed, and Chip hadn't been the first—or the only one. Chad wanted to work it out, though, and even with Chip, he had hoped, hadn't wanted the divorce to happen. Then, finally, when the dalliances hadn't stopped, Chad just hadn't cared any longer.

For it to be laid out so baldly in front of his son, in front of the world, was to rip away his self-respect, leaving him once again the broken man he'd tried to live with the past three years. He looked at Chaddie, the boy crumbling under Wally's assault, and he didn't know what to say. He felt his mind shutting down, and he knew he'd be a mess if this kept up much longer. He cringed when Wally jacked his tirade up a notch, sending Chad reeling even more.

"That woman you've been with is waiting for you. I was just there. She said you're just another john, so be sure to bring her money. She'll be looking for you. She said something about coconut, too. Shampoo or body lotion or something. What was that about, Chad? I'd be more specific, except my great-grandson is listening, and he doesn't need to know any more details concerning what you intend to do with that loose woman. You know, now that I see the picture as clearly as I do, it might be better if you and Ms. Reinhardt just wait until I take Chaddie home tomorrow. Then you can do whatever you want to that bimbo without the boy having to know what you do or how much you pay her."

A deep voice rumbled from the bathroom, "I can't listen to any more of this." Ben stepped into the room, his massive bulk shifting the tenor of the conversation, and it grew quiet. He looked at the three faces turned to him. "Chaddie, do you know where Lou and Stinky are?" When the boy nodded, Ben said, "Go there. Your father will come for you when he's ready. Tell Lou that."

When the red-eyed boy was gone, Ben turned to Wally. "You are a tyrant, sir, and this rig'll be better when you're gone. I have no place to send you except out of this room."

Wally snorted his derision. "I don't know you, and you can't send me anywhere. Leave if you want, but I don't intend to."

Ben groaned and muttered to himself, "Why do old, white men always think they rule by right?" He walked up to Wally and looked down at him. "Sir, you need to leave now, and I'm asking you to do so without another word." The closer Ben edged to him, the more Wally backed up, until he finally turned and stormed out the door, slamming it after him.

Chad sat hard on the bed, barely getting out, "Thank you, Ben." Wally, he now remembered, had been a large part of the problem all those years ago. Chad had boxed up all that with the other issues from the divorce and put it far away in the back of his mind. He'd refused to look at it since. Yet, when Wally had started his tirade, that first tug at the lid of Chad's box had caused it all to erupt as fresh as the day of the divorce.

Now all he could see was Wally, and Chad was trapped with the most hateful person he'd ever known. The worst part? There was no escape, and his son had been forced to watch the lashing begin.

BEN ONLY saw that Chad had caved under the old man's assault, and he'd seen the hits the boy was taking. He liked this man, and he liked his son. Ben had also seen that Lou

168

more than liked this man, and that meant Ben was involved.

"What was that all about?" Ben's kept his voice low and mellow, but he also put steel in it. "You let that man say mighty awful things about you, and you didn't deny a one of them. Are they true?"

Chad didn't look up. "Some of them. The ones about my son's mother. All that happened at the end, and I couldn't stop it." He sat looking at the floor, and then he continued in a whisper, "About Lou? I wasn't going to . . . I mean, we haven't made those plans . . . Ben, she wouldn't have told him that, would she?" He looked up, and Ben just shook his head in disgust.

"I know you don't know Lou like I do, but for you to even doubt her is too much for me to listen to. If you can't trust her, then you need to leave her alone. She doesn't deserve that. Your boy needs you, though. He needs you to stand up for him against his grandfather. That man's quite a piece of work for your boy to have to live with."

Chad coughed and continued, his voice drained of emotion. "I can't defend what he just did, but he's not always this bad. Yeah, you're reading him on the money, and he does run over people, but something's set him off." Chad stood. "You're right, though, about my boy. Thanks, Ben. Gramps threw me for a loop, and I cannot believe I just stood there." Then, as if a switch were suddenly thrown, Chad grimaced and hit his forehead hard with the heel of his palm. "Chaddie! How could I do that, let him stand there and listen to all that? My God, I'm an idiot!"

Ben grasped his arm, and the steel in his voice stopped Chad's tirade. "No, man. Don't beat yourself up. You're not an idiot. An idiot doesn't know he's made a mistake. You already know it, and you're on the way to fix it. Get your boy, and I'll do what I can with his grandfather. I can't promise, but I'll do my best to keep him away."

A frown crossed Chad's face as he moved towards the door. "And if you can't? What should I do? Gramps bested me just then, but he is Chaddie's great-grandfather. I don't want to hurt my son any worse than what he just endured."

Ben rumbled out his best advice in a kinder voice. "Family. Your son comes first. Don't lose that boy, no matter what else you have to give up."

"THANKS, BEN," Chad said, letting out a long-held breath, as he remembered the past three years. He put his hand on the safety gear still resting in his helmet. "I should have learned that already, and I'm glad you put me back on the right track." He took a deep breath, wishing he had put Gramps in his place in front of his son. He couldn't go back, though. He had to fix this while moving ahead. "You'd make a good friend to anyone who crossed your path, and I hope I didn't mess up the chance for you to be mine. About Lou, I didn't mean—"

"You said it quick, though. It was there in your mind, and you can't love someone you can't trust." Ben looked hard at Chad, and the iron was back in his voice. "It'll be best if you let her alone during your time on the rig."

Chad chewed his lip for a moment, feeling a rush of denial, then he reached and shook the big man's hand. "I understand," and then Ben was alone.

WITH A QUICK shove, Ben pushed the mattress under

the table, and he paused to look around the room. "Sorry, Lou," he said to the emptiness around him. "I thought this one might be the man to crack through your shell. I thought he had, too. He doesn't believe in you, though. You can't love a man who doesn't believe in you, no matter how hard you try. Let this one go, Lou. If you can hear me, let this one go. He's not the one for you."

Ben stepped out and shut the door behind him. He had errands to complete. He had to warn Lou, and he had that old man to keep under control. What a mess this day had become! Now all he needed was for the weather to get worse. Then, they could all go to the bottom of the ocean in a handbag, and no one would be able to put the sky back together again.

Sorry, Chicken Little, Ben thought. *That's just the way life plays itself out, sometimes.*

THE FACT is that a dog's love can't be bought. It has to be earned. Some dogs give it easily, and others, well, they don't like to give it at all. The big black Rottweiler was the first kind.

Stinky was easy to love, and Lou could see the animal gave the love back just as easily. She sat on her bed and pressed the black dog's backside down with her hand.

"Sit!" The command came smoothly to Lou, and after only a few tries, the big dog did exactly as she asked. She was so willing to obey, and all for a few words of praise.

In the supply room, Lou had been incredibly insulted by Chaddie's great-grandfather. As she returned to her quarters, she'd been furious with all those on the ship who didn't belong, and that included Chad and his son.

Then, the boy had brought the dog by for her to watch, and she'd prepared to spew out the sharp retort already on her tongue. In that moment, she realized that the boy hadn't been the one to proposition her. He was still the bright and charming thirteen-year-old who had come aboard just the day before. He had smiled at her, and his eyes had been infectious. His quick tale of his enthusiasm at getting his own bed in his father's room had softened her anger, and she had readily agreed to keep the animal while they retrieved the missing mattress.

The old man had also said several very harsh things against Chad. Even as she played with the dog, teaching her some simple commands, she evaluated just how she needed to move forward on this. Should she trust the old man's words, words she couldn't prove, or should she trust her heart, and possibly put herself in harm's way? She had a good life, and she had a family back in Oklahoma. She still prayed sometimes, although not much since Tracy was killed. Her family continued to pray for her, though. They told her so every time she talked with them.

After one especially complicated command was obeyed correctly, Lou simply knelt and wrapped her arms around the black dog. She buried her face in the animal's fur, and she held on for several minutes, needing the feeling of warmth against her skin. It wasn't quite the touch that her Tracy had given her, but it was the best she had at the moment.

When she pulled back, she laughed and looked the dog in the eyes. "Girl, you're better than people think you are. You've helped me decide. I should let the man prove himself. I've been able to trust everything else about him. The old man that insulted the both of us is the bad seed, isn't he?"

When the knock came at her door, it was Chaddie, and he was nearly in tears. At first he didn't want to come in, and when he finally did, he kept his head turned from her.

"Chaddie, what's wrong?" The boy acted as if *she* had done something. She couldn't think of what, but there was certainly something that had gotten to him. "Chaddie, is it your father?"

He did look at her then, and his eyes were tormented. Red rimmed the skin around them. He looked like he was about to cry, perhaps even had been crying, and Lou was crushed. In one day, she had learned to love this boy, even as she'd seen his emotions vacillate wildly. In that time, he had never refused to talk to her. She'd been able to make a comment or suggest a series of humorous actions, and he'd come right out of his mood.

Then came another knock. Walking as if pins and needles covered the floor, she brushed Stinky's head for comfort and stepped to the door. When she saw Chad, she was certain he could explain.

"Something's wrong with Chaddie." She turned to look at the boy standing in the room with her. "He won't talk to me, and I don't know what's the matter. Come in and see if you can help, Chad. Please." She stepped back to let him in, but he just stood and drew in a deep breath. Releasing it in a heart-rending sigh, he called to his son.

"Chaddie, do you have Stinky?" He turned away. "We need to get to my room to work things out."

She was shocked. He couldn't just walk away from her. She stepped into the corridor to force him to talk to her. She'd been accosted in the supply room, and her inner reservoir of strength was cracked, and severely, too. She was barely holding herself together, and her determination to give Chad the benefit of the doubt against the old man's words was fragile at best. It had taken her five years to begin to open her heart to another man, and to be rebuffed so soon was taking the life from her.

She placed her hand on Chad's arm. "Talk to me. Is it something I've done? If so, I don't know what."

He just shook his head, his mouth pressed in a tight line. Then he turned his head away before speaking. "My son and I need to talk in private, that's all. Ben can explain everything else to you. I hope we can still work together after all this is done." Then the boy and the dog stepped by her, and she was left standing alone outside her room.

She leaned her back against the wall, and the tears began to flow. Closing her eyes, she whispered, "What have I done, God? You took Tracy from me, and now this. What have I ever done to deserve this?"

A deep, melodious voice resonated in the air around her. "Nothing. You've done nothing to deserve this. I am here for you, though, and I'll help you through this."

Lou opened her eyes. When she saw Ben standing at her side, she broke into nervous, tittering laughter. "My God, Ben. I thought I was actually getting an answer. It's just you. You don't know what's happened." Her laughter faded from her, and her tears began to flow once again. "Oh, it's so horrible that I can't describe it."

He laughed. "So, it's just me? How do you know I'm not an answer to your prayer? How does your Baptist Bible verse go? *God works in mysterious ways.* Is that close?"

Wiping her tears from her face, Lou smiled. "You know it is, you old scoundrel. Ben, today is falling apart faster than fast. How do I manage all this? Chad and Chaddie. This grandfather, and a dog, Ben. A dog here on the platform. Ooh, and that grandfather!" She felt her anger rising again, and her temples begin to throb. "If I told you what he did, you'd throw him over the side."

He smiled, and his teeth were brilliant against his skin. "I've heard things he's said, also. The words I heard weren't pretty, either. Promise me that if I don't tell you what I heard, then you won't tell me what he did. We'll both be better off. Is that a deal?"

She stepped to him and put her head against his chest just for a moment. When she lifted it, she placed her hand where his heart was located, and she whispered, "I do love you, Ben. More than all others."

His deep voice comforted her. "I'm here to protect you, Lou. Just trust me. Can you do that?"

She patted the hand that still rested on his chest, and her next words were almost too soft to hear. "I have since the day I arrived. You saved me then, and I have no reason to doubt you now."

He put a big finger under her chin, and he lifted her eyes to look at him. "This will be hard, something I haven't said, yet. Do you really want to hear this?"

She nodded, although she wasn't sure. Ben had never, ever talked to her in this serious a tone. "I'm listening."

"Leave this Chad alone. He doesn't trust you, and you cannot love someone without trust. Please, Lou. I know what I'm talking about in this. Can you trust me?"

HE DIDN'T get an answer, at least not aloud. She did wipe her tears on his shirt, one side of her face at a time. She could do that, and in that action, Ben knew he must accept Lou's response as if she had answered him in words. He had to believe that she would keep her distance from this man. He might be aboard for another month, and they would have to work together, at least until the next rotation off the platform. However, together and *together* were two different things.

He whispered to her, "Two weeks, Lou. Less than two. We can do this, you and me. Trust me. He won't be here forever."

As she laid her head on the big man's chest one more time, she murmured her heart, and this time it was too soft for Ben to hear.

"That's what I'm afraid of, Ben. That scares me to death."

CHADDIE SAT on the bed, and then he stood and ran his fingers through his thick, blond hair. His green eyes jumped restlessly around the room, and the tall boy, slender almost to the point of lankiness, crossed his arms over his chest, not moving.

"Dad?"

There was a very long pause during which Chaddie kept his eyes anywhere but on his father. The room was completely still, except for the eyes of the dog as they shifted between the two men on either side of her. Chaddie didn't really want to ask his question. He couldn't even turn to face the man he called his father, as he pressed him for the answers he needed.

"Were you really going to pay money to Lou . . . would you sneak out in the night . . . um, she wouldn't do that with other guys, too, would she?" His youthful voice broke with emotion.

At the sound of anguish in the boy's voice, Stinky rose to her feet and went to him, brushing her body against his legs. When he reached his hand down, she licked his fingers with a soft tongue. After a time, with tears flooding his eyes, Chaddie turned to his father, upset that he hadn't answered. His mother always said that no answer was as good as a guilty answer. He didn't want his father to be guilty of this. What he saw when he turned was a father who couldn't speak. Chad sat in the one chair at the end of the workspace that had been made from a door, and his eyes were on the floor. His face was ashen, and his hands were in constant motion, flexing but grabbing nothing. Finally, his eyes looked up, and they were burning with tears.

"Chaddie, I didn't stand up to Gramps, did I? I'm sorry, Son, for letting you down. I just found you again, and I learned something I'd forgotten during the past three years. I remembered I love you very much, and when Gramps started to talk, I lost that all over again. I should have stood up to him. I should have been the father you needed me to be. I'm so sorry, Chaddie." He reached to his face and brushed at his eyes. "Can we try again?"

The boy chewed his lips for a moment. He wanted to keep what his father was offering. For a day it had been his, and he desperately wanted to hold on to that. He had to know about the other, though.

"Was that true with Mom? Did Chip . . . did you know

177

they were ... together while you and Mom were still married?" He liked Chip well enough, but sometimes only a little. However, to think of his mother in this light was entirely new to him. He didn't like what Gramps had said about her, either, or that his father hadn't been man enough to keep his mother. He wasn't sure exactly what that meant, but it sounded like Gramps was calling his father a sissy.

It was too much for him to take, and he felt the tears flood his eyes.

CHAD NODDED. "I always wanted to work it out with your mother. I wanted to be with you, and I always hoped that things would get better."

He watched his son's face. He could tell him about the other men that his mother had been with, if he wanted to traumatize the boy. He wouldn't, though. There had been a lot: the officer at the Naval Air Station in Fort Worth who used to meet Diana at the house in Westover; the athletic instructor she saw when they were skiing in Boulder; that surfer who had been giving her surfing lessons in California; then Chip, who was now Chaddie's stepfather; and once, during her affair with Chip, even the stock boy at the A&P.

The stock boy had been the final straw. He'd been in high school, still, and on the junior varsity team, sixteen or seventeen at the time, Chad supposed. He graduated captain of the basketball team two years later, and with academic honors, too. Diana hadn't been able to deny that one like she had all the others. Chad had come home from a business trip a day early, and when he stepped into the living room, the curtains had been open to the backyard. Out on the chaise by the pool, he'd seen the boy, and underneath was his wife. Furious, he'd beat his hand on the window, shattering the glass.

The boy had jumped up, startled and guilty, but Chad hadn't watched to see whether he had pulled on his clothes or just run. He'd turned away, and there on the kitchen counter sat the sacks of groceries the boy had delivered. Diana hadn't even bothered to put them away before taking her latest conquest out back.

That was when Chad truly knew it was over. He'd told Diana she could have whatever she wanted, even Chaddie, if she'd just go. She had, too, marrying Chip less than a year later and moving to Boulder. It had taken Chad three years to find his son again, and he didn't want to lose him this time. Ben was right. Family first. Chad had to hold on to his son, no matter what else he had to give up.

Sitting there in front of this young man who looked so much like him, Chad also felt guilty for his question to Ben about Lou. Of course, he wasn't just a john to her. That had been a crazy old man speaking, one Chad had known was crazy even when he'd been married to his grand-daughter.

He stood up, and in his heart, he was infused with a new resolve. He wasn't married to the old man's grand-daughter anymore, and while Chaddie might be related to the old reprobate, that didn't mean the boy had to endure his abuses any longer. He moved to his son to throw an arm around him.

"I'm sorry, Chaddie. I'm trying to make things right. It's a slow process, though. Will you help me out?"

Chaddie turned to his father, and they looked at each other eye to eye. "How, Dad? How can I help?"

Chad smiled. "First, be patient with me, Son. That's mostly what I need. Next, I need to find Ben and apologize, and maybe to Lou, too. I need to make sure Gramps hasn't made too big a mess of this. This is our oil rig, not his. Gramps needs to go back to Dallas and stay on his golf course. He's safe there." Chad chuckled. "Better than that, *we're* safe when he's there."

Chaddie's arm finally found his father's shoulder, and they stood forehead to forehead, a son's head pressed against his father's. "I like Lou, Dad."

"So do I, Son. Let's find her and keep it that way. Maybe then she can begin to feel the same way about me."

Chaddie backed away with a laugh. "I think she already does."

His father smiled. "So, you think so? I like that idea. I sure hope you're right."

A knock at the door drew their attention away from each other, and Stinky backed under the bed, barking. Chad motioned for his son to answer it while he quieted the dog.

"Chaddie," a resonant voice rumbled. "Is your father here with you?" The boy nodded and turned to look at Chad kneeling by the table and holding Stinky.

Chad chuckled and called out, "Come in, Ben. I'm glad you're here." This was what he wanted to do next, to apologize to this man. He stood and reached a hand to shake.

Ben looked at it hesitantly, and then after too long of a pause, reached his own out. Chad was perplexed at the response, and he pointed to his son. "Chaddie and I are good, Ben. We got our issues worked out. Thanks for the advice. You know people, how to work with them, and I appreciate your help."

Ben took a deep breath and looked to the dog. He knelt and clapped his hand quietly. Stinky bounded to him with her tail wagging.

He turned to Chaddie. "Can you take her for a walk, son? She can't play on a rig like this, and she needs to be outside."

Chaddie looked to his father. "In this weather?"

Chad could see that Ben's visit wasn't a social call, and it must be something he didn't think the boy needed to hear. "Go ahead." Chad reached for the leash. "Ben's right, and I should've already sent you two out for some exercise. You get your gear on, and I'll hook up the dog." He took his time, too. He needed to occupy his hands, because with what he had seen so far, he wasn't sure this visit of Ben's would turn out to be a good thing.

Dressed, Chaddie turned to his father. "Dad, are you sure I shouldn't stay?"

Ben clapped him on the shoulder. "I like you, boy, and a lot, too. With that dog, there's no better pair on this rig. Have a good walk, and you might take the steps up to the helipad and back down several times. It'll be good exercise for the animal." Then he gently pushed the boy outside.

Chad stepped to close the door, and he turned to the big, black man. "Thanks, Ben. I meant that earlier. However, this makes me nervous. What is it that the boy couldn't hear?"

Ben put his hands in his pockets, and a sheen of

moisture on his forehead told of his own trepidation at what he needed to say. "It's Lou."

Chad laughed. "Chaddie and I were just going there to see if everything's okay with her. I remember what you said earlier, but I have to make sure everything's all right." When he realized the other man wasn't laughing with him, Chad's demeanor tightened up. "What, Ben? Tell me. It's not Gramps, is it?"

Ben's voice rumbled, "Yes and no. You've got to promise me to keep away from her. I said that to you earlier, and that hasn't changed."

That got his attention. Surely, Ben's earlier admonition had been an impulsive remark, one made in the intensity of the moment. Chad thought the big man had been helping. Now, he was telling Chad to do something he didn't want to do, to keep away from Louinda.

Chad smiled as he tried to bridge this chasm. "I was wrong, Ben. I knew that as soon as I got back here with Chaddie and the dog. I was so wrong. Gramps just threw me for a loop, and my brain went dead. I know she wouldn't do anything like the old man suggested. It was stupid of me to think so."

Clearing his throat, Ben paused. "Maybe so. However, what's done's done. I took Lou under my wing when she showed up on this platform, and I can't let anything bad happen to her."

"She knows? About what I said?" Chad twisted around and hit the heel of his palm to his forehead. "God, how could she know?" Then, in sudden realization, he turned back to Ben. "You told her?"

"Close enough," the big man said. His face was set,

and Chad knew he was serious. He watched the muscles tighten in the big man's jaw.

Chad ran the palms of his hands over his eyes and made to head out the door. "I've got to tell her I didn't mean it." When the big man grabbed his arm to stop him, Chad tried to twist away. "Get out of my way. She'll think I don't care. Let me go!" He finally tore loose and stood there, panting with the effort expended. Chad wasn't a small man, but just that one victory had exhausted him.

"Chad." The word was like golden honey, deep and thick, and a person could drown in a sound like that. It was also an iron cage, resonating with impenetrable honesty. "She already does. Lou's strong, but this has cut her deep. For now, she needs lots of space. Give her that. Once all the rest clears, maybe you two can start again. Not now, though."

"Ben," Chad started, but there was no strength in it. His foray back into life had been too brief to give him real reserves of fortitude. He'd had that once, the ability to stand against the disappointments of life, to try until he had what he wanted, until life, until *love* was his. He'd had that, and he'd used his reserves to try to maintain his marriage to Chaddie's mother.

She'd taken all he had, though, and no one else had come along to stoke those fires back into life. That was, until Lou. Just this one day had changed him inside, made him feel alive again.

Yet, those internal fires, that strength he had once felt, had only begun to glow with warmth, and this disaster that Gramps had brought upon them was the icy chill of winter once again. What he felt for this woman was intense, but it had no firm foundation, yet. Without that foundation, it couldn't help him stand against the battering Gramps had thrown against him. Trust had to be built for a relationship to stand.

Trust. With that word, Chad sat on the bed. He knew Ben was right. Trust had to be in place for love to grow, and he hadn't trusted Lou. If he had, he would have immediately stood up to the words Gramps spouted. He would have shut him up, railed at him, hit him if necessary. He should have stood for Lou's honor, and he hadn't. His first words to Ben had been ones of doubt, and he could never take those back. Never.

Chad felt broken all over again, just as he'd been for years, and the fight was gone from him.

"I understand." He squeezed his eyes for a moment at the burning he felt. "I'll keep my distance." He glanced into the big man's face. "If I'm to do this, I can't see her. Not tonight. I want too much to apologize to her and let her know I care."

"She wouldn't listen. Don't try to apologize over this. Not now when it's fresh. The wound will just go deeper. You should stay here in the accommodations block for a time, I think." Ben paused as if realizing something before clarifying his instructions. "Yes, inside your room. That'll be better. She'll have to be in and out of the accommodations block, and you're correct. You shouldn't see her. You're a good man, and I know you want to do what's right for Lou. This is it, and I'm glad you see that." Ben's face was calm, but his words drove his iron cage tighter around the younger man.

"I'll do as you ask. For you, and for Lou. However,

what about food?" Chad smiled, and the expression was sour, even to him. "I might need to eat. When Chaddie returns, he will, too. A growing boy, you know."

As if in apology, Ben smiled. "That I can do. I'll bring it here, as well as for the boy, and something for the dog. You're a good man, Chad. Your son is lucky to have you. I'm sorry this turned out as it has."

Chad just smiled bitterly and motioned with a wave for Ben to make his exit. He didn't need someone else to tell him he was lucky to have his son. He knew that. However, it wasn't the boy he was thinking of. It was the feel of soft skin against his, and the smell of coconut in a woman's hair that kept his mind busy. It was a night spent in her sheets, and the feelings that had coursed through his body as he had lain there surrounded by her smell.

No, he didn't do those things Gramps had accused him of, and he wouldn't have, either. Not as the old man had outlined them. However, right now he wanted to. Whether that came from the old man's suggestions to his love-starved mind, or whether it was because those things were no longer accessible to him, Chad didn't know. He didn't care, either. For Ben, though, and for Lou, he'd stay away. He didn't see how, but he was determined he would keep his promise. He looked across the room at the door. It formed a prison cell, one he could leave anytime he wanted. He could. He should. However, he just watched it hold him in, and there he sat, thinking of Lou.

This love thing was hard, and he wanted it to be easy. It had been at eighteen. Now, it wasn't easy, and Chad knew there wasn't anything he could do about that.

Chapter 10

THE WIND whistled until it became a screech that Lou could no longer ignore. She sat on the bed with her legs crossed beneath her. Her arms were wrapped across her torso, one hand on each side of her neck, and her chin rested on her wrists as a cushion. At thirty-one, sitting this way was no longer as easy as it had been at fifteen, but she no longer cared if her back hurt when she got up. Her heart hurt, and that was even worse.

Yet, the noise was very distracting, and it pierced the silence of the room. Untwisting her body, she stretched her legs and placed her feet on the floor. It had grown darker in the room, and in August this far south, the darkness meant it was getting very late.

Stepping to the window, she felt around the edges until

she located a ribbon of moist air whipping in underneath the lower pane. Placing her hands at the edge of the frame, she raised it several inches and slammed it down hard. She was gratified to hear the keening stop. Turning, she looked around the room, and it was only emptiness she saw.

She trusted Ben. He had saved her, protected her, and been her closest friend during her time on the rig. He wouldn't do her wrong. Yet, he was telling her to stay away from this man who had put his hooks into her heart. She didn't even know why.

Chad had been in this room. That was part of what pulled at her. He'd been here just that morning. She had stood outside that door with his son, and she hadn't walked through. She hadn't wanted him to feel uncomfortable, to feel that the space he had been given wasn't really his.

Now she wished differently, that he was with her here. She would look at him as he stood in front of her mirror, and he would be unaware of her eyes. Shaving, his arm would reach to his face, the muscles in his broad back flexing with the repetitive movements, as the razor stroked his chin. She wouldn't look away, either. In fact, she would step to him. That chest she had brushed against, she would place her hand there, and he would know that she wanted him. She did, too, and she knew why after only one day. It wasn't just that leonine grace of his, his way of stepping through a room as if aware of each item in the space. She had watched him do that, move fluidly around each chair and table, as if they were his to command, his supple body shifting as it stepped towards her, moving next to her as if he knew exactly her position in relation to his own.

Lou knew it was more than that. His son moved that

way, and the boy didn't bring out these feelings in her. She had come to love Chaddie, but it was the love of a big sister for a younger brother, of a mother for a handsome son. Chad made her twist inside. Perhaps it was because he'd shown that he could be human, that he could make mistakes and still be someone she could find sweet and charming and adorable. Perhaps she found him charming because he made mistakes. Perfection would have made him unapproachable. His flaws made him hers. At least, she'd hoped he would be hers. Now, she didn't know.

This day was no longer endurable for her. She reached to the window once again, and before pulling the shade, she looked at the waves thrashing the surface of the sea. Somewhere in the back of her mind, she knew that if the storm continued to get stronger, there would be no way on or off this rig by tomorrow night. She hoped someone was watching the weather. She'd been preoccupied with other things today. She had missed the latest updates, and right then, she didn't even care.

She turned in the near darkness and pulled flannel pajamas from a drawer. Dropping her clothes where she stood, she held the pajamas in her hand. She felt the warm air of the heating system kick on, and she tossed the items of clothing at her bed. They would be there if she wanted them later. She wasn't cold now. She climbed under the covers and pulled them over her head. She couldn't bring herself to even take a shower tonight. She could barely stand to be on this rig. Then, as her head rested on the pillow, she knew an aroma she had smelled before. It was in her bed and her sheets and in her pillow. It was the same as when she had brushed by that awful man, Chad

Dickson. He'd left his aroma in this bed she had to sleep in. It was with her, surrounding her, and in that moment, *he* was with her. Then she knew he wasn't, and sobs began to wrack her body.

She pulled her legs to her chest, and she wrapped her arms around them. She needed warmth right then, and it wasn't warmth that the bedcoverings or the warmed air from the vents could supply. Her heart needed to be warmed, and that could come only from a man. The only man who could do that was somewhere in another room, and he wasn't coming to her tonight. He was far away, and Ben had told her not to trust this man she needed so very much.

"It's hard, Ben, when I want him with all my heart. I want to believe you, but it's very hard." Her tears began to flow, but as the light behind the shade began to dim, so did her tears. At last she was asleep, and in the long moments of her heartbreak, she was unaware that she hadn't thought of Tracy even once.

"HEY, I DON'T care." Torch laughed dismissively. He had no intention of giving in to this man. To tease him, though? Sure, he could do that. He continued, his voice suggesting a carefree nonchalance, "Besides, I'm off here as quick as a supply boat comes. Sooner, if I get a chance."

"Tell me, then." Wally leaned across the table. "You say everybody knows which room is hers, so what's the big deal?"

"There is no big deal. It's just that most of us here on this rig like Lou. We don't want to see her hurt." Torch had taken a liking to this man when he first met him, but

189

he didn't know if he could keep on liking him or not. He already knew he didn't trust him.

"Hurt? No one's getting hurt." Wally waved away his concerns with one hand. "She invited me down. I told you that. To her room. Just for a nightcap. I'm an old friend of her grandmother's from way back. High school, in fact."

Torch leaned in to meet Wally's gaze, tapping his hand on the table between them. "Nightcap, huh? Why didn't you ask her to meet you up here?" Then he looked down to see Wally's hand over his. With a small movement, there were two hundreds pressed firmly in between.

Wally chuckled. "For old times' sake?"

Torch's eyes glanced to see that no one was watching, and he took his hand away, the bills firmly wrapped inside. He didn't like this, but Lou didn't have to let the man in if she didn't want to see him. She was a strong girl. What could telling hurt?

"You know where the sleeping level is?"

When Wally nodded, Torch gave him a quick series of directions to find Lou's room. Then, without looking back, he was gone, leaving Wally alone, the anticipation already rising in his blood.

GRINNING, the old man stood, and then he froze, holding onto the edge of the table. For a moment the burning was back in his chest, and then after several motionless seconds, it faded. That was all right with Wally, the fact that it faded. It was probably just the rush of arousal at the thought of getting under this woman's clothes. He *was* aroused, and his face felt the heat bleeding up from the rest of his body. He'd do this tonight, and then tomorrow he'd fly out. He'd never see her again, but he'd always remember how he'd finally gotten revenge. That'd feel good after all these years, and more would feel good than just the revenge. He'd enjoy her smooth skin, those firm breasts, and taking her as she fought him off. He'd had a few women that way, by force, and the feistiness just made the rewards that much sweeter.

Wally made his way out the door, once again refusing to wear any safety equipment. He did put on the rain gear, only because he intended to step out into the weather for a bit—but that concession was for his comfort, not to conform to the rules of this damned oil derrick. Putting the rain gear on tired him out, though, and that *was* unusual. However, he knew arousal gave him weak knees, and he didn't think he'd ever put on rain gear when he'd been this aroused.

Stepping outside, he walked to a place where he felt he wouldn't be seen. Reaching into a pocket, he pulled out a slender package of exotic cigars. Putting one under his nose, he drew in the aroma. He wanted a smoke badly. He knew what that woman had said about lighting up. He had to be in the approved smoking location. However, just to be out here alone, and to draw in the heady flavor would be so much better. Yet, when he went to that woman, she would smell it on him. Ever practical in such matters, Wally knew he could wait until he'd taken his revenge before lighting up. Moving back to the accommodations block, he slipped the cigar back in his pocket and ripped the rain gear off. Suddenly breathing hard, his eyes blurring out of focus, he steeled himself and grabbed a wall for support.

Ouch, he thought with a chuckle. *If I'd known I'd get this jazzed up over getting revenge with this woman, I'd have found where she was a long time ago. I want her so badly, I can barely see or stand.*

He could do this, though. After all, he'd be lying down soon enough—right on top of this woman he'd discovered. All he had to do was find her room, and with the directions from that idiot Torch, that would be easy enough. Who called a man Torch, anyway? What sort of name was that? Wally chuckled, then coughed, the small motion tearing at his chest.

Finally catching his breath, he pulled out two stiff pieces of wire. These would be his key. Doors everywhere worked pretty much the same, especially old ones, ones that had real keys. He could trip this woman's lock in the dark. Counting numbers on the doors, he stopped. He stood in front of the one that was hers. Looking left and right to make sure no one was around, in a smooth motion, he went to one knee. Grabbing the door handle to steady himself, he felt it give, and twisting it, the door swung open.

He hissed, "Good God, woman! Invite me in next time."

He grinned, but getting back up wasn't so easy. Just that small motion winded him, and Wally had to catch his breath once more before he could step inside. The interior of the room was dark, and before closing the door, he glanced around and located the bed. In the darkness, it seemed unoccupied, and he knew he might have to wait for some time for her to return. However, it was already getting late. It shouldn't be too long.

After Wally closed the door, it was quite dark. Breathing hard, gasping really, he began to remove his clothes. He felt his way to a chair and sat to untie his shoes. Then he pulled his socks off.

Leaning back for a moment to rest, struggling to get enough air, he finally found the energy to unbutton his shirt. His left arm had begun to tingle, and it was difficult to extricate the buttons from their small, sewn slits. However, a little at a time, he worked it off his shoulders and let it fall into the seat behind him.

Undoing his belt, he let the pants fall as he stood up. As they slipped down his legs and hit the floor, the buckle jangled against itself.

Wally's chest was burning again by then, and he could barely lift his legs clear from the fabric where it bunched around his feet. Then, a sharpness cut through his chest that he thought would tear his body apart.

"Arrgh!" The sound was torn from him, and he couldn't have contained it if he'd wanted.

Then a hand scrabbled on a tabletop, and a small lamp lit the room. A startled voice barked out, "Who's there?"

WHEN LOUINDA saw the bleary outline of a man in her room, at first she thought it was a joke. Then reality hit her, and the memory of her first night on the rig flooded her with fear. Her blood drained with the realization that she'd been so distraught she'd forgotten to lock her door. Everyone on the rig knew which room was hers. There was no way to anticipate who this was. She considered what she could grab to defend herself.

Then he moved, and she recognized the intruder as Chaddie's great-grandfather. She saw he was stripped to his underwear, and that made her angry. Finally, she noticed his hands grabbing at his chest, and she understood. This was a heart attack. While he'd been inexcusably crude and vile earlier, this unfolding drama meant he needed immediate medical attention. Her prior disgruntlement with him was set aside, and the questions she had about why he was in her room wearing only his underwear could be answered later. There were matters of priority here, and helping this man was number one.

As she threw back the covers and stood to offer her assistance, she was only vaguely aware of the fact that she hadn't dressed completely for bed. Her underwear didn't concern her. This man and his medical issues did. She had to get the medic here, and quickly.

"Sir," she called to him. "Mr. Saunders." When he just looked panic stricken and pawed at his chest, she tried again. "Gramps, can you hear me? I need you to lie on the bed." He nodded, and as she stepped to him, he gasped violently and flailed his hand at her, grabbing at her for support. In that motion, his fingers grasped the front of her bra, and as he crashed to the floor, it pulled from her, snapping the back wide, and sliding painfully down her arms and into the floor, still clutched in his hand.

"Gramps," she cried as he flailed, knocking against the desk and sending items to the floor.

As she knelt to him, the door burst open, and a voice called out, "What . . . Lou! I heard the noise. What's this?"

She looked up to see the radio operator, Yolanda. The look on the woman's face said she didn't believe this could possibly be what it looked like. Lou took in that disbelieving look, and she shook her head. "This isn't what it appears, Yolanda. Get the medic. This man's having a heart attack. Go."

Yolanda took a deep breath, and her eyes were wide. "That old man in here with you, and your bra in his hand! Girl, you've got it going on! A little tête-à-tête with an old guy. How interesting! A heart attack, you say. What'd you expect, girl? You being so beautiful, you shocked his heart to death." She laughed like she didn't believe it.

"Yolanda, stop it!" Lou was suddenly aware of her exposed chest. However, it wasn't the most important concern in the room. "This man's dying. Go for the medic."

"YES, MA'AM." Yolanda turned to run that direction, but on the way she took the time to stop by another room first and knocked. She knew who that old man was, and she knew who he had come to harass, that good-looking Chad Dickson. Word traveled fast on the platform, and she knew the geezer'd not put on his safety gear even once. She also knew where his great-grandson was staying—with his daddy, on the mattress Ben had pulled out of storage—and she'd be danged if that boy needed to see what her eyes had taken in.

When a bleary-eyed Chad came to the door, Yolanda hissed, "I'm headed for the medic. The old man's had a heart attack. He's in Lou's room, but don't take the boy. It's not pretty. Go quick. I've got to radio for emergency medical evacuation, if he's not already dead. That's standard OP for something like this." She glanced up and down the corridor furtively. "Go!" Then, without waiting to answer questions, she was gone, the urgency of the situation finally tightening around her chest.

CHAD STOOD, flummoxed, only turning when the dog growled. He quietly snapped his fingers.

"Quiet, Stinky."

The radio operator's words confused him. Lou's room? Gramps? He tried to push past the fog of sleep, hoping the old man hadn't gone there and picked a fight. He grabbed his pants and pulled them on before fastening the catch. Then, forcing a shirt on, he slipped his feet into his steel-toed boots, dropping the laces inside. He tried unsuccessfully to button the shirt as he ran, and after several attempts, he finally gave up, letting the tail flap around his hips.

Several people, including the medic, were entering the room as Chad arrived. When he stepped to the door, he saw Gramps on the floor in his underwear, and his clothes were strewn around the room as if the man had been undressing for bed. What disturbed him was looking up and seeing Louinda. She sat on the bed, and she was also in her underwear. She held a sheet over her chest, a makeshift covering that didn't quite hide the fact that she had no bra on.

When she saw him, her hand flew to her mouth, and panic filled her eyes.

YOLANDA'S WORDS came back to her. *"A little tête-à-tête with an old guy. How interesting!"* With those words, she saw this as she knew Chad must. Her eyes dropped to the floor, where she could see Wally's hand tightly grasped around the front of her bra.

"Chad," she called. She looked to see shock on his

face. He mustn't be allowed to believe she was bedding his son's great-grandfather. Dear God, no!

"Chad," she called again, attempting to stand. Several people in the room looked to see who she was talking to, and noticing the visitor at the door, they quickly turned their attention back to the man they were trying to save. However, her sheet was still fastened at the foot of the bed, and she was unable to successfully extricate herself. She tried to talk to him anyway, calling out the door. "This isn't how it looks, Chad. Let me explain."

He closed his eyes and took a deep breath. Opening them once again, his fierce blue gaze quickly silenced her attempts to speak.

"DON'T, LOU. How much more damage can you do to one family? Don't say anything. You can only make this worse." He stepped in and knelt at Wally's side, relieved to see he was still breathing. No matter how harsh the old man had been earlier, he was still Chaddie's relation, and Chad didn't wish for his son to be forced to endure the death of his gramps while out here on this rig.

Chad watched the medic work for a moment, attaching medical equipment to the old man and poking him with needles. He did feel a little guilty at his words to Lou. He did want this man to live, but not because he loved him. If the old man died here, not only would his son be heart-broken, but the old man would surely be deified in the boy's eyes. Chad didn't want that.

There was something else, too. If the circumstances of this came out, this old man dying with this woman's bra tightly grasped in his hand, Chad knew his son would link

Gramp's death through Lou directly to his father. Chad would bear the brunt of this. That was how a thirteen-year-old would think. Chad knew, because at thirteen, that's exactly what he would have done.

Then a familiar and unwelcome voice came faintly through the door. "Dad? Where are you? What happened? Is Lou okay? I heard Stinky growl, and then suddenly you left." The words arrived in a rush, and Chad stood and headed back through the door, hoping to catch his son before he entered the room. The boy hadn't even taken time to dress. All he had on was his sleeping pants, and he was rubbing his hands up and down his bare arms nervously as he tried to force his way through the growing crowd of onlookers in the corridor.

"Don't go in, Son." When Chaddie started forward anyway, Chad threw his arms around the boy's shoulders to hold him back. "Everything will be all right. Go back to our room. There's been a medical emergency, but there's nothing we can do. The medic's already taking care of everything."

"Dad," he insisted. "I don't need to be sent back like I'm a kid. I'm grown, now." His eyes opened wide. "Medical emergency. It's Gramps, isn't it? I can take whatever it is."

His father snorted. He knew better. The boy didn't know what was through that door. He wouldn't be able to understand his great-grandfather holding that woman's bra. Then, he noticed that there was no dog. He saw his opportunity and seized it.

"Chaddie, my God, you didn't leave Stinky, did you? She'll be frightened. Go get her, quickly. I'll see if you can go in when you get back." He was relieved to see the boy's eyes turn frantic at having forgotten the poor animal.

"Dad, I'm so sorry," Chaddie apologized. "I'll go right now. Please, Dad. Wait right here. I'll be right back."

Chad breathed a sigh of relief to see the boy run from him and disappear around a corner. Then, when his feet could be heard pounding on metal stair treads, headed to their room, he turned back to get this situation under control.

"Lou," he hissed, stepping through the door, his voice dripping acid. "Chaddie was just here, and he wants to see Gramps. Please get your bra out of the old man's hand. Put it back on, if you would. I sent him on an errand, but the boy runs fast. You need to move quickly unless you want him to know you were bedding his great-grandfather."

Everyone in the room looked at Lou a second time, and her eyes danced across their faces. Most of them turned away, but the implication was there.

"Chad," she called, tugging the sheet and forcing it all the way off the bed with a vicious yank. Wrapping it around her, she dragged the train of cloth after her and followed him into the corridor. "Surely you cannot believe I would have an affair with that horrid man. Give me that much credit. I hated every minute I spent with him."

He looked at her, and there was no mercy in his gaze. "Of course, I believe you. However, that means you have to explain why this old man, one whom I equally hate, is in your room wearing only his underwear and holding the bra that you should have on. You were even in your bed wrapped in your sheet. What? Did I also see his clothes strewn about your room where he disrobed for you? Yes, I did. So, you can easily see that it's obvious I have no reason to believe you intended to take him to bed with you." His eyes glanced to the side to see his son and Stinky coming, and then he looked back to her face. "Time's up. Think quick, Lou. Chaddie's here."

He stepped around to catch his son, grabbing the leash from his hand. "The leash, Chaddie. Is it tight?"

"Dad! I'm not stupid. Of course, it's tight."

"Check it, Son." Chad handed the leash back to the boy. "She mustn't get loose." He glanced at the woman standing wrapped in her sheet. She looked to him in despair and just covered her face with her hand.

THIS WAS worse than horrid. Lou knew Chad must be busying the boy to give her time, but she couldn't think. She knew what must have happened by now. She thought she did, anyway, although she couldn't be entirely sure. If she said what she thought, no one would believe her, though, not with her bra in the old man's hand.

He had come in to ambush her, to rape her. There was no other explanation. His suggestive words. The way he had grabbed her breast earlier and pressed his arousal against her.

Still, aside from proving rape, such a dalliance, itself, wouldn't be illegal, although it would be viewed as rather shady under company policy. They were certainly both of consenting age. Yet, for her to be involved in this travesty, especially if he died, would rankle with corporate execs. That only compounded the atrocity.

She now knew she should have said something to someone earlier about having been accosted. She hadn't, though, and this was the price she was being forced to pay. Her word against the obvious facts. She'd be found guilty, and there would be no leniency given her. She could very well lose her job over this. She cringed at that, but she also knew it could be worse. Chad was planning on taking her job, anyway, so what were a couple of weeks? Her family, though. They would vilify her. Oh, they'd say they loved her and felt sorry for her, would even pray for her, but she would always be the elder sister who had gone bad.

She looked to see Chaddie in the act of standing as he finished checking the dog's collar, and his father was glaring at her. She had to think before she spoke. She had to think *now*.

"Lou, is someone hurt in your room?" Chaddie looked directly at her. "I thought it might be Gramps earlier, but now I'm not sure. Dad didn't say." The boy led the dog up to her, and she knelt to rub her fur.

She whispered to the animal, "Sit," and the dog immediately dropped her hindquarters to the floor. "Good girl," she said.

Chaddie looked at his father. "Dad, did you see that? Stinky never sits for us."

"I saw it, Son." He sighed and looked from his son to the woman wrapped in her sheet, kneeling on the floor. "You're here, Chaddie, and you might as well know. It's Gramps in the room. Lou has the answers you need. Ask her whatever you want. She'll explain it all."

When the boy turned to her, Lou looked at Chad in desperation, her eyes pleading with him. However, she knew he wouldn't help. Her only option was to lie, and to lie well and elaborately. She prepared herself and started slowly. She was being forced to make this up as she went.

"Chaddie, I was in the shower, and there was a loud knock on my door." She glanced at Chad's face to see him roll his eyes. She had started, though, and she couldn't stop in mid-story. "It was your gramps knocking, and he was desperate for help. I asked him to wait, but he said it was a heart attack."

Chaddie's face went white. "Is he dead?"

Chad interrupted, "He's not dead yet, Son. Let the yarn continue. Go on, Lou. Make it good."

Chaddie looked to Louinda and back to his father. "Dad?"

"Just listen, Son. You'll like this next part. Just listen."

Lou glared at the man standing next to his son. He was making this into a joke, and she had done nothing wrong, nothing except not tell about the old man's earlier harassment.

"I had fresh sheets out to put on the bed, and since I wasn't dressed, I grabbed one to cover with. When he fell in the room, well, I couldn't lift him."

"And, Lou, why does Gramps have your bra in his hand?" When his son frowned at his father, Chad just put his finger to his lips for him to listen. "Questions later, Son."

Lou cleared her throat. "Well, I couldn't let go of my sheet to put my arms under him, and I had to find something Gramps could hold onto. The only thing I could see was my bra. He grabbed it, but I still couldn't get him up. Then, when I yelled for help, Yolanda ran to get the medic."

She was defeated. This man had forced her to lie to his

202

son, and she felt horrible. This man believed one thing, and the son, if he were either gullible or very innocent, might believe the other. However, neither one knew the truth.

Chaddie pleaded with his father, "Can I go see him?"

His father hugged him. "Sure, Son. Just don't talk. I think I heard someone say an emergency medical transport had to be called."

"CareFlite. Possibly MedEvac. They'll radio out of Galveston or New Orleans." Lou held very still as the boy stepped inside. After he was gone, she hissed to Chad, "I lied to him. You know it didn't happen that way. It didn't happen the way you think it did, either."

He looked at her for a moment. "Sure, Lou. It didn't happen the way I think it did. Okay. That's fine. I'll go with that. Later, we'll talk about the finer points of May-December romantic dalliances if December in there lives. How does that sound?"

"Ooh!" she said, shaking in fury. She turned, and grabbing her sheet, she marched off to get away from this man. She couldn't even go to her room because it was full of helpful medical personnel—and everyone else who could fit inside.

That made matters even worse, but there was nothing to be done about that. Nothing at all.

Chapter 11

IT WAS DARK outside, and the rig was lighted like a Christmas tree. It was raining, although it was a light, pelting nuisance instead of the driving rain that often comes with excessive winds. Wally was bundled and on a gurney. His machines were attached and running, but he wasn't coherent. A medical evacuation was under progress, and the helicopter was on the way.

Chaddie stood next to his father, both in full rain gear. They were outside watching for the lights that told the helicopter was approaching.

"Dad," the boy yelled over the noise of the oil rig and the crashing waves. "Do you really think Gramps did all that?"

"Did all what, Son?" Chad knew exactly what his son

was asking, but the boy would have to work out his version of the events on his own. Chad wasn't about to clarify either Lou's lie or her dalliance with the boy's great-grandfather.

"You know, Dad. Knocked on the door. Tried to get up like Lou said." He looked straight ahead. The set of his jaw told his father he didn't want to catch a careless expression on his face, one that he might wish he hadn't seen. This didn't seem on the up and up to the boy, and it was pretty obvious his father knew more than he was telling.

"You heard what she said. Why do you ask?"

"It's Gramps. He wouldn't ask anyone for help. You know he wouldn't. He'd fall down and die rather than ask for someone's help. Do you think Lou was trying to make us feel better? Maybe she found him in the hall, and she was helping him. Maybe she wanted to make it look like Gramps would ask for help. That's what most people would do, after all. They would ask."

"Do you think it happened that way instead?" Chad didn't think it had, but then he had seen a version of the events that his son hadn't been privy to.

"Maybe. She could have been in the shower and heard Gramps fall, but her hair wasn't wet. Did you notice that?"

Chad chuckled. His son was sharp. He hadn't missed a trick. "I was too worried about Gramps to pay attention to her hair. Maybe it dried really fast."

Chaddie looked at his father, and the look was one of disbelief. "Mine never does. Why would hers?"

Chad was relieved to see a light coming in from the distance. His son was pushing hard, and the only answers Chad had were ones he didn't want to give. This was the diversion he needed.

"Is that the helicopter?' Chad pointed at the blinking light in the distance. "I don't hear anything, though. Can you?"

His son nodded. "I think I can. It sounds like the one we rode on. The one Gramps came in on was whiny-sounding. This one's deep."

Chad clapped him on the shoulder and pulled him toward the steps. "They've probably radioed in that they're arriving already, but let's go check below, anyway. How about that? Maybe we can help Gramps out."

Stepping inside, once they were out of the continuous thunder created by the oil rig and the crashing waves below, they pulled their earplugs, and finally they could talk without yelling. "Dad," Chaddie started in, "I was supposed to stay with Gramps back in Dallas. Do you think I should ride back on the helicopter with him? I could be there for him when he wakes up."

His father smiled at the boy. "He might like that. However, I don't think they'd let you. Weight means fuel consumption. Extra weight means more fuel is used. More fuel is more weight. Less fuel carried means less fuel is used."

"Okay, Dad, I guess." Chaddie frowned at the explanation. "What does all that mean?"

He chuckled. "They calculate the fuel they need, and that's all they carry. I'll bet there's not much of a reserve, either. An extra person might make them run low on fuel, and they wouldn't make it back in. That means you're stuck with me, so get used to it."

He was pleased to see that Chaddie looked relieved at the prospect, and not the other way around. He was also pleased to know Gramps would be off the rig, even if this wasn't the way he would have chosen. The damage the man had already done was incalculable. Who could tell what else might happen if he stayed longer?

Then, the gurney was on the way. Chad and his son stepped back to let them through, and at the door, they were met by the MedEvac team.

"This is the man with the heart issue?" A man with *Red* sewn on his shirt stepped forward.

The rig's medic stepped forward. "Yes, sir. About two hours ago, we think. I have him stabilized, although he's in pretty serious condition."

Red frowned as he looked at Wally. "He's an old one. I thought there was a cut-off age on these rigs."

The rig medic laughed. "He was with us just for a visit."

"Haven't seen that tour. *Sunshine Gulf. For the Vacation of a Lifetime.* I guess when the oil is gone, you guys can still make some money hosting paying guests. Great job security."

The medic laughed again. "Okay, you comic. Get him to shore. He needs real medical attention."

"Like you're just a trainee," another transport team member grinned.

"Get out," the medic said with a laugh. "Stay dry." He stepped forward to hold the door, and the gurney passed through. "Return my gurney once you get him loaded!" He shook his head at the medical crew taking his surprise patient away, and he glanced at Chad and his son. "You guys going up to see him off? They'll go quick. Then you can bring the gurney back, if you would."

Sticking in earplugs, the two raced for the door. The team on the helicopter had Gramps just about fastened in, and the rig's gurney was standing off to the side.

Red leaned over to be heard. "Good. I'm glad to see someone came up to get the gurney. Take it back down, if you will. We won't need it."

"Sure," Chad replied. "By the way, this is my son's great-grandfather. Thanks for coming out to get him."

"Sure." Red ducked his head Chaddie's direction. "Sorry about what happened, son. Hey, when are ya'll evacuating?" Red looked between Chad and his son expectantly.

Chad looked at his son. Then he frowned at the man in the copter. "Evacuating?"

The man pointed all around into the darkness. "This storm. This is the edge of a hurricane. Another hour, and we couldn't have made it out. Regs, you know. Wind speed and all that. Most of the other rigs around here have already evacuated. Pack your stuff. If they don't pull you off, you're dead." Then Red slammed the door, and the machine began to rise into the air.

Chaddie pulled on his father's arm. "Dad, he didn't mean that, did he?"

Chad turned to his son. "I don't know. We can find out, though. Someone will know." He hoped they would, anyway. From what he knew, if this rig were to be evacuated in the next twenty-four hours, shutdown procedures should have already been initiated. Even though that wasn't his area of expertise, he wasn't sure he'd seen any sign of shutdown procedures being run. He also knew that his entire day had been thoroughly disrupted, and after his bruising morning, he hadn't been keeping track of much on the rig, much except what Gramps kept stirred up.

"HEY, LOUINDA. Glad to see you're actually wearing clothes." It was Yolanda. She held her helmet in her hand, and her safety glasses dangled around her neck. She was laughing. "Toolpusher needs you. No hanky, now." She winked, and Lou growled as the radio operator moved on past her open door.

"No hanky, my foot. There never was any hanky, and there wasn't going to be, either." If Lou knew Yolanda, she was already spreading it around the rig that the pretty safety coordinator had been very accommodating to the needs of that older man. Just thinking of that made her growl once again.

Donning her safety gear, she headed out the door, this time making sure it was locked. Hers was a private room, and keeping it locked was her prerogative. It would be from now on. Stepping to the pipe deck and tapping at the door that said *Toolpusher,* she opened it a crack. It was late on her personal schedule, but rig life went on twenty-four hours. The toolpusher, the general manager of the rig, was a night owl. When she saw him at his desk, she knocked on the glass, cracked the door, and called to him.

"Yes, sir, John. Yolanda said you needed to see me." When he motioned, she opened the door and stepped inside.

"You've been a hard woman to catch since that watch-dog got on board. I hear there's been some trouble. Medical type." His eyes looked up from his work.

"Yes, sir. However, it's already resolved."

"That's what I like about you, Lou. You're on the ball, and I never have to worry. Here's what you don't know. We're shutting down."

"Sir? It's windy outside, but shutting down?"

He studied her face. "I know it's late, but are you all right, Reinhardt? You look rough. Anything I need to be aware of?"

She laughed. "No, sir. The trouble just shipped off in a helicopter. MedEvac. I'm good. I was asleep earlier, though. I guess my eyes are still puffy."

He chuckled. "Sorry for getting you up, then. However, this couldn't wait. That storm out there changed directions again this past hour. We've been running initial shutdown procedures the past twenty-four hours, keeping it at a minimum, hoping we could bring the rig back up if the storm bypassed us. That's not going to happen. Everybody goes this time. Not even a skeleton crew gets to stay."

She cleared her throat. "Everyone? Will this storm really be that bad?" She'd just been out in it. It was windy, and sure, it had started to rain. However, evacuation?

"It's that man you've been babysitting. U.S. government. He's got all the power. Not him, actually, but the fact that we're under direct observation means we don't get to decide in this. The U.S. of A. has already done that. You know our emergency escape equipment is inoperable. Thank goodness Coast Guard ships with copters will be here in the morning. You'll be on the first team to return when this blows over, though. Three days off, five tops. We'll need you back out to see where we stand as soon as possible and to tell us if repairs are needed. You know the skinny on that."

Lou nodded. There was no "if" to the repairs. This was an old rig, and it wasn't in the best of shape. "Torch McGee. He's here now, sir. Can we keep him? He's good as a welder. If I've got someone familiar with the rig, it'll speed us up getting back on line."

The toolpusher nodded his assent. "I'll see what I can do, get the requisition in. Make sure everyone reviews muster points, Lou. Check with Yolanda for muster lists, too. I want copies posted as well as extras for the Coast Guard."

"Yes, sir. Anything else?" When he shook his head and turned back to his work, she knew she was dismissed. Stepping from his office, she looked both ways and saw no one. A full shutdown was a big deal. That meant it would take days to get everything back up and running once the storm was past. It was this Chad that was the problem. If he weren't here, then a full shutdown wouldn't be happening. Only nonessential personnel would leave.

He was, though, and she needed to see Ben and about sixty other people. It had been a very long day, and it was shaping up to be a very long night, too.

BANKS OF LIGHTS glowed along electrical boards, and that's where Lou found Ben. He was opening panels and tripping switches, causing a number of the lights to go out. A smile broke across his face when he saw his friend.

"Lou! You are my best treat tonight. So, they finally got you involved in the shutdown, too." His rumbling voice was just what she needed to hear after what she had endured since she saw him last.

She looked at the clipboard she was carrying. "Ben, I

guess I should have attempted to find you listed under *electrician*." She knew he could do almost anything on board the rig. He was motorman because it was what appealed to him at that moment.

He chuckled. "Lou, check under *assistant*. That's what I'm doing right now, being an assistant to the electrician. A rig this size doesn't have enough electricians to go around during a shutdown. You know that."

She leaned against one of the cabinets, looking at the big man, a smile on her face. She shook her head, but she didn't speak immediately. She needed him to give her the time she required to get a grasp on things. The shutdown would go on all night, and that meant there was no hurry for her. The entire crew would be in their muster positions at dawn, and Sunshine Gulf would be left to weather the indignities of the storm on its own. Then, they would all return days later to restart all these machines and get the lifeblood of America flowing once again. Finally, she took a deep breath.

"You heard about the heart attack earlier?"

His eyes looked to her out of his black face, and there was no smile breaking across his lips. "I heard you were part of it."

Lou frowned at that. "Part, how?"

His voice was the ominous thrumming of a distant train on a track as he murmured his words. "Close that door, Lou, and we can talk." Seeing it was done, he quizzed her in a low, gravelly voice. "Some are saying you were with him when his ticker blew. I'm hoping you can tell me how it really went down." Ben turned to her, leaving his electrical panels to themselves for a moment. He pulled a

212

large tool chest from the wall, one just the right height for a bench. He pointed her to it, then he joined her. "Just the facts, Lou. I was there when he made some of his threats. I'm on your side. I just need to hear it straight."

She laughed hoarsely. "It went down bad, Ben. It was very bad, and I might lose my job."

"Your job? That's pretty serious doings."

"The old man grabbed me. I didn't tell you that. In the supply room when I was getting his safety gear. He walked up behind me, grabbed my breast, and he forced his crotch into my backside." She took a deep breath. It was okay for Ben to know about this. She wouldn't have told anyone else. He was the only one who wouldn't see her words as whining. She was simply telling, and he would accept it as such.

"Did you report it?" She shook her head no. "Did you tell anyone?" Again her head moved in the negative. Ben chided this woman he loved and protected. "You should have, you know, to have it on record. However, even that wouldn't take your job. What's the rest of it?"

She laughed and shook her head. "I don't know for sure. Not all of it, anyway. I was asleep, and there he was in my room, stripped to his underwear, and having a heart attack. I tried to help, and before long, I was the wanton woman seducing an eighty-year-old man. It also seems that in the process, I was also the one who caused him to have that heart attack."

Ben's big black face began to smile, and he couldn't keep his chuckles inside. "You knocked him dead, huh? I knew you had it in you, girl. Five years in oil, and you've still got the sex appeal to knock the man dead."

Lou looked at Ben for a long moment, and then she smiled. "I guess you're right, except he's not dead. At least he wasn't when MedEvac arrived. It got worse, though." God help her if the man's eyes didn't twinkle, and then he winked.

"How can it be worse?" His honeyed voice reached around his good friend and comforted her, as his big lips fought a grin.

"Chad walked in—"

"I told him to stay away from you."

"—and the old man had my bra in his hand. I was on the bed and he was on the floor—in his underwear, Ben."

Ben was actually laughing, now. He reached to wipe the tears from his eyes, laughing and saying that this was the funniest thing he'd ever heard.

"Tell me it gets worse, Lou." He looked at her, daring her to say more.

"Oh, I can do that for you. Then Chaddie came running up, and I was there wrapped in just a sheet."

Ben snorted in mirth. "Did the grandfather still have your bra in his hand?"

"Yes. Of course he did, and all the medical team were in there working to keep the old geezer alive. I was praying he'd die, and one of the girls was praying to God for his recovery. I wanted to hit her." She reached and took his hand. "Ben, and by God, I'm serious, Chad made me lie to the boy to explain why his great-grandfather had my bra in his hand."

Ben roared, and in his deep, melodious voice, he crooned, "We've been making passionate love, your great-grandfather and I." His eyes glinted at his own humor.

214

Lou could resist Ben's mirth no longer. Breaking down, she chuckled, then she slapped her leg with laughter and tried one of her own. "I did a strip tease show, and Gramps caught the prize."

Ben hooted, "It was only a dollar. But he wouldn't pay up."

"He's a heartless fool."

"You can't stop time, but you can break a heart."

"My prince was nothing but a frog."

"And he croaked."

The comments had been silly, but the tension that had wound Lou tighter than a spring had broken. In the aftermath of the jokes, both people, one large and dark, and the other petite and light, wiped their eyes as they sat in silence. Finally, Lou turned to the mountain of a man across from her.

"Marry me, Ben. You're the only man I love."

He reached for her hand, and it was small in his. Raising it to his mouth, he kissed it. His deep voice melted warm butter over her as he spoke.

"You'll find love, Lou. It's out there for you, if you can take the time to let it find you." The whites of his eyes glowed warmly in his face, and his teeth flashed as his words wrapped her. "Don't ever take seconds where your heart is concerned. I love you, but I'm not your love."

She sighed, pulling his hand to her face to return his kiss. "I know. You're here, though. That counts for something."

"That counts for a friend. You can't marry a friend. You can care about a friend and stand up for them. Once in a while you lose them, and occasionally you find them again."

"Can you hug a friend?" She looked at him with impending tears in her eyes.

His smile was wide as the Grand Canyon. "Of course, you can. If they're a really good friend." He pulled her close and let her wipe her tears on his shirt for a second time that day. Then, separating, he whispered, "Better? We do have a storm on the way, and all the hugs out there won't get this rig shut down."

"I know. Thank you. I feel I might actually be able to get through this now."

BEN HAD no doubt she would. Lou was tough as nails, and that's what it took to survive on an oil rig. Soft people got chewed up and spit out. On days like today, Lou might need a little foundation repair, but then she would be all right once again. He was glad to help out, too.

After all, she *was* his friend.

"DAD, WILL IT get worse?" Chaddie held onto Stinky's leash, and he kept turning around to walk backwards. "We won't have to evacuate, will we?"

"Son," his father cautioned, "watch for the dog. You've nearly tripped on her several times."

"Dad, you haven't answered me. Will it?" They were at their room, and Chad twisted the knob to swing the door wide. Chaddie pushed for an answer. "Dad?"

"Sit," Chad said, as he swung the door closed. Turning around to see Chaddie on the bed, and the black Rottweiler on the floor at his feet, he laughed. "It works!"

"What?" The boy reached a hand and ran it down the

dog's back.

Chad smiled and ignored that question as he knelt in front of the dog. "Good girl, Stinky. You do learn when someone works with you." He let his fingers grab her ears, and he rubbed the flaps of skin between his fingers. She immediately began to pant, letting her tongue hang from her mouth.

"Of course, she does," Chaddie said.

Chad stood. "She's a good dog, Son. Did you see that?" Chaddie watched his father, though. He understood what he was doing. He didn't want to answer his question, and that was an answer in itself.

The boy stood and reached to pick up the clothes he'd taken off the night before. They were scattered across the room where he had tossed them, and now he wanted them packed away. *If* they had to go, or probably *when* they evacuated, he wanted to be ready, even if his father didn't want to talk about it. He folded several items, but instead of putting them into a drawer, he pulled out his bag and laid them inside.

"What are you doing, Son?"

"Remember yesterday when we got here? I was stupid and said to Lou that I'd like to be here during a hurricane. She said almost everyone evacuates. I didn't think I'd want to leave, even if everyone else did. I've changed my mind."

His father walked up to him and put a hand on his shoulder. "So, you're packing for the evacuation."

"Yes, sir. Just in case." His hand picked up the plaid boxer shorts he'd just put inside, and he slowly unfolded them and began to refold them more neatly. It was nervousness, although neither of them mentioned it. "Is that okay?"

His father squeezed his shoulder and then patted him on the back. "Sure. It's well past bedtime, and we're both too wound up to sleep. Packing just in case is okay. Then let's go try out one of those game consoles down below. It seems you were pretty good at auto racing when we used to play. Are you still?"

Chaddie looked at his father, and he let an eager smile flash across his face, the offer needed and welcomed. "Racing? Sure. If they've got combat games, I'm even better at that. Can we do one of those, too?"

CHAD PULLED his son to him in a quick hug, and he laughed at the boy's sudden enthusiasm for the diversion he'd offered. The shift in scenarios was just the thing to bleed the tension that had been building as the storm outside gathered its strength. The boy's emotions were quick to shift, both up and down, but he was also quick to recover.

Now, if he could just do that himself. As harsh as he'd been to the woman who had gotten hold on his emotions, he knew the situation as he had perceived it hadn't felt on the up and up. When he'd seen the old man and Lou in that compromising situation, he'd been shocked, to put it mildly. She'd been adamant about how it wasn't as it seemed, but in his anger, Chad hadn't given her the benefit of the doubt for the second time.

Chad knew Gramps, or at least well enough. He'd been married to the old man's granddaughter for twelve years. There were almost forgotten things starting to stir in the back of Chad's mind, old memories and events that had never seemed connected before. Now that he was calmer, he could see them from a different perspective. He'd had some time to think about it, and, well, it just didn't seem quite right, not even a little bit. It was more than just Lou, too. It was a lifetime connected with the old man that didn't square.

Now wasn't the time to deal with all that, though. His son had things to pack, then the two of them needed to check out the gaming systems. This night didn't have to all go to waste. Not every bit of it, anyway.

Chapter 12

DEEP WITHIN the massive Coast Guard Medium Endurance Cutter *Dauntless*, over two hundred feet of it, powerful engines roared to life. The big ship had been prepared especially for this evacuation. U.S. Coast Guard Station Galveston also roared to life. On a screen at a desk that had been manned just moments ago, a message blinked, and it matched the one scrolling across the bottom of the television monitor sitting in another room in the building.

"Mandatory evacuations have been ordered for Galveston County and all surrounding low-lying areas. Twenty-six manned oil platforms directly in the path of the oncoming storm should be in shutdown mode by dawn. Ninety percent of those personnel are hoped to be on Coast Guard or other rescue vessels by mid-morning. Do not

delay. This is a mandatory evacuation."

"Tucker. Johnson. Abramski."

The responses were just as succinct.

"Sir."

"Sir."

"Sir."

The officer barked his next words. "Let's go, men. We have lives to save."

They did, too. Oil production was important to the United States economy, and shutting down an oil production platform was an involved process. It wasn't like flipping a switch. Each of the men stationed here knew that. Getting each platform back on line was equally involved, more so if the storm damaged the machinery. For both reasons, ones diametrically opposed to each other, the platforms wouldn't be shut down until the last possible moment. For those same reasons, the evacuation procedures required the men on the platforms to be pulled off in the worst possible storm conditions. On twenty-six platforms, that meant there could easily be two thousand men still waiting for evacuation. The Coast Guard officer sending these three men outside was glad his wasn't the only ship preparing for rescue tonight.

Stepping out of the building, the men were hit by the rain that had already begun to lash the coast. This wasn't even the storm yet, at least not the brunt of it. They would hit that once they pushed through the stiff chop that had already begun to build all along the Houston shipping channel. Even the Intracoastal Waterway was already showing signs of wave action. There would be no protection for anyone anywhere, and even the Coast Guard would want to hunker down when the heaviest weather hit.

Tucker, Johnson, and Abramski jumped aboard the cutter, completing the complement of crewmembers already aboard. The men were thoroughly energized, too. This was what they'd trained to do. For most of them—Tucker, Johnson, Abramski, as well as others on board—they thrived on adrenalin-rush adventure. Being close to death was what made life possible. This was no sailboat search, digging through lockers and bulkheads for contraband. This was life-affirming *action*.

Lt. Tucker would pilot the helicopter in the storm. It was an HH-65 Dolphin, and it had twin Turbomeca turboshafts that would blast through any weather, on autopilot, if necessary. Lt. Johnson would man the deck, pulling men aboard, settling them as efficiently as possible. He was also Tucker's copilot if needed. Petty Officer 3rd Class Abramski was the big man, though. As the rescue swimmer, he would go in the water if needed, attaching drowning men to harnesses and baskets, waiting in the maelstrom until the last civilian was aboard the helicopter. There were normally four crewmembers, but it had been decided to run one man short to leave room for as many civilians as possible. Rapid transfer of evacuees was paramount.

These three men didn't plan to let anyone die. If there were people on a rig, and they wanted off, these three men would see to it. Of course, there were always those workers that never evacuated. They made up the skeleton crew, and while being part of that crew was very dangerous, it was one more part of the life of an oil rig worker. Anyone who joined the Coast Guard understood that. Some men evacuated, and some were the last on the rig. Those that remained on board just hoped it didn't sink. They hoped that like crazy.

The big ship rocked against its mooring, and Tucker ran up to Abramski. Ducking his head to divert the water from his cap, he slapped the man on the back.

"Gonna get wet, Bram. You ready?"

Abramski reached out to yank at the tie-down straps holding the Dolphin in place, making sure they were secure. He laughed, "Too late for that, Tuck. I done got wet when I stepped out the door."

Tucker came back, "Damn right there. Think one of these jokers will get blown into the water during the evac like that guy we had to pull out during Ike?"

There was no hesitation in the reply. "One always does. That's why I'm along." He looked up into the blowing rain. "Are they going to cover the flight deck soon?"

Tucker slapped his shoulder before moving on, "Yeah. It'll roll out before we get underway. They'll take good care of the copter. You're a good man to have aboard, Abramski."

Abramski watched the pilot's back, his quick footsteps carrying him away, before moving to check the next strap. His next words were to himself, but he would say them to anyone who wanted to listen.

"We're a good *team* to have aboard, Tuck. That's even more important." He knew it was, too, even aboard the *Dauntless*. It was the *team* that was important.

CARS SKIDDED across city streets, and in a fiery explosion, a rain of death showered onlooking pedestrians.

"That was so cool, Dad! We *both* crashed and burned."

Chaddie lifted one of his headphones and turned to his father. His green eyes sparkled with excitement. Except for his height and his broad shoulders, he could easily have been ten years old again. Inside, he was.

His father grinned, and instead of answering, he held the remote high in the air. Then, with a dramatic flourish, his thumb pressed the reset button. With a flash of light on the screen, both cars shimmered onto a fresh city street, and they were instantly at full speed.

"Wait, Dad. Pause it. I wasn't ready." Chaddie laughed as he fumbled for his headphones.

"Sorry, Son. You snooze; you lose." With a flickering of his thumbs over the remote, his car skidded around a corner and began to increase in speed. With blinding movement, it hit a drawbridge and flew off the end. It seemed to float, and the back end shifted until glowing, neon lights could be seen outlining the undercarriage. Then, with a slapping thunk, it skidded back onto the road surface and was off again.

The father and son were the only ones in the recreation room. They had gathered in the back section that was separated off for die-hard gamers. Everyone else was catching a few hours' sleep before the evacuation, either that or in the process of finalizing the shutdown proce-dures. For the rest of the rig's crew, no one could imagine the game consoles being occupied at a time like this. A storm was coming, and a shutdown was in progress. Who would play video games during a hurricane?

However, this man and his son had just reconnected after three years apart. They were excited with each other's company, and when immersed in their video games, the time passed unnoticed.

Also passing unnoticed was the increasing fury of the winds just outside. The waves were hurling huge fists of water at the rig, attempting to smash it into the sea. It couldn't reach it just yet, but it was trying. It also knew a bigger series of brothers were on its way, and bigger brothers meant more power and larger waves.

Inside, there were only small windows in the games area of the recreation room. The occasional shuddering of the floor could easily be the cars on the television monitors as they slammed into each other. The father and his son grinned at each other over the realism of this gaming setup. Who knew it would have vibration modules built right into the floor? They expected that in the remotes. All they ones they'd played with for years had that. In the floor, though? It was great, and if the vibrations didn't always match the action on the screen, then what of that? It was a game, wasn't it, and games were just that. Games. They weren't perfect, and they weren't real life. They were fun, and that's all they were supposed to be. This one was, too, vibrating floor and all.

In the corner, Stinky opened her eyes for a look, and seeing something reassuringly familiar, a video game in progress, she rested her eyelids again. There was nothing to worry about for her. Life was going on as usual, and she was safe. That was the extent of her worries, and that meant she could sleep. She did, too. Just like that.

THE TELEVISION flickered off, and the room was silent. The morning sun streamed in thorough broad windows, and the lined woman jerked her head sideways, painfully

225

sitting up. Nearly eighty wasn't the same as nearly thirty.

"What's going on here?" Granny Reinhardt looked at the black surface of the television in front of her. "Who turned that off?" She fumbled on the table at her side for the remote, and then she spied it on the coffee table. She called to her son, "Bill!" She knew he should be here. He had been when she dozed off.

It was her grandson who poked his head in the door. He was staying with her for the day, and he could bring it to her.

"Willie, get me that remote."

"Where, Granny?" He was eating again, and his attention was focused on his peanut butter sandwich. She was glad to see that. He needed to eat. She'd been there when he'd lost his suit in his sister's pool, and if he had more meat on his bones, he'd be able to keep his clothes on. He'd just grown so much in the past year. Six inches or more, she thought, and none of the growth had been on his backside.

"It's right there on the coffee table. See it?" She pointed. "I must have hit the sleep timer by accident when I turned it on. The TV went off by itself."

"Oh, sure. I've done that before." He picked up the remote and handed it to her. "What were you watching?"

"Weather." She peered at the small numbers on the control. Brushing up against seventy-nine, she didn't see as well as she used to. Pushing one that seemed to say *power,* she smiled to see the television light up, a weather map the first thing on the screen.

Willie grabbed the remote from her hand and flicked the television back off. When his grandmother slapped the arm of her recliner in frustration, he laughed.

"Granny, you don't need the weather on. Look outside. The sun's shining. You mean you can't predict that it might be hot with a good chance of sunburn?" He flopped down on the couch and held the remote up in the air. "So, what else do you want to watch?"

She leaned forward and grabbed the remote from him. She'd found the power button once, and she could do it again. When the television flickered back into life, she settled into her recliner, letting it lean back to her favorite position. She looked at her grandson, thinking how handsome he was. Skinny, yes, but she loved him anyway. Skinny and handsome. Buck naked in the pool just last week, but handsome, anyway. He was a wild-child rascal, too.

"You ornery fool," she muttered.

He grinned. "What, Granny? Horny mule? Is that what I heard you say?" He reached and patted her hand. "Slow down, old girl. The pasture's just fine on this side of the fence."

She slapped at his hand, and he jerked it away. "You're the horny fool, you scalawag. I know that word. Horny. You're almost nineteen, and you chase girls. That's what boys do. I was a teenager once, you know."

"GRANNY, YOU were born old. Look at you, watching the weather for entertainment." He looked at her with a grin. "Besides, how do you know I'm horny?"

Willie loved teasing his grandmother. She could give as well as he could throw out. She never got offended, either. She just came back with another gibe that was often as good as his.

She snorted. "I had a boyfriend once. It was back in high school. I got away before he trapped me, and I was glad to be gone."

Willie laughed at her words. "Trapped you, Granny? No one could trap you. You'd figure out the lock and be gone before they could see your shadow."

"I was, too, Willie. He kept wanting in my drawers, and I wouldn't let him." She looked at him with one raised eyebrow. "You stay out of girl's drawers, Willie."

He rolled his eyes. "Granny, I didn't need to hear that. Let's not talk about anybody's drawers, especially yours. Mine, either."

She snorted. "I'll talk about anything I want, young man. When you were two and your mother died, I offered to take you. No, your sister said. He's my brother. He lives at my house. Well, you did, too, but I came over and changed a few of your diapers, boy. You've got nothing I ain't seen before."

"Aw, Granny," Willie said, covering his ears. "I just ate. Please."

"Don't you *Aw, Granny* me. I saw you in your sister's pool just last month. Grow it up, Willie, before some girl laughs at you." Seeing his discomfiture, she laughed. "I love poking at you, grandson. Everyone else in this family's too proper except your eldest sister. I miss that Lou being around. She's feisty like me. I always liked that in her."

"Me, too, Granny. What about that boyfriend? Can we talk about that instead of me?" He grinned at her as he eyed the remote in her hand. "I get that remote from you, and

I'm changing the channel. You better start talking, now."

"I thought I'm marry him."

"Not Grandpa? Granny! I never knew you had two loves in your old heart."

She wagged her finger at him. "Be glad I didn't, boy. You might have been just like him. Then you wouldn't have been so good at controlling that male member of yours. You do keep it tucked away when you date those girls of yours? Tell me, now." She looked at him, and it was clear she was serious.

"Granny! Bethel Baptist, remember? We both go there. What do you think I am? A backslider?"

She snorted again. "That's not what I asked, grandson. This is important. You haven't let any girls at it, have you? You're not married, yet. Not for a long time, I hope, either. If they ask, you tell them to keep their hands out of your drawers and to go take a cold shower. You, too, Willie. Take lots of cold showers, you hear me?" She looked at him. "Well?"

"Well what, Granny?" Willie drew in a deep breath. This was no longer discussion territory for him, and if she was going to chase this answer, he wasn't going to make it easy for her.

She leaned forward and slapped his arm. "Have you kept yourself under control, William Reinhardt? Do I need to be more specific?"

That broke Willie up. He slapped the couch with the palm of his hand as he laughed. "You're a hoot, Granny. I'll keep it under control whenever I'm on any of my dates, no matter how wild we get. Does that make you happy?"

She settled back in her recliner. "I was to be prom

queen. All the votes were counted, and I won. I know it."

"Prom queen, Granny? I thought this was about your boyfriend."

"He was the king, Willie. Prom king, and he was standing up there with his crown on his head. Captain of the football team. All the girls wanted him. I thought I loved him."

"Thought, Granny? You always tell me that when I fall in love, I'll know for sure."

"It's not that easy, boy."

GRANNY PAUSED and closed her eyes as she remembered the humiliation of all those years ago, seeing Wally up there on the stage, and him looking at her as he called her his love. However, it seemed she hadn't been his only love. There had been thirteen others. She knew, because she counted. When she saw them, things had fallen into place for her. Stories he told her about why he was late. Looks from the girls on the cheerleading squad. Times his parents had called looking for him, and she'd been home for hours already. It all made sense that night.

"Granny," Willie interrupted. "You asleep?"

She opened her eyes and peered at him. "Remembering, grandson. That boyfriend, the king of the prom, always wanted me to put out for him. I never would, though."

"Put out, Granny?"

She patted his hand. "Male member games, Willie. Think about it. You'll understand." She smiled to watch him turn red. "I was pretty then, Willie. We were *people*, too. Teenagers. I'm sure you can imagine it." He sank lower into the couch.

"Well, what happened? Why didn't you marry him?"

"He stood on that stage and called for the girl he loved to come up and be his queen. He looked right at me. Before I could move, thirteen other girls ran up on stage to stand beside him." She remembered one that had jumped in his arms, too.

"Thirteen, Granny? What about you?"

"Willie, do these phrases mean anything to you: two-timing; sleeping around; cheating?"

He laughed sourly. "Yeah. An old girlfriend."

"I didn't even know until that night he'd been doing that to me for three years. More, maybe. It's been a long time for me to remember exactly. I remember that night, though. I never saw him again."

"Good for you, Granny. What happened to him?"

"He ran his daddy's business in the ground. Moved to Dallas. Stayed rich. Turned into an old fool." She let her eyes rove to the screen on the television. Her interest in Wally was fading. It had been over sixty years, and she had made a point of keeping that time of her life pushed far into the back of her memories. Willie had one more question he wanted answered, though.

"What business, Granny? I have to know."

"Business?" Her eyes flickered across the television screen, looking for interesting bits of weather information. "Oh, you mean Wally's business. The building's still there. You've seen it, though it's closed down now. Saunder's Tool and Die out west of town."

Willie jumped up, and he stood between his grandmother and the television. Excitement was all over him.

"Old Man Saunders? Granny, I know about him. Sam from school, my best friend. You know him. He's, like, Saunder's great-nephew by, like, the old man's third wife. Saunders's richer'n God with all these big houses all over. You almost *married* him?" He danced in a circle. "Wow! We'd have been so rich. I could've had a new Corvette for graduation."

When he danced close enough, Granny slapped him down. "You would have been a grandson from his *first* marriage, and he'd have forgotten all about you. Besides, no one's richer than God. A good Christian boy shouldn't say things like that." She looked at him to see that more of his boxers were showing than she liked. "Pull those pants up, Willie. You're about to be showing again."

He grabbed them and tugged. "Sorry, Granny. I'm eating peanut butter like you said. My pants just won't stay where I put 'em."

"I forgive you, Willie. Besides, someday when you get married," and she emphasized the word *married*, "your wife'll be glad to hear you say that every night. Now just sit with me and watch this for a bit."

"Granny," he complained. "It's the weather, and it isn't even for here. It's for Texas and Louisiana. What do we care about down there?"

"We care because your sister's down there. Lou's on that well down there in the water, and I love that girl." She looked at him with a frown. "More than you, Willie."

He laughed and jumped up. With a twinkle in his eye, he planted a kiss right on her forehead. "You don't love anyone more than me. I'm going to get me another sandwich. By the way, Dad left an hour ago. You were asleep, and he had to be at the church. I told him I could borrow your car later if I needed to go out on a hot date with some wild girl." He grinned as he pulled his pants up with one hand and headed into the kitchen.

Granny called after him, "Don't bet on it. Remember, when you were a baby, I saw you play with it, and I slapped your hand away. I can still slap, you know."

He yelled back, "I don't play with it anymore, Granny."

She mumbled too low for him to hear, "So you'd like me to believe. You shower in my bathroom, grandson." However, she did love this boy, even more than Louinda, if that were possible. Now, she needed to watch the weather. She might not be able to help her granddaughter, but she could certainly worry about her.

She could say a prayer, also. Prayers worked. She knew that. She hadn't married Wally, had she? That one thing alone proved that prayers worked very well, indeed.

LOU HUNG onto the rail as the wind and rain buffeted her. It should be morning, and the sun should be up. However, the day was barely there against the glare of the platform's lights. Most of the equipment was shut down, but the illumination on the outside of the rig had to guide the evacuation efforts.

Yolanda had been in contact with shore, and it was the Coast Guard coming for the workers on this rig. A big boat, too, they said. A cutter with a helicopter. Lou was glad for that. She didn't want to force men into a basket to be hoisted to sea level. In this weather, there was too great a risk for someone to be dumped into the sea. However, she also knew the helicopter would have its own risks. The pilot would have to be an expert at landing in high winds, and it would take a number of repeated trips to get everyone to the ship.

She wondered if she would see people she knew on the cutter. It would be evacuating other rigs, also. There was Tom from over on Yellowfish No. 5, and she thought Brandon was still working Manta Ray. He might be ashore, though. He'd been rotating off when she was in Galveston last. Some rigs would leave a skeleton crew on board, and others would do as Sunshine Gulf was doing, especially the older, smaller rigs. Everyone would go. She hoped Cracker's Barrel evacuated everyone. She knew too many people on that rig, and she wanted them safe. Torch was there before coming to Sunshine Gulf. He might have heard.

Lou looked up at the helipad. Surely it had been more than two days since Chad and his son had come aboard. She'd been furious that her rig had been invaded. She'd thought of it as an invasion of her privacy, and she knew that feeling hadn't changed in two days. He'd come to invade her rig, and then she'd been thrown off her feet when he stepped from that helicopter. His movements had shown such assurance, and there was grace and fluidity in his walk. She had seen her Tracy in that.

His son had been the unexpected surprise. She had seen that youthful face and had prepared herself to hate him. She'd been unable to do so, and that boy still had a hold on her heart. So did that man who had brought him aboard, but she didn't have that man. She'd placed her trust in Ben, and Ben said to stay away from him, to let things alone.

She dared not think about the old man who'd been airlifted off. She just shook her head and put her thoughts of him aside. She'd have to work out all that later. Now, she needed to go up to make sure all the preparations for the evacuation were complete. The helipad was her next stop.

With a determined tread, Lou grabbed the rail and placed her foot on the first step. She looked down at the placement of her boot on the tread, careful of a misstep. It was a long way up, and in this storm, it was an even longer way to the bottom. She didn't dare make a mistake at this point, not in something so simple as making her way to the landing pad. She couldn't afford to be distracted, not by Chad or that wicked old pervert who had come to harass him. It was too windy, and that wasn't a good way to die.

Chapter 13

TUCKER WRESTLED the throttle as he struggled to keep the helicopter steady against the gusting wind. He knew the Dolphin would hover on autopilot by itself. It was that good a machine. However, a hover wasn't what he needed just now.

He peered down to where Abramski could be seen hooking a harness around a fool oil rig worker who had fallen off the helipad. Tucker groused to himself as he waited for the signal. *Cracker's Barrel, my lovely backside! This rig ought to be renamed Barrel of Crackers. All the man had to do was stand still. Instead, he backed right off the helipad. Was he scared of the rotors? Old Tuck here knows how to fly this thing.*

Then his headphone crackled. "Take her up, Tuck.

Abramski says he'd like us to hurry back. He's getting more than a mouthful of water, and it don't taste so good."

Tucker laughed. "Sounds like Abramski. I'll do my best, Johnson."

With a roar of the machine's motors, the rotor blades shifted, and the Dolphin lifted into the air. The idiot who had forced Abramski to jump in after him hung at the end of a long tether. Tucker cringed at the image that suddenly jumped into his mind, one of Abramski enduring his back-wash while in the sea. There was no way to avoid it, but Tucker knew what it felt like to have seawater thrash his skin. It was like a thousand needles, and he hated to be the one to do that to his friend.

Abramski, however, would have to wait. If Tucker couldn't nail this man's delivery, it would be that much longer that his friend would be out there, so it was to everyone's advantage for the pilot, and that was Tucker, to be as focused as possible.

His headphones crackled on. "You're there, Tuck. Down twenty feet, fifteen, ten, slowly, slowly, hold. Wait. Lift now. Hard." The helicopter surged into the blinding rain, and Tucker was pressed against his seat.

"How's that, Johnson?" He chuckled into the micro-phone. In the back of the helicopter, Johnson wasn't in a seat like Tucker. He knew to hang on, though. "Hard enough?"

"God, Tuck," a breathless voice answered in his head-phones. "You nearly lost me there." The fury of the storm just outside the copter crackled through the 'phones.

"Anchored in, aren't you?" He was enjoying this.

"Yeah, but—"

Tucker snorted. "No buts, Johnson. If you'd fallen out, you could have climbed back aboard by the tether. You didn't take a dive, did you?"

"I'm still here in the chopper, aren't I?" Johnson's voice was very unhappy, but that was fine with Tucker. Surprises were the spice of life, and that was what emergency rescue was all about.

"If you'd gone over, I'd have just looked for a new partner. You know. Variety, and all that. A new face for a copilot." He chuckled. "I knew you wouldn't, though. I trust you. Do you trust me?"

"Yeah, man. Let's just not let Abramski sit out there any longer than necessary. I'd hate to lose him."

"Won't happen." Tucker jerked the throttle sideways to line up the helicopter with his target. "I'm the best there is." He cackled his laughter into his mic. He repeated himself just to hear those words again. "I'm the best there is."

THE SOLDIER leaned over the wall. The barrel of a long rifle could be seen as his eyes jumped from target to target. Deep in the woods, a movement could be seen behind a tree. The soldier's rifle jumped, and with a distant *oomph*, another man in a different style uniform fell to the ground. Blood covered the side of the tree.

Suddenly, with a scream of pain, the soldier jerked to his feet. The rifle he was holding shot off multiple rounds as his hand convulsed. Bullets riddled his body, splattering the wall with red. Falling, his hands released the gun, and it fell at his side.

Chaddie yanked his headphones from his head. "Dad! I was just about to get to the house. I cannot believe you took me out!"

Chad slapped his son on the shoulder as he pulled his headphones off. "You got close this time. Real close, Son. Good job!"

When his father reached to eject the game, Chaddie pulled on his arm to stop him. "One more time, Dad. I can make it this time. Please."

Chad chuckled. "You like to die, do you? I brought you into this world, boy, and I can take you out again. Are you sure you want to do this?"

Chaddie looked at him with concentration in his eyes. "You're dead, Dad. Plan on it. No more sniper rifles for me. I'm taking the machine gun this time."

"Okay, Chaddie. Best man wins."

Chaddie grinned and caught his father's eye. "No, Dad. Best *boy* wins!" He slipped his headphones on, and when he hit the reset button, the game was on.

"BEN SAYS we're ready. Muster lists are up, and I've spent the night talking to fifty-nine men. They know what's up, every one."

The toolpusher smiled at her. "Fifty-eight, Lou. You haven't talked to me."

She reached to her hair and ran her fingers through it. She was tired, but not too tired to make a joke. Or, perhaps she was willing to joke because she was tired. She no longer knew. The joke just seemed right.

"Sir, we are evacuating at first light. The rig must be non-operational before the last man is off. No crew will remain for the duration of the hurricane." She smiled. "Sir, I've now talked to fifty-nine."

He laughed. He was as tired as she was, but they would be away soon. Then he could let this go until the storm was over.

"It's going to be close, Lou. That storm's at hurricane strength just east of here. Take a pair of glasses and let me know when the copter's in sight. I've got Yolanda working the radio, but the signal's bad. Lots of static keeps messing up her broadcasts. I trust your visual report. I'll put the alarm out when you get back, get everyone to their muster stations."

She reached and took the binoculars. "Sir, I certainly will. They've already cleared Cracker's Barrel. Took every last man. It shouldn't be long before they get to us."

"Thank you, Lou. You're a good woman."

She nodded in recognition of the compliment, then turned, and picking up her safety gear, she was gone, closing the door after her. She was soon at the steps to the helipad once again, and she could tell the difference. The wind *was* stronger. She dreaded seeing any craft land in this. What if the machine just blew overboard? It was certainly possible, she supposed. She knew from experience, however, that military helicopters had the ability to turn the rotor blades and force themselves down on the landing deck. She'd been ferried out before in winds nearly as stiff as they were facing now. If the pilot was good, once the helicopter landed, it wasn't going anywhere until the pilot told it to.

Putting the glasses to her face, she scanned what she could see of the sea. It was all gray rain, roiling water, and more gray rain. She dropped the binoculars to hang by its strap and began to climb. At the third level up, she caught a glimpse of something off to sea. Moving more quickly, she reached the landing deck, and she lifted the glasses back up. Holding them to her face, she scanned once again, and there it was, white and black, with a helicopter visible on board. Satisfaction surged through her. The men on board this rig would be safe.

With a smile across her face, she headed to the pusher's office. *Hit the alarm, John. The ship's here. It's time to go home.*

IT WAS, too, for the sixty people on the muster lists. Lou had talked to fifty-nine, and she made it a round sixty. However, two people weren't on those muster lists; they were in the recreation room with headphones on, listening to soldiers shoot-'em up. Lou hadn't talked to them, and in the tired fog of her mind, it never crossed her thoughts.

When the alarm went off, lights could be seen blinking off in rooms all over the accommodations, and soon the offices went dark as well. As switches were flipped, computer monitors went black, and the power for the HVAC units went off line. Exterior lights were manually extinguished all over the rig. Only the landing lights remained, with a backup generator left running to power those until they were no longer needed. As safety-suited men covered in rain gear gathered at their assigned muster points, no one could see that the recreation room lights were still on. Those windows were off down the side towards the sea.

With the helipad lights blazing God-knew-how-many foot-candles into the darkened sky, Tucker had no problem landing his craft. Abramski jumped from the Dolphin and counted out six men. Johnson pulled them aboard, and they were away. Six was crowded, especially for the Dolphin, but Tucker was skilled. When he first landed, a mountain of a black man told him there were sixty workers to ferry off. Tucker had nodded and known he needed ten trips, eleven if some of the rig workers were big. He'd like to make it nine, but there was no way. Abramski would remain on the rig to organize the evacuees, and Johnson would stay with the copter to move them onto the ship. Abramski would be taken off with the last man.

On the next to last trip, Johnson jumped off the copter and pulled the black man aside. He yelled to him over the fury of the storm, "Hey. You've got some lights on below. Two windows, center level. You sure everyone is up here?"

Ben knew which windows those were. He yelled back, "If they're not, they will be when you return. Thanks!"

"Gotcha," Johnson yelled back, giving him a thumbs-up signal and a grin. Then he turned and was on board the helicopter. Ben stepped back, and the machine was gone to deliver its load of men.

Ben ran to find Lou. It was difficult to tell one person from another under normal circumstances, with the safety gear they wore. With the rain gear everyone had on over their safety gear, it was near impossible. Her size was her only giveaway. Grabbing her arm, he yelled, "Lou. Lights are still on in the recreation room. Are you sure everyone's out?"

Before she could answer, Abramski stepped up. "Is there a problem?"

Ben turned his eyes to him. "Lights are on below. Your

man on the copter saw them. We need to check on it before he gets back."

"The rig's powered down, already." Abramski looked up and across the monstrosity, mostly dark. Only the landing lights were operational now, and they wouldn't be pulling from the platform's main power supply at this stage of shutdown. All platforms had reserve batteries for the helipad lights, just in case of power failure. He grasped Lou's arm to get her attention. "Lights below?"

Ben answered him. "There's a backup generator running for the helipad lights. The helipad and accommodations block are tied in together. Our reserve batteries for this are down." He motioned with his hand at the lights blazing just where they stood, a brilliant beacon in a sea of darkest gray.

Abramski looked at his watch, and then he held up a white board and a grease pencil. "Go. I'm keeping track. If you're not back, I'll know. I've loaded fifty-four. What's the total again?"

Ben looked to Lou and shrugged. She was the one who bore that responsibility. She called, "Fifty-eight, plus us."

Just then a gust of wind hit the rig, and Abramski tapped his ear. As the wind continued to whistle, he yelled a number for confirmation. "Fifty-eight?"

Lou shot him a thumbs-up signal and yelled back. "Plus us."

THE WIND upped its game, letting out a vibrating screech just then, tearing her words away. Abramski shot her a return thumbs-up, turned, and wrote the number down, then looked to find where Tucker was. He wanted off this rig as much as these men. The adrenalin rush was what he lived for, but after a time, all that's left was the tired feeling, and he was about there.

He looked at his board. Fifty-four across to his cutter, and four people still to go. He didn't stop to check that there were already four standing behind him. His numbers didn't account for the two headed down the steps, and there were two more besides those that no one had thought to warn. That meant four people weren't on Abramski's board. Five if Stinky were to be saved.

HALFWAY DOWN the steps, Louinda froze, and she grabbed Ben's arm. In the howling wind, she looked in his face. It was growing light enough to see each other, and he stood out against the tormented clouds that were closing in.

"Ben. I forgot to warn them. How could I have done that?" She was rooted to the step, her stomach knotted with dread.

"Don't know what you mean, but we need to hurry. I don't expect anyone's down there, but we must verify everyone's off. C'mon, there's no time to waste."

He motioned her along, but she resisted, turning to look back up the steps. Indecision engulfed her: to race for the rec room, or to return topside to question the rescue personnel.

"Lou, the recreation room. We need to get back up top. Come on."

"Ben, did you load Chaddie and his father on the helicopter already? I must know. The dog, too. I couldn't have missed the dog. They wouldn't have been on the muster lists. My God, Ben. It's got to be them in the recreation room. I never talked to them."

Ben closed his eyes, the whites going dark in his broad face. "Two days and all the trouble with the boy's great-grandfather. I bet no one thought to get Yolanda to enter them into the system."

"Then with the rig's shutdown, it's thrown everyone off. The boy wasn't supposed to be here, and I'd hoped he'd be gone today. They weren't being tracked, and they've been overlooked." Her gut churned with the implications.

"Lou." He opened his eyes, zeroing in on her face. The gravel was back in his voice, and it got her attention. "That means we must go faster. You must move." He looked up to find the helicopter to see it already returning. He pointed. "Now, Lou."

She looked up at the blur of blades flinging storm water out in a great circle. "They know we're here. They'll wait for us. You're right, though. We must hurry. In this storm, I wouldn't trust this place. I never knew that before, but I do now. We cannot let a boy die just because we were careless."

Slamming open the door to the accommodations block, she reached and palmed a switch on the wall. Lights flickered on. She looked at Ben. "Thanks for not tripping those breakers."

He grinned. "I did, to the main power panels, anyway. The emergency generators won't run for long, though. I kept the fuel at a minimum, just enough to juice the jennies until we were off." He came to a set of steps. "Here." He ran up and flipped open a door, and sure enough, the lights inside were blazing away.

Lou called for the missing visitors. "Chad! Chaddie! Are either of you in here?" When there was no response, she breathed a sigh of relief. Looking at Ben she smiled. "I guess they loaded, and I missed them, somehow. In this rain gear, I can't tell one man from another."

Ben let a smile break onto his face. "Even me, Lou?"

She called back as she turned to the door, "Oh, I'd know you, Ben. You're unmistakable."

As her hand reached for the switch, the lights went out, and the sharp report of a barking dog echoed in the room.

"Lou," Ben started. "Did you hear that? Turn the lights back on."

She whispered, "I didn't turn them off. I think the generator's fuel is gone. What about that dog, Ben? You heard her. She's in here."

In the dimness of a room lighted only with small windows, the grayness of a storm-clouded sky didn't give much illumination. However, she could just make out the animal as Ben knelt and clapped his hands together.

"Stinky," he called. There were several more sharp barks, and then the big dog flew into his hands. "Lou, they must be in here. We have to find them."

Suddenly this was no longer about just finding two people she had forgotten to notify of an evacuation. This was also about a helicopter that would have no lights on the helipad. Perhaps the morning had brightened enough for it to land and take off. She could only hope so.

Her voice cracked as it came out, "Ben, we just looked, and we didn't see them. Do you think they would have left the dog by herself?"

At that point, a loud boy's voice called out of the darkness, "Who turned the lights off? I was about to kill Dad. I was finally to the house this time."

"Chaddie? Where are you?" Lou felt relief rush over her. "Is your father here with you?"

She saw someone step from the gaming area, and in the dimness, she couldn't tell if it was the father or the son. In the smoothness of his fluid, leonine movements, she recognized Chad, and as he approached, his grace twisted at her heart, and relief flooded her. It was as if the storm were no more than a summer shower, and she'd found the cure to her heartache. What he'd said to her earlier was gone as if it had never happened, and all she remembered was that she wanted this man. He had become real to her, his faults had made him approachable, and he had made her feel alive again.

She ran to him, and she grabbed him. "Chad, I'm so sorry." She was, too, and she would do anything to right their misunderstandings.

The person in her grasp laughed. "I'm Chaddie. Dad's tangled in his headphones. When the televisions went off, we couldn't see, and he got his wires twisted." He turned at a noise behind him, and another person walked in from the back of the darkened space.

A man's voice called out, "Chaddie, did anyone say what's wrong with the power?"

Embarrassed at having mistaken the son for his father, Lou's response was sharper than she might have intended, and she emphasized her words by using his last name. "What's *wrong* with the power? There's a storm, Mr. Dickson, and you're endangering the lives of both yourself and your son. We must get both of you up to the helipad immediately." She could take no more time to explain. She realized that.

They must go now.

IN THE UNEXPECTED darkness, Chad tried to put Lou's words in perspective. It had been a long night of high-energy gaming, and he hadn't eaten. He also couldn't imagine they had played until morning, even though they had done that frequently when the boy was small. Here on this rig in a storm? He could see dim light coming through the windows. Morning was on its way.

But the helipad. Why did they both have to go? If a chopper had arrived for his son, only Chaddie would be leaving. The storm didn't have Chad worried, not when sixty other people trusted the integrity of the platform.

He turned to his son. "Chaddie, I suppose you don't get to stay." Lou must have set this up, and she knew he'd want to see his son off. If the helicopter was here, there was nothing much he could do. He did feel regret for the refreshed bond that had begun to solidify between them.

"What are you thinking? No one's staying." In the darkness, Lou turned for support. "Ben?"

The big man stepped in with his strong, rumbling voice. "Chad, you seem to be unaware of what's going on right now. We're evacuating, and the last helicopter is waiting on us. We must go now."

"Evacuating? You're serious?" Chad stepped through the door to peer into the corridor. "I need to get my things. My son started packing, but I haven't. Are *all* the lights out?"

Ben barked, and his words were dark with insistence, "There's no time, sir. We must go to the helipad directly. The evacuation team won't wait longer. Chaddie, you, also, must hurry."

The boy's mind shifted gears faster than his father's, and his words were high-pitched with sudden anxiety. "That's why the power's off, isn't it? Can Stinky go with us?"

Louinda gripped his arm and began to urge him on. "Of course. She can absolutely go with us. Please, though. We must head up now. We don't want to be left." This had been pressing before, and now it was urgent.

The four remaining souls on board headed out of the accommodations block, together with one frightened dog. They hurried, too, or as fast as they could stumble in the near darkness. They had to make up the lost time, and the helipad was a long way away.

"WOULD YOU look at that, Johnson? They've already shut down the power to the helipad. I'm glad the sun's up, if you can call it that. You'd think they'd wait until I'm down." The radio crackled as he talked. Lights blazed from his copter, illuminating the driving rain.

Johnson called to Tucker, "As ready as us to get to shore, I bet. You think this rig'll still be standing when this storm blows over?"

Tucker sighed and spoke into his mic. "Probably not. Sometimes these old platforms can't take the wind, and down they go. At least we'll have all the people off this one. I don't know why they don't all evacuate."

"Suckers for danger. That must be it. They should play

249

it safe like we do." He laughed at that.

"I'm setting down. Quiet, Johnson." The radio went silent, and Tucker worked the controls as he fought the blinding wind. It took more than one try, but eventually he was down safely. He looked up to see Johnson jump to the pad.

"Abramski, you got 'em all?" He looked to count four flapping sets of rain gear.

Abramski looked at the numbers on his board. "I got four more to check off." He turned and called out, "Let's load the final parties. Up this way, gentlemen. I'm marking each of you off my list." He did, too, making a tally mark for each body that stepped aboard. When they were finished, he turned to Johnson. "Four to go. Four loaded. Let's head out." When he started to jump aboard, Johnson grabbed his arm. He remembered two of the rig workers specifically, and he hadn't helped either of them aboard yet.

"The big man and the woman from earlier. Did they load?"

Abramski was tired. He'd counted his total, and besides, the rig was dark. How could anyone else be aboard? He answered as best as he could.

"I've got fifty-eight tallied, Johnson. The rig's powered down. Let's go."

"Abramski, did they?" Johnson wasn't so sure, and he needed to be. He remembered those two very well. They were polar opposites: tall and dark; short and light. "You couldn't have missed them."

Abramski blinked his eyes with exhaustion, insisting, "I saw them get on the last run. We got everyone." After all, he figured. Someone had turned the lights out. They must be on board. Who would hide on this rig in a hurricane?

He pushed Johnson on the back to let him know to give it up, and when the man finally moved forward to climb in, Abramski jumped in after him. With a thumbs-up sign, Tucker had them up and off the rig in a heartbeat.

Chapter 14

WHEN THEY opened the outside door, the sound of the thrashing rain assaulted them, and Stinky yelped and pulled back. A swiftly spreading odor of urine permeated the room. Chaddie looked compassionately at the poor animal whimpering beside him.

Kneeling, he rubbed her head. "Good girl. It's okay. We have to go outside, though."

Lou glanced at Chad in frustration, and she pressed on the boy's shoulder. "We have to move, Chaddie. Drag Stinky if you have to."

His father frowned. It was clear what was happening, and the lights *were* all off. He could see that, but the urgency was beyond him. Surely the stability of the rig itself wasn't in question.

He knelt beside his son and looked up at Lou. "The dog's frightened. Can't you see that?"

She hissed at him, her eyes leaping to Ben's face and back again. "We must move. Can't you see that?"

He was about to speak when Ben moved up, and the big man called to the dog. Lou was relieved to see the animal move forward. Ben was able to coax her out the door and into the rain.

"Lou, Chaddie and I don't have our safety equipment or our rain gear." He turned to the boy standing beside him. "Son—"

She interrupted with her own set of forceful instructions. "Chaddie, you're going to get very wet. So is your father. I know you don't have your helmet or your safely glasses, but just make do. It's only the distance up to the helicopter. That's as far as we have to go. There's the door. Out."

Her voice this time left no room for negotiation, and seeing his son step out the door, Chad braced himself and followed. It only took moments for his face to sting, and moments more for him to be drenched to the skin. Almost immediately, Ben came back down, meeting them with a very soaked Stinky, the two blocking their way. After a moment fighting the lashing rain, he worked his way to where Lou waited.

As they stood on the steps, rain and wind blasting the five of them, Ben described the very series of events Lou had hoped beyond hope wouldn't happen. The lights were off on the helipad, and there was no helicopter to pick them up. No, Ben didn't know what happened. Yes, he looked for the ship, and no, it wasn't there.

The clammy hand of defeat swept over Louinda. This man had now stranded her on a dark rig in the middle of the Gulf. No matter what she did now, there was no way to get away from him. In fact, she was *responsible* for him, and that was the worst-case scenario. She had to interact with him, and she still didn't know just why Ben had told her to stay away. A day ago, she'd been willing to allow Chad time to connect with her heart, or maybe she'd realized she was the one who needed the time to connect with his. Either way, she'd been willing to allow that it was possible for something to happen. Now, it seemed she was to be stranded *because* of this man.

Reaching to the pipe railing in front of her, she wiped it free of water only to see it immediately beaded with a mixture of sea spray and rain once again. They should be on that Coast Guard ship headed to safety, all four of them. Five, if she counted the dog, and Lou intended for the dog to be saved, too.

Yet, even in her rush of despair, she remembered her promise to herself from just a day ago. Twenty-four hours. She'd vowed to give this man a full day before writing him off her books. As she looked across the roiling water, sheets of rain coming in to throw themselves at the drilling platform battered their small group; and as her face felt the sting of the water, she reminded herself that the hours might be gone, but she also remembered the other numbers she had said. Thirty hours. Then thirty-six. Five years of loneliness wouldn't allow her to throw away her chance at happiness without at least that.

Her eyes glanced up to see Ben in his rain gear watching her. The water poured off his head in rivulets, and his concerned eyes peered out of his dark face. Then, behind him, her gaze shifted, and she saw the two men they had returned to rescue.

Men. This man and his son were so much alike in height and looks. There was that same blond hair, those eyes that a woman could fall into, and the way they moved, that assured grace that assumed command of everything around them. It was uncanny.

No, she knew better than to say it was uncanny. It wasn't uncanny. It was father and son. One was thirteen, and while he might have the body of a man, he was still a boy in his heart and mind. They were drenched. Their hair was plastered to their heads, and water dripped from their faces. They had no gear of any kind on, just thin shirts and pants, and the soaked fabric clung to them. Underneath, visible through the fabric, involuntary shivering of muscles told how cold they were. They looked tired, pathetic, and entirely vulnerable.

It was up to her, now. She had to make the call on this, and she harbored no doubts how bad this would get. This storm was growing worse as they stood here. Then, thunder reverberated across the landscape, and there was a brilliant flash of lightning that hit the top of the derrick. The report was sharp and loud, and everyone on the steps involuntarily ducked. Stinky tucked her tail between her legs, and she began to whine.

"Lou," Ben began in his resonating voice. "Standing here won't bring the ship back. Rampart Oil has let the escape pod maintenance go for years. They won't even release from their berths. We can't get off that way. We have to deal with this. Can we start with going inside?"

She brushed water from her face, and she realized she was getting wet even inside her rain gear. She couldn't imagine how Chad and his son felt. The dog, too.

As she pointed to the door, she watched Ben lead the others ahead, and Chad walked directly in front of her. Even in this maelstrom, there were things she could imagine that had little to do with the wild weather around them. They concerned the wild emotions roiling inside of her; and seeing Chad's shirt glued to his torso, and his pants clinging to his legs, revealed this man in a way that not even her imagination had been able to achieve. The quivering of his muscles as he shivered in the cold only accentuated his masculinity, his grace of movement, and the sudden rush of attraction that had overcome her in that moment he had stepped from the helicopter two mornings ago.

To focus, she placed each element of her current predicament in a separate box in her head. Stranded on this platform, they were in a potentially deadly situation, both for their lives as well as for her heart. Box one. In a wild jumble of thoughts, she also knew she'd been warned away from this man. Box two. He had a son and a dog he was responsible for, and that made up box three. The authority to take this rig down fit perfectly in box four. She felt a wild and inappropriate humor surge through her thoughts, and knowing her face couldn't be seen, she let herself smile in desperate abandon. Perhaps the storm would collapse the entire platform, and she could overlook that last item. It would be out of Chad's hands. If that were so, then maybe she could give this man forty-eight hours, or sixty, or whatever it took.

She would have to press Ben to answer for his concerns. There had to be a reason for the big man to come between them, and it had to be more than just this horrid Gramps character who had forced himself on board the rig. She was determined her friend would talk to her and explain.

Now, though, there were other concerns. There was a boy to take care of. He was bound to be frightened. His dog needed to be warmed up. Dry clothes would have to be found for his father. There was also the matter of the rig, itself. It was powered down, very dark, and it would soon begin to grow cold, frighteningly cold indeed, even here deep in the Gulf of Mexico.

JOHN MOVED about the Coast Guard cutter. People from his rig were on board, and as toolpusher, he knew they were people he was ultimately responsible for. There were also many others from other rigs, and that made it difficult to keep track of everyone.

He knew what the helicopter crew had told him. They'd gotten everyone off. When John had asked whether they'd checked off names using the muster lists, he'd been told it had been wet and windy, and they hadn't been able to work off the paper. However, they'd kept a tally with a grease pencil. Alas, the tallies had been wiped after clearing each rig, so, no, they didn't remember just how many they'd pulled off. Sunshine Gulf was one of many rigs they had been to during the night. John's rig was the last, and one of the crew, Abramski, had told John that he should be glad to have gotten off when they did. Another hour, and those on Sunshine Gulf might have had to ride it out.

Things were already that bad out there.

It was Lou that John was worried about, her and her friend Ben. He seemed to remember they were with him to board for the last copter ride off. Then, with everyone wearing rain gear and the lights failing at the last minute, the final loading of the rig's crew had been in the dark with only the copter's lights to guide them. John had been freezing by then, and once seated, he'd laid his head back to say a prayer of thanks. Everyone had sat quietly, trying to warm up, and there'd been no conversation.

It was only aboard the Coast Guard vessel that he'd noticed he hadn't seen Lou or Ben for some time. As the shortest and tallest people on his rig, they usually stood out, too. No one he talked with had seen them, either.

The ship was large, though, and there were bound to be places he hadn't checked. Besides, he'd been awake all night. Even for him, that was exhausting. He found an empty spot on the floor—just for a moment—intending to look more once he got his energy back.

However, while John was a night owl, even those wise old birds need to sleep during the day. Once his eyes closed, John did, too, soundly and without waking. They had a long way to travel, and even the ship's struggle against the raging waters of the Gulf didn't jar him from his sleep.

Others from Sunshine Gulf saw him and smiled, and one man even threw a coat over his boss. Because of him, they knew, there had been no one left behind, and for that, each one of them was profoundly grateful.

"GRANNY, DRYER'S done. Do you want me to bring the

clothes in here?" Willie leaned into the living room to where his grandmother was sitting in her recliner. "Granny, you awake?"

She waved the remote at him. "Willie, come in here. You want to see this."

He stepped into the room and threw himself on the couch. "What, Granny? It's just news. Can't you find any good action movies?"

She held the remote high and pressed the sound up. A green bar crawled across the screen as the newscaster's words grew louder. The image showed a man being off-loaded from an ambulance as lights on top flashed. The surrounding sky was still dark.

"There have been numerous reports of miraculous rescues that have come out of Hurricane Thomas, even as it lashes the Gulf Coast. Just last night, as the weather was taking a turn for the worse, this seventy-nine-year-old man was evacuated from an oil production platform in the Gulf of Mexico. It seems he was visiting his great-grandson, and he suffered a heart attack. I believe we have the name of the rig here. Yes, Sunshine Gulf Platform No. 9. No, I'm sorry. That's No. 6. Sunshine Gulf Platform No. 6. We have news that Sunshine Gulf Platform No. 6 has since been completely evacuated, and all personnel are safe and aboard a Coast Guard vessel. We wish them well. The man who was evacuated with the heart attack is none other than one-time Oklahoma City industrialist Wallace Fountaine Saunders. Good luck to you, Mr. Saunders, and to your great-grandson as well. In other news . . ."

Willie sat up, and he poked his grandmother's arm. "Granny, how'd you like that? It's your old boyfriend. He has great-grandchildren, now. Ha, that's funny." However, his interest in her old boyfriend was fleeting. He'd never have any of the old man's money, and surely, there was a movie on. "Give me the remote. I want to find something good to watch." He reached and snatched it from her.

She chided him. "Willie, you be careful. I still know how to slap your hand away. That's your sister's well down there. She's on that one."

Willie laughed. "Slow down, Granny, and turn your hearing aid up. They got her off, and the Coast Guard never lets anyone drown. She'll be here tonight, and you can tell her how worried you were. Look!" He had flipped through the channels, and there was a sudden explosion of blood on the screen. "They just killed that guy. That's so cool. I want to watch this movie."

Granny finally stood from her recliner. She looked at her grandson lying sprawled on her couch. He was a treasure, skinny legs and all. She guessed she'd keep him.

"I'm going to get the dryer, Willie. Do you want me to bring you a sandwich?"

He muted the sound and looked up at her. "Peanut butter?"

"If you want, grandson."

"Sure, Granny. I like peanut butter." Then, the sound from the television blasted the room once more.

"BEN, CAN we do anything about the lights?"

They were at least inside, and Lou had opened a door to get access to a bathroom and towels. Chaddie and his father were toweling off, and she was attempting to get the dog as dry as possible. It might take more than one towel for an animal this size, though.

She called out, "Chad, do you think Chaddie would mind getting another towel for Stinky?" In the dimly lit space, it was hard to tell who she was looking at, and she was relieved to see the man she thought was Chad raise his head to look her direction.

"Sure," he said. "What about dry clothes? I'm freezing, and I'm sure the boy must be, also." His voice shook, clear evidence he'd yet to warm.

Ben answered, "First things first." The big man was almost invisible in the near-darkness. "Son, you go back into that room where Lou found the towels. Root around. There should be more. Me? I'll work on the lights. Chad, you need out of those clothes, that's for certain. Pneumonia is not an option right now. You and your son can wrap in towels until we can get to your room for dry pants and shirts. Lou, are you okay with that?"

She held up her hands and shrugged. Just a few minutes ago, she'd walked behind Chad, seeing his wet shirt and pants clinging to his body. She'd imagined what must lie underneath those clothes, and it had left her giddy inside. Now, Ben, the man who'd warned her away from Chad, was asking her permission for him to strip to just a towel?

It was Chad's voice that interrupted her thoughts. "Lou? An answer, please? I'm freezing. After all, it's Ben's idea, not mine. Or should I just sit here and become a block of ice? When you want a cold soda, you could chip the icicles off my cold, dead skin."

Chaddie laughed in the background.

She spoke up, her voice filled with an unexpected

surge of emotion. "There you go again. How do you do that?" However, there was dampness in her eyes. This man was getting to her, charming her with his words once more, and she wished she had the strength to fight against him.

"What did I do this time?" Exasperation tinged his response. "Please, whatever I'm saying, I don't mean to offend. May I take my clothes off? I promise you'll be as safe as new mown grass. Chaddie'll bring towels, and he can chaperone every moment of our time together."

Ben's deep voice chuckled at that. "Lou, are you okay with this? These two cannot afford to get sick during this storm. You know that. I remember what I said to you earlier, and I haven't changed my mind. However, safety now is the important thing."

Before she could answer, Chaddie already had his shirt over his head. At first she thought it was his father, and her heart leaped in her chest. She knew she wouldn't see anything intimately revealing in the removal of his shirt, no more than she'd seen in the glimpses of him the night he had come upon her when the old man had been in her room. His shirt had been unfastened then, but he had also spoken harshly to her. In those moments, she'd known only her desperation that he hadn't understood what really happened.

Now, though, that raising of his arms, and the movement of fabric sliding over his skin, was as if this man were reaching toward her to take her in his embrace. Then, when he stood and began to remove his pants, she knew she should turn her eyes, but she couldn't. His boxer shorts were all that kept him decent, and even that seemed overdressed.

Then she heard Chaddie's voice. "That's better. I'm not nearly as cold with my wet clothes off. Dad, I'll get us towels, and then you'll feel warmer." She watched the boy-man duck into the room they'd opened earlier, and after a few moments of fumbling sounds, he reappeared. A white towel wrapped around his hips stood out in the darkness. "Better, even. I'm barely cold, now." He threw his father a towel. "Here's a dry towel for you, Dad."

Lou grabbed her throat and pulled her hand down her chest between her breasts. With a ragged breath, she realized she'd been watching the wrong person. That left her feeling silly, and she laughed.

Chad called in an exasperated tone, "What can be funny now?"

Her voice was unsteady as she spoke in an unmanageable rush. "You and me and your son, and taking clothes off in the dark and wearing towels. All of it."

His words bit at her. "Well, it seems to me you're not taking any clothes off. Perhaps you should give me your rain gear and go stand outside. Then you can come back in and take your wet things off. I'm sure my towel-clad son will be glad to get you an extra from his terrycloth stash."

"Dad," Chaddie began, "that was the last one."

"I'm not going outside, Chaddie." Once again, she'd come across badly in this man's eyes, and she knew it. "I didn't mean any offense, Chad. It just seemed funny then. It's the stress, I guess." She put her hand to her forehead and leaned back against the wall. "I'll keep quiet."

She would, too. The platform could fall into the sea, and she wouldn't say another word. At least until Ben fixed the lights, and she hoped it was soon.

Chad sat and leaned against the wall, several feet away from Lou. "I'm sorry, too. I'm tired and cold, and I haven't eaten." He sat for a moment, and then, suddenly unable to take anymore, he said violently, "I'm also freezing, and I want out of these clothes."

In a frantic series of motions, he stripped his shirt from his torso and flung it to the far wall. Then, as he sat, he worked his pants down his legs, and with a toss, they landed wetly next to his shirt. It was when he stood to wrap the towel around his waist that Lou noticed one thing he'd done differently than his son. This man had not gone into the adjacent room to remove his shorts. They had come off with his pants.

Oh, my God, she thought, turning her head away.

Ben knelt by Lou, and he whispered to her softly, "Lou, you've seen it all, now, and I mean all. Are you satisfied?" There was a chuckle in his voice.

She reached and pushed his face away. "Go fix the power, Ben. I need to be able to see."

He wasn't through, yet, and he cleared his throat. "Don't get too close to this man. You don't know every-thing about him. Remember what I told you."

She remembered, and that was what made it hard. He moved with grace, and he had charmed her with his words. Now, he had shown her a shadowy glimpse of more anat-omy than she'd seen on any man except her Tracy. She knew she didn't need light to see that she was deeply attracted to this man. She remembered Ben once calling it love. Perhaps it was. What she did know was that she didn't dare try to stand. Her knees felt weak, and her head felt light. If she stood, she would probably fall into this man's arms, and that wouldn't do.

Then she smiled in the near-darkness. Perhaps that wouldn't be so bad. She might fall into his heart, also. He was wearing only a towel, and with what she'd seen, perhaps . . . perhaps. Then, she pushed at Ben and put that thought from her mind.

"Go, Ben. I remember your advice, and I'll try to follow it. Don't forget, we have a chaperone."

Just then Chaddie walked up, his towel around his waist, and his body long and tight in the way boy's emerging bodies always are. "Ben, how are you going to get the power back on? I thought the whole rig was shut completely down."

Ben stood, and he reached to place his hand on the boy's bare shoulder. He chuckled, and then his voice rumbled. "It is, son. However, out here, we're our own power company. We pump fuel from the ground, and fuel is what we use to get our power." He laughed, and the sound of his voice was rich. "Of course, it's not quite that easy. We were running off a backup generator. We didn't know it at the time, but while the rest of us were evacuating, you and your dad were playing the gaming systems, helping use all our fuel, I guess."

Chaddie hung his head. "All night, too." He snorted, and then it turned into a chuckle. "We didn't even know it was morning." The sound of his renewed enthusiasm bubbled in his voice, "I was winning at the last. Dad just wouldn't let me get to the house."

Ben, a head taller than even the tall boy, used one arm to pull him to his side just for a moment. Just as quickly, he released him and laughed again. "Fathers should have fun with their sons. You needn't be ashamed of that. However, your fun did put a strain on the generator, I'll bet. The recreation room was the first thing I took off the power grid. We just need to add a little fuel to the tank. We won't have heat, but we will have lights, at least in this part of the accommodations block."

The boy's face brightened. "Can I help?" He looked at his father. "Dad? Then we'll be able to see, and we can get to our room and find dry clothes."

Chad called out in frustration, "You're our chaperone. I might try to expose myself in front of our good hostess, here. Ben can do this alone."

Lou knew it was too late to keep her from being exposed to this man, and her heart hadn't settled down yet. If he was saying this just to irk her, she could return irk for irk just fine.

"Chaddie, just go with Ben. When your father threw his wet clothes away, he forgot that it's not all that dark inside, and he showed me there's nothing underneath his towel that I need to be afraid of. Your father's safe with me. If I need another towel for poor Stinky here, I'll try my best not to grab the one your father's wearing." She looked away as she finished, although in the dark it was an empty gesture. Her words had an icy bite to them that she hadn't intended, but once they were out, it was too late to gather them back.

"Dad?" Chaddie stepped forward to find his father's arms on his knees and his face in his hands. He leaned to him and whispered, "I think she still likes you."

Chad waved him away. "Not likely. Go with Ben, and see if you can bring us light."

"Lou? Are you sure? I see more sparks flying in here than fireflies on a summer night." Ben paused for a moment.

"Go, Ben. We're safe together."

He rumbled quietly, "Are you sure?"

She wasn't sure. All she could think about was the fact that he was sitting right there close enough for her to touch, she could see him, and he was wrapped in a towel. That made it hard to focus on anything else, and with those thoughts, she had already forgotten about the storm raging just outside.

It had not forgotten her, though, as advertised by the wailing just beyond the walls. To judge by the sound, big brother was almost there.

Chapter 15

"I'D GET lost in the dark if I had to find my way around in here. How about you?"

The corridors were dimly lighted, and Chaddie danced along in his bare feet, sometimes in front of the big man, his steps often taking him backwards down the darkened corridors, and at other times looking where he was going. His hand was sometimes holding the towel at his waist, and once he had to grab at it as it slipped loose and started to fall. Glancing down, he pulled it snug and worked the loose end tight where it wrapped his waist.

With Ben at his side, the boy's enthusiasm had returned, and his words tumbled from him.

"Ben, do we get to go outside? I was there before, you know, when the helicopter didn't wait, and I'd go out again. I want a raincoat or a poncho, though." He stopped at every window, grinning at the smallest slivers of light in the darkened passageways. "That lightning that hit was cool. I bet that happens all the time out here. No one ever gets killed, though, I bet, and I'd like to see it hit again."

Ben stopped and smiled at the enthusiasm bubbling over in the boy. "Do you ever stop talking?"

"Sometimes. Now, though, I want to know if we're going outside. Is that where the generator is? I'll wear my towel if you want. It'll get all wet, but I was wet before, and I survived. I'll be cold, but I can take that. Surely other rooms have towels also, and I could get another dry one. Please say we're going outside, Ben. Please. This is a hurricane, and no one ever gets to say they went outside in a hurricane." Chaddie put his hands together in a prayer-like temple and half bowed as he pleaded.

Ben started off again, and there was amusement in the sound of his voice. "Son, you'd go outside and be dancing naked as soon as the door closed. That storm'd rip that towel right out of your hands." His good-natured teasing continued. "Is that what you want, to dance naked in a hurricane? There are no girls out here to watch you, so it sounds rather pointless to me. Dancing naked requires girls to watch."

Chaddie felt his face flush with warmth. "Of course not. I don't *want* to dance naked. I'd do that, though, if you'd let me go outside, dance naked, but I'd rather have clothes on. Clothes and rain gear, too, maybe a poncho." His voice bounced from idea to idea with the excitement. It seemed possible that this might actually happen. What a story this would be to tell back home!

269

Ben laughed and grabbed the boy on the back of the neck. "Sorry, son. No naked hurricane dances today. The generator that serves the accommodations block and the helipad is inside the building. However, there might be a need for us to search for fuel. That you can help with. Let me show you our last resort." He came to a window where another part of the rig could be seen just across an open catwalk. The light was eerily gray outside, and sheets of rain lashed everything they could see. Ben pointed. "There, boy. See across that catwalk? There's a cradle, and there's a red, plastic fuel can inside. That's where we have to go if we don't find any extra fuel at the generator."

Chaddie grinned. "Will that be when I get to do the hurricane dance?"

Ben chuckled. "I like you, boy. There's no part of life that's not interesting to you. In answer to your question," and he shook his head, the motion barely visible in the dim light that filtered in through the window, "we'll look inside, first. Hurricane dances are dangerous on an oil rig. Just being here's dangerous. I want you safe."

Chaddie laughed. "I want to dance." He did, too, just for a moment raising his arms in the air in a parody of a wild fete with plenty of footwork. Then his towel started to come loose, and he grabbed at it, laughing.

Ben slapped him on the back and moved on. "See, boy? That's what happens when you dance with a hurricane." He laughed loudly at the picture his words generated. "It takes everything you've got, even the clothes off your butt."

Chaddie thought that was funny, and he laughed, too. He was thirteen, there were no girls around, and he thought this was all really good fun, especially since he might just get to do that hurricane dance after all.

CHAD SAT in the dimness and rubbed his hands over his knees. The drilling rig around him was alive with the onslaught of the storm. One moment it was silent, and then the repeated lashing of rain came through in a low-pitched, driving echo that drummed and hammered throughout the structure with a vibrato that was both eerie and ominous. Dimly, metal could be heard as it pulled against metal in the vibrating hum of the wind. The floor shivered under his feet.

He was vividly aware of Lou sitting just down from him. Her presence was like a toxin, a sweet toxin, killing him as he sat there. He was out of breath, and he could barely think. He wanted to be at her side, and he couldn't force himself to make that move, not after the past two days. He'd pushed women away—all women—for too many years. Now he was unsure how to bridge the gap.

He was also well aware that this was the first time he and Lou had been alone together. Repeatedly Chaddie or Gramps or Ben had been at their side, or perhaps they had been expected to return at any minute. There had been no opportunity for that slow time, for one of those moments when the rest of the world faded away so attraction had the chance to blossom into something more.

Now the world was far away, as far away as a hurricane could drive it. There was no one who would be coming for them, and the only other two people on the rig who might know what went on between them were off exploring the far reaches of the platform. Their only chaperone was the dog that lay beside Lou, breathing in slow, sleepy draughts of air.

Chad rubbed his hands over his knees, and the motion had nothing to do with the growing chill in the air. It was because he desperately wanted to have them touching the woman who sat just down from him. He had thrown his wet clothing to the far wall, and he had stood in the darkness, so cold that he hadn't cared whether he was dressed or not. It hadn't been intentional or well-thought-out. Perhaps stupid, but in any case, he'd done it, and then he'd wrapped himself in the relative warmth of the towel.

Now, he had nothing other than his towel, and he felt very exposed. A beautiful woman was here with him, a woman he found very attractive, if somewhat mystifying; and he wanted the lights to stay off, so he could hold her while the storm raged around them. He'd been married before, and he had no illusions about what else he might want if he were to sit at her side and hold her. He wouldn't be able to resist the demands his body would make on him, and he knew that if he took her in his hands to make violent love to her, it would offend her. It was certain to, because everything else he'd done in the past two days had offended her. Besides, they might get caught. Who knew how quickly Ben and Chaddie would return?

He decided he could speak to her, though.

"Lou?" Chad broke the silence in the room. "There's a hurricane outside. What'll happen now?" That was a stupid question. He mentally kicked himself and cringed at what he imagined her response would be. She wouldn't be here now if it weren't for him and his son. However, he couldn't take it back. "Will the rig be okay?"

After a moment, he heard movements from where she sat, and he closed his eyes in dread. She was probably angry with him and moving away. Then, there was a strong smell of wet dog, and Stinky moved to curl up beside him, placing her head on his lap.

Without looking at the animal, he reached to rub her ears. "At least someone wants to sit with me."

"Two someones," a voice said in his ear. "May I?"

Chad looked up, his heart pounding, and there she was, kneeling at his side. He smiled and reached his arm up, and she moved in next to him, leaning her head against his shoulder. The rig shuddered under a new onslaught from the storm, and he pulled her tight.

He chuckled. "Should I be frightened about now?" In actuality he was, and he knew he must be strong. He was the man, and tough was what made a man. However, he knew any "tough" he showed right now would be false bravado. Deep inside, he was barely together. He looked at her, serious now, and pressed her for an answer. "Lou, should I?"

LOU REACHED her hand, and in a brave stroke, she brushed it against his chest, letting her fingers run across his skin, pausing before dropping her hand to rest at his waist. That's what she'd done so many times with Tracy when she'd lain next to him, stopping there if she wanted to just snuggle.

Resting against Chad, she knew those times were so long ago, and the feeling wasn't quite the same. Tracy would have seen that movement of her hand across his chest as an indication that she knew he'd worked out, or that she could tell he'd eaten too much pasta the week before. Tracy never made the first move. He always waited for her signal that she wanted more, for her to rest her hand on his lap, or on his leg, something to signal to him what she needed. The second touch was always up to Tracy, however. The motion of her hand on his body would be a dance of touches, a dance he would quickly take control of, and when he was ready for it to end, he simply removed her hand and turned from her to fall asleep.

Chad just let her dance. He sat there, and her fingers moved against his skin, running along the fold of his stomach just where the towel was tightened around his waist. She let her hand run up his ribs, and she gently traced her finger along each one. Finally, reaching under his arm, he squirmed at her touch and chuckled.

She whispered, "Do you want me to stop? I don't want to make you uncomfortable." Chad's proximity—as well as that of the raging storm—made her more than willing to throw away all her reservations. Besides, she *was* scared.

He reached to place his hand around her wrist. "Want you to stop? No. Never. However, perhaps you should. I'm not dressed, and now I'm also not able to stand without embarrassing myself. We have company—other than this dog—that will be returning before long." He reached and touched her face with his hand, and he kissed her forehead. "It may take some time before my body returns to a more presentable state, and my son would be mortified if he knew what's going on in my head right now." He chuck-led. "Well, actually, it's not my head I'm worried about."

"I understand." Lou shifted slightly, moving to put a small space between them. "I have a brother, and he was just younger than Chaddie is now when I married. He found everything Tracy and I did either amusing or horribly embarrassing."

CHAD REMEMBERED her earlier comment to Gramps. *"My husband was killed."* Perhaps she would be willing to talk about it now if he were tactful. He took a deep breath and tested the waters.

"His name was Tracy?" He let it go at that. She would either answer or not, and he couldn't force her response.

She sighed. Reaching down, she partially unzipped her coverall, and then she smiled. "I know how this might look under these circumstances. However, I'm not getting undressed. It's hot in here."

He leaned his head against the wall, closed his eyes, and smiled in the dimness. "I understand. I'm not dressed, and I'm feeling entirely too warm, myself. About Tracy? Is that a hot topic I should let alone?"

"Two days ago, yes. I would've said to leave it alone. Now I can at least talk about it. We were married a year. Then he was gone. That's about it."

Killed. He wanted to know about that scrap of information. She'd told him only part of the story. Perhaps she would say more. He persisted gently, "Gone how?"

She reached a hand to his leg and touched the skin just where it extended out of the towel. Then she put her hand back on her own leg.

"This is pulling deeply painful memories from me, but in this unusual and oddly intimate situation," she chuckled nervously, pulling at the front of her coveralls as if trying to cool down, "I feel it's right to give you an answer. He

275

was found downtown. A highway runs through Fort Worth, and his rig had a flat there. He was changing it, apparently, on the side of the road, and he was robbed. At least that's what the police think. His wallet was gone, as well as his money. He always carried cash, and quite a lot. I told him not to, but he did as he wanted."

Chad opened his eyes long enough to place his hand on hers before closing them again. "I'm sorry." What else could he say? He was glad she was free, but what a horrible way for it to happen!

She turned her hand over and worked her fingers into his. "I've grieved for five years. It's time I move on. Everyone I know tells me that."

He smiled. His eyes were still closed, and he was enjoying this woman's company, really enjoying being with a woman for the first time in years. The feeling was nice, and he wanted it to last.

"Who's everyone?"

That got a laugh from her. "Ben. Ben tells me that and tries to set me up. He told me I was in love with you. I laughed at him."

"He did, did he?" Chad's heart pounded at his next question. "Are you?"

If she *were* in love with him, then there were a lot of unanswered questions. If she wasn't, why was she sitting next to him, telling him all these things? Was it just fear at being stranded on this drilling platform during a hurricane? She might die, and, as they say, any port in the time of storm is better than no port at all. Was he just a last resort, and if this was the end, the man she was with didn't count?

"Ben loves me, a lot, you know."

276

He knew, then. She and Ben were the ones who were a pair. Perhaps he loved her more than she loved him. A one-sided romance.

"Ben loves you, huh? Do you love him?"

She laughed softly, working her fingers more deeply into his. "Immensely. Ben takes care of me in every way I can be taken care of, except intimately, of course, and he's the best thing next to a lover I'll ever have."

That made Chad laugh. She asked him what he was laughing at, and he told her he was picturing a one-sided love affair with Ben as the pursuing half. She slapped his stomach at that, causing him to flinch.

"You're terrible, Chad. Ben and I are best friends. The first night I was here, he rescued me from an assault. I would've been raped, if he hadn't come along. He's been there for me ever since."

"I'm sorry." Chad thought for a minute. "What has he said about me?" He was pretty sure he knew what she'd heard, although not the actual words. Ben had told him, *"Stay away from Lou."* He wanted to hear it from her lips, though.

She took a long time before answering. When she did, her voice was very quiet, almost as if she didn't quite want to say what needed to be said.

"Ben said that you couldn't love me because you didn't trust me. He wouldn't tell me what he meant by that, either."

Chad's heart pounded. He knew this might be his only chance to rectify this misunderstanding. He might never convince Ben of his good intentions, and in fact had tried already, very unsuccessfully. However, he might convince

Lou. She was the important one.

"I can explain. I can try, at least, that is if you want to hear it." The room felt suddenly cold to him, as if she might not want him to explain.

"Please. Ben said to trust him, but it's been hard. He asked me to stay away from you, and I didn't want to. I need to know why he told me I loved you, then warned me away from you."

Chad squeezed her hand and cleared his throat. It took him a moment to gain control of his thoughts. He cleared his throat one more time before risking his voice. "I was married to Chaddie's mother for twelve years, and divorced for three. I always thought it was my fault we couldn't work it out." He remembered the boy from the A&P. That had been only part of it, though. "Gramps was part of the reason for the divorce. I didn't realize it then, but when he began accusing you of some horribly untrue things, I remembered incidences I'd never put together before. I was suddenly back three years ago, and the divorce was happening all over again."

Chad sat for a time, silent, remembering the last months of his marriage. Gramps had made things worse than they had to be. He saw that now. On this rig, he'd done it again.

"I was stupid, and I responded the way I used to do when Gramps said things like that to me years ago. I even asked Ben if the things Gramps said about you could be true. I knew they weren't, and I told Ben that immediately afterwards. He said I should have stood up for you, and he was right. I couldn't even stand up to that old man in front of my son, Lou. I was a fool."

He ducked his head, not responding even when the storm outside shook the building in an especially violent lashing, causing it to shudder and groan. Quietly, he continued, "I made it right with Chaddie already, but Ben told me to keep away from you. I've tried to do as he asked. I would have, too, if this storm hadn't stranded us here. I really would. It's just that now with you here, I feel like I've found someone who's real for the first time in three years. It's like I'm alive again."

She reached and put her hand to his lips. "I've heard enough. I believe you."

Chad couldn't respond. He'd let his emotions bleed to the surface, and all he could do was sit in the dim light and let the beautiful woman he was with help sponge them away.

Meanwhile, just outside the walls, the storm continued to beat at the rig, attempting to tear it from its foundations. It was growing stronger, too, and it seemed as though big brother was knocking on the door.

CHADDIE RATTLED the fuel can. They found it in the generator room, hoping for enough to get the power back on, but it wasn't to be.

"It's empty. You've got to let me do this." The boy's voice sparkled, and with his free hand, he held his towel as his words danced a chorus of excitement. "Ben!"

The big black man looked at the backup generator. He couldn't read the fuel level in the near-dark of the room, but he could hear the few ounces in the can the boy was holding. There wasn't enough in there to line the inside of one cylinder.

He stood and sighed. "It's my duty, boy. You think it's fun, and I know it's dangerous. Going outside for that fuel is taking a chance on death. You don't want to die, do you?"

Chaddie was so excited about this that it made everything else he'd done on the rig pale in comparison. "But Ben, I can do the hurricane dance. I *can.* I know it. I can bring back that fuel, and I can be safe." When Ben didn't reply, Chaddie challenged him. "Were you ever thirteen?"

Ben laughed. The sound was rich and washed across the room. "Boy, I was thirteen once."

"Then you'll let me do the dance?" Chaddie's grin was from ear-to-ear.

"I didn't say that, boy. I just laughed and said I was thirteen once. However, let's start that direction. We won't get there unless we're walking our feet along the floor. You can leave that fuel can, too. It's empty."

Chaddie set it down and used both hands to loosen his towel and pull it tighter before tucking it in once again. Then he danced around Ben as he moved out, as usual walking backwards as often as he walked forward.

"So, Ben, did you ever do anything at thirteen that was so big that no one else had ever done it? Something that scared you, and you did it anyway? Did you, Ben? Huh? Tell me, Ben. Did you?"

That was what Chaddie wanted, to claim the biggest prize there ever was, and nothing was bigger than a hurricane.

BEN STOPPED. His massive body was merely a black shape in the dark, and he smiled at the blond-headed boy wearing no more than a white towel wrapped around his hips. Ben *had* been thirteen once, and he had done something that had changed him forever. It had also been dangerous, and he'd thought he might die. After that, he'd never been afraid of anything ever again.

He'd also never told anyone. It had been his secret for fifty years. Not even his wife, God rest her soul, had known. Ben always thought of the adventure as nothing more than a stupid stunt by a foolhardy kid, and it embarrassed him. Now, with this boy vibrating with excitement over the possibility of going outside to dance in a hurricane, he was proud of what he'd done, and he wanted to tell this boy about it.

He took a deep breath. "I jumped off a bridge when I was thirteen. Thought I would die." He chuckled, and the sound rumbled in the darkness. Outside, the blistering wind grabbed a cable somewhere and sang with a high-pitched keening wail. The two men froze for a moment, and after a bit, silence reigned again, broken only by the brittle sound of the pounding rain. The sound of their breathing seemed loud in the dark space.

Chaddie chuckled with relief and barged ahead with renewed excitement. "You said you jumped, Ben. How? On a bungee cord? Or did you parachute off?"

Ben laughed again, grabbing Chaddie around the shoulders and pulling him close to his side. "I like you, boy. I like you a lot. Not even a hurricane puts you off. You're more like me than you know. A little shoe polish, and your daddy'd never tell us apart. Neither, to answer your question. It was a train bridge over a river. I was all alone, and it was at night."

"You did it at night? What, you snuck out? I'd have to if I did something like that at night."

Ben just squeezed Chaddie's shoulder. "I went out in my underdrawers, straight from my bed. I didn't dare get my clothes wet, and anyway, I was afraid if I did, they'd pull me under. I'd heard tales of wet clothes drowning people. Before long, there I stood on that bridge. I was scareder'n a deer in a car's headlights." He paused, his voice dropping an octave, telling of a moment that still struck a deep chord in his emotions. "I heard that train whistle, and I tell you, I peed my drawers right then and there." He chuckled. He still remembered the warmth of the urine running down his leg. "I didn't move, though. No, sir. When that train got to that bridge, the light shown across that track. I looked down, and in the light, I saw the dark stain I'd made on my drawers. I knew there was nothing but the water under my feet."

The old man's voice grew quiet for a moment, remembering the intensity of that moment. Only the sound of the raging storm outside broke the silence. Ben breathed deeply as he gathered the next part of the story. "That bridge shook like a clothesline on a broken pole. If I'd had anything to eat that day, I would've done my business in the back side of my drawers right then and there. I didn't, though. I'd been planning this. All day I'd been too nervous to eat, and right then I was sure glad."

He paused, and Chaddie's eyes were bright. "The train saw you and stopped? It wouldn't hit you if it saw you there, would it?"

Ben looked at the youth under his arm, and he smiled. "Look at me, boy. Can you see me in here?"

"Only your teeth, Ben. Your eyes, too. Not the rest of you. Why?"

"Think, boy. That train had a light, but my skin's the color of midnight. I was a shadow in the dark, and he never slowed down. I tensed my muscles to jump, but I couldn't make myself. Sometimes I think the wind from the front of that train pushed me off that bridge. I never told a soul, either. In all my life, you're the one person that knows what I did."

Chaddie's chest heaved with the excitement. "You gotta let me do this, Ben. This is my bridge. I can dance with the hurricane like you danced with that train. You gotta, Ben."

Ben chuckled, and he let his big hand run up and over the boy's head. "We all should be thirteen at least once, son."

"Everybody is, Ben."

Ben let his hand fall back to Chaddie's shoulder. "Not everyone, boy. Some people go past thirteen and never get it. I got it, and it changed me. It might just change you, too."

Chaddie made a fist and pumped it. "Yes!" Then, just as quickly, he grabbed his towel as it fell from him, and he wrapped it around his waist once again. "Thanks, Ben. I can't believe you're going to let me dance with the hurricane."

"I can't believe I'm doing it either, boy. However, everybody needs to be thirteen at least once. Today's your day."

JOHN WOKE with a start, and he wrestled with the coat

that covered him. There was the steady churning noise from the belly of the vessel, and he knew they were underway. From time to time, the boat lurched, at times violently, and then it churned steadily ahead again. Shaking his head to clear it, he tried to focus on what he'd been doing when he sat to close his eyes.

Then, the dawning realization of what he'd not finished washed over him. He hadn't found two of his people, yet. He lurched to his feet, and seeing Yolanda sleeping off to the side, he went to her, shaking her arm to wake her.

"Yolanda, open those eyes. It's John. This is important." When he saw her start to come to, he spoke with greater intensity. "Have you seen Lou?" He looked at her, waiting impatiently for her to wake. She blinked her eyes to clear the sleep, and then she took a deep breath.

"Sir, she's on the muster list. The Coast Guard would have checked her off."

He shook his head. "I talked to someone named Abramski. They couldn't use the muster lists because of the weather. He said they just tallied everyone until the rig was clear. Ben, too. Ben Tosh. I can't find him."

She reached to rub her eyes and yawned. "Big Ben? Yeah, I saw him on the helipad. Surely he's here somewhere." She smiled. "You can't miss Ben. Don't worry, sir. The rig was dark when we left. We're all here."

He began to search with his eyes. "Yeah, well, I'll believe that when I see their faces. Do you have copies of the muster lists with you?"

She smiled again. "I'm surprised you even ask. Of course, I do." Reaching in her satchel, she pulled out a packet. "Here, sir. Everyone's listed. Would you like me to go around and start checking the names off?"

John was relieved, and he felt it as a tingling of antici-pation in his limbs. "Would you? I'd appreciate that. I know you were sleeping, and I apologize, but this has been eating at my gut." He ran his fingers through his hair. Not knowing where they were just didn't seem right, and it bothered him, too, that he hadn't already resolved this. Instead, he'd been napping!

"Sure, sir. I don't mind. With the rig shut down for the storm, I'll have several days at home to do nothing but sleep. I'll get caught up then."

TAKING A pencil from her pocket, Yolanda stood. The first thing she did was find her name and John's. She put little checks in the boxes by them. Two down. Now she just had to find the other fifty-eight. Easy, easy. After all, this was a boat, and it was a good sight smaller than the rig. She might even have time to get more sleep before getting to shore.

Just then the boat jerked wildly, and she stumbled. She chuckled, deciding sleep might just have to wait.

"Bill," she called to one familiar face, making a check on her paper. "Have you see Josh and Jeromy? I'm marking off everyone on the muster list."

He pointed to a group of sleeping men leaning against a bulkhead, and she headed that way.

Chapter 16

TUCKER GENTLY slapped the side of Abramski's face. Then he laughed. "Johnson, look at that. Abramski always sleeps like a baby after one of these evacs. His wife must love that. She just steals his wallet and goes shopping."

Johnson smiled as he sat down and pulled on his boots. The dry socks were a boon to his feet. He always brought an extra pair, and he was glad he did. He couldn't sleep, though, not until he got home and showered. Then he'd crash.

"We're almost in. Poor baby's gotta wake." Johnson reached down and shook Abramski. Hard. When the man jerked, Johnson slapped his face firmly several times. "Wake up, Bram. We're home." He grinned to see the man jerk his head to clear the sleep away. Johnson called to

Tucker, "That's the way it's done, Tuck. Learn from the best."

Tucker wiped his hands on a damp towel and reached for a candy bar. Breaking it open, he called, "Men, did you see that big, black guy on that last rig? I don't think he had a scared bone in his body. He stood there next to that little lady the whole evac. He never flinched once when the copter put down, and he made sure to put everyone else on first."

Johnson slapped Tucker on the shoulder. "Got another candy bar?" When one appeared, he broke it open. "Yeah, on that next to the last trip, I told that guy there were lights still on below. He said he'd check it out. Never hesitated. He's a man I'd want on my watch." He bit into the bar of candy, then held it up to peer at it closely. "Peanut butter?" At Tucker's nod, he smiled. "Good stuff." He paused, taking another bite and chewing slowly. "I never saw him load the copter, though. Guess I missed him, somehow."

At that, Abramski sat up with a frantic look on his face. *Plus us.* He remembered, and he scrambled to his feet. "My God, I've got to get to the captain."

Johnson called, "What is it, Bram?"

Abramski turned as he reached the door, his face flushed with the knowledge of what he'd done. "We left two behind!"

CHADDIE LOOKED out the door, and rain swept across the catwalk in sheets. His heart was in his throat, and he felt sick to his stomach. He looked at Ben with trepidation.

"You peed your pants?"

Ben smiled, and it was broad and white in his face.

"You don't have to do this."

"Yes, I do." Chaddie held his towel at his waist. "I have to dance the hurricane. You danced a train. I've got a standard to live up to, now." He was scared, though, and he knew if he were wearing undershorts, he just might pee them as he waited, trying to gain his courage.

"That's not why I told you that story, boy." Ben placed his hand on the boy's shoulder. "You don't have to go. It's still my responsibility."

Chaddie shook his hand off. He was thirteen, and he had to prove this to himself. It had been a lark at first, and then he'd heard Ben's story. Now, nothing would stop him.

"I want the red can, right?" He looked up to catch Ben's eyes.

"Plastic can, boy. Red plastic. It's inside that cradle right there. It'll be heavy."

Without turning around, he held his arm up with his fist clenched. "Feel my arm. I have muscle."

Ben chuckled. "I can see that."

Chaddie turned to look him in the face, insisting. "No, feel. It's not real unless you feel it. I want you to know."

Ben placed his hand around the boy's arm and let out another laugh. "Boy, you surprise me. You do have muscle there. You're so skinny, I'd have never thought."

"I surprise a lot of people. You gonna hold my towel?" He put his hand on the door.

"Boy," Ben said, reaching out to stop him, "I can give you my rain gear."

Chaddie snorted. "Did you have floaties on when that train was coming at you? No, sir. I bet not."

"Well then, boy. Out there, the wind can blow you

right off. Hold to the rail."

"I tell you what, you just hold my towel." Then the door was open, and the boy was gone before Ben could step aside to stay dry.

Ben grabbed the door handle with one hand, ready for the boy's return. In the other hand he held the white towel. Outside on the walk, the boy was soaked instantly. He did hold the rail until halfway across. Then, he raised his hands over his head and did a victory dance. The wind whipped through at just that moment, and Ben drew in a sharp breath as the boy was slammed sideways against the rail. Ben watched him stumble and pick himself up, holding on once again. He smiled in relief to see the boy's arm lift in the air to shoot him a thumbs-up hand sign.

Coming back across, the red can at his side, Chaddie struggled, and when he reached the door, he stepped inside and collapsed to the floor, gladly taking the towel from Ben.

"How was it, boy? You made it, didn't you?" He watched the teen run the towel over his head.

Then Chaddie's face appeared, and his eyes glowed. "I did it, Ben. Did you see? I danced the hurricane. It tried to take me down, and I danced it anyway. That was the coolest thing, ever. It was so cool. I can't wait to tell everyone."

Ben helped the boy to his feet. "You do that, son. You got to be thirteen today, and that's something not everyone gets to do. I'm proud of you, boy. Now, let's go make us some light."

"Yes, sir," Chaddie said. "Just let me get my towel on."

Ben's laugher rang out. "You do that, boy. Those two

adults down there might appreciate it more than you know."

"GRANNY, ARE you watching this?" Willie stood in front of the TV and bit into his peanut butter sandwich. Making a face, he ran his tongue up around his teeth. Granny had put on the peanut butter extra thick this time.

She stepped in from the kitchen. "How are your pants fitting, grandson?"

He looked at her. "Same as this morning. Why?"

"That's your fourth sandwich today. Thought you might've put on some meat. You need some right about here." She reached to him and patted his backside.

He stepped away, dropping onto the couch. "Granny, are you *watching* this?"

"What, Willie?"

He pointed. "It's a well out in the Gulf. You know, like Lou's well. They missed some people. They're fixing to tell who."

"Oh, Willie! Somebody's stranded there?" She stepped around to her recliner. "The dishes can wait for something so heartbreaking." She sank into the chair's generous cushions, adjusting herself until she was comfortable. "I hate this. Some poor people out there are going to be sad. We should say a prayer for them."

He reached and handed her the phone. "Here, Granny. I've already dialed the number. It's Daddy at the church. If Bethel Baptist can't pray those people home, then nobody can." He raised the remote and increased the volume as the announcer began to speak.

"Two names have come in from that oil production

platform in the Gulf that left two crewmembers on board when it was evacuated. The name of the platform is, no, let me double-check this. Yes, it's the same one that we reported earlier as completely evacuated. That was clearly in error.

"Sunshine Gulf Platform No. 6 had been running shut down procedures for over thirty-six hours when the Coast Guard arrived to evacuate the crew. However, when the evacuation boat left this morning, thinking the platform was cleared, two crewmembers were accidentally left behind. One is veteran crewmember Ben Tosh, 64, who lost his wife on a platform off the coast of Kuwait several years ago. The other is one-year veteran and safety coordinator for the rig, Louinda Reinhardt, 31, of Oklahoma City. It's unclear how a mistake of this magnitude could occur, but these are experienced hands, and we are assured the rig should be standing once the storm has passed.

"In other news, long-time Dallas resident Wallace Saunders, formerly of Oklahoma City, passed away in a Houston hospital today. The apparent cause of death was ruled a heart attack. Mr. Saunders at one time ran the now-defunct Saunders Tool and Die just west of downtown. Services will be in Dallas.

"Back to you, Clarinda."

Granny dropped the phone. "My word, Willie. Lou out there in that storm. Who'll take care of our Lou? You better call your daddy. I don't think I can."

"Sure, Granny. Hand me the phone."

She sat and rocked in her recliner, and the phone lay on the floor at her side. Her face was flushed, and tears glistened in her eyes. "I don't think I can, Willie. I just don't think I can."

STINKY WHINED, and then she put her paws in Chad's lap.

"What is it, girl?" He looked around. Things didn't seem much different to him. There was a strong vibration in the rig, but it had been doing that off and on for some time.

"She's scared. Just run your hand on her head." Lou reached out to do just that when Stinky barked.

Then, the overhead lights glowed for a moment as if they were attempting to come on, and just as quickly they went dark again. Finally, with stuttering alacrity, they snapped on and up to full brightness. The windows that had been filtering in light from the day outside suddenly appeared completely black.

"Lou?" Chad looked at her for information. "Are we on line again, up and running? We have power."

She laughed softly, and she shifted her position in preparation to stand. "No, it takes more than Ben and a thirteen-year-old boy to get this place back on line. We wouldn't want that to happen during a hurricane, in any case. We spent the past thirty-six hours shutting it down."

"They did fix something, though. Ben said something about a generator. Is that on line?"

"I think so. That's what he went to check on. It runs on fuel, and it operated longer than intended. It would seem he was able to refill the tank and restart it." Finally standing, she reached for Stinky's wet towels and absently began to fold them.

"Our fault, I guess, mine and Chaddie's. We never went to bed. After Gramps had his heart attack, I wanted to divert Chaddie, and we headed down to play games." Still on the floor, Chad ran a finger through hair that was nearly dry.

Finished with the towels, she looked at him and shook her head. "There are two things I don't understand. You can actually play video games all night? Don't you get tired?"

His hand still in his hair, he looked up at her with a grin. "You have to play to understand. Gaming can be very intense, and hours can go by before you notice. Yeah, to answer your question, I can actually play all night, especially with a teenage son pushing my skills. He's better than when he was ten, too. That's the last time I really played against him."

Lou leaned against the wall and crossed her arms. "Ten. You're serious. What did you do when you were together over the last three years?"

This time he looked away. It was hard to admit this. "Nothing. I hardly saw him. I wouldn't have seen him this time if he hadn't shown up on my doorstep. Literally." He turned back to her. "Number two?"

"Number two. Oh, yes. How did you miss the muster? It was my fault leaving your names off, and I apologize I never talked to you specifically. I did with everyone else on board, and I take full responsibility for that. However, John, that's the pusher, he did sound a general alarm. There's nowhere on the rig that the alarm can't be heard. Why did you ignore that?"

He looked embarrassed and pointed to his ears. "Someone bought really good-quality headphones for the gaming systems. Both Chaddie and I were wearing them the whole time."

She slid down the wall to sit again. The air was cooling in the space, and she zipped her coveralls back up a bit. She never considered that she might be feeling the coolness that had been there all along, and that moving away from Chad was why.

She murmured, barely audible over the sound of the storm, "Surely you could hear it in spite of the headphones. The alarm's very loud."

"In retrospect, we probably did. I wondered once or twice why the sounds we heard didn't really match the action in the game." He paused, leaning his head back with a grin. "We could hear a little, enough to talk to each other during lulls in the game play. With machine gun explosions and car crashes in our ears, well, one of those sounds that didn't fit could have been the alarm, I guess. I'm sorry about that."

She snorted and then laughed. "Well, at least we've worked two things out. We might wash away in the storm, but those two things are no longer a problem."

Chad looked at her as his finger toyed with the bottom edge of his terry wrap. "I laughed a while ago, and you asked me what was funny. Now it's your turn. What's amusing about washing away in this storm?"

She let her eyes map out the ceiling for a moment and found a small rivulet of water tracing its way rapidly along the bottom edge of one beam. "That's not the amusing part, actually. When we found you, I thought you must be an idiot to be playing video games during a hurricane.

Everyone else on board was scrambling to get ready to evacuate, and you sat there and played video games with your son. Surely you were an idiot."

He smiled. "And now?"

Her hand reached to her face, and she wiped moisture from one eye. Then she turned her head and wiped it from the other. "I see you were being a good father. There's no idiot in you. That relieves me of a lot of worry." She smiled at him and sniffed.

"Oh," he said, "there's plenty of idiot. I was an idiot for three years, and I nearly let my son grow up without me. Trust me. Idiot abounds in the Dickson clan—at least in this Dickson."

"True idiots never figure that out. It seems to me you've come a long way towards fixing that problem."

"Yeah, I hope so. You know, I had a very smart man tell me that exact same thing not so long ago."

She looked at him. "Smart man?"

He chuckled. "Your friend, Ben. You two must be in cahoots."

She laughed. "Sometimes I think we are. That's what good friends do, think alike."

After a minute of silence, Chad said, "There's a third thing that you didn't mention." He looked at Lou hesitantly, not sure if he wanted to talk about it. She'd said she thought he might be an idiot. Bringing this up might prove it. "Gramps."

LOU'S STOMACH twisted. It all came crashing back on her, the man in her room and his hand holding her bra, the lie she had forced to tell to this man's son, and the humil-

295

iation. She had let that fade against the intensity of the past several hours. Now, Chad had brought it back up, and she didn't know where he intended to take it.

"Gramps. It wasn't what it seemed—"

Chad stopped her. "No. You don't need to say another word. I was shocked and angry, sure, but my idiot came out, also. Afterwards, things I knew about the old man began to click into place. I know what was happening in there, not all the details or the motivations he had, of course, but I trust you. He's a wicked old reprobate, one with more money than morals, and he likes to push others around. Money lets people do that sometimes."

"Chad," she began. His apology, or confirmation, perhaps, she didn't know the right word to use, but his charming admittance of his faults had opened her heart once again. She was certain now that Ben had been right, that she definitely had been falling in love with this man when events on the rig had conspired to shatter that for her. She could just reach his feet, and they were bare. She placed her hand on one of his ankles, and she saw him smile at her. She had to tell him how she felt.

"Chad," and she hesitated again when her voice cracked with emotion. He had to be told how her heart was swelled up inside of her as if she couldn't breathe, how she had fallen in love with him. A third time, she called his name, "Chad—"

Just then, there was the scramble of footsteps, and a completely dressed Chaddie burst in. Excitement sprinkled his face like a starburst of freckles, and he held fresh clothing in his hand. He ran forward, sliding to a stop in front of his father and Lou.

"Here, Dad." He was out of breath, and he dropped the clothes on his father's lap. "Clothes. For you." His face was animated with something else, though, and he leaned over, resting his hands on his knees to catch his breath.

"Son, what's going on?"

A grin opened up on his face, and his green eyes sparkled. He turned his gaze to include Lou. "I danced the hurricane, Dad, Lou." He stood and pumped his arm as he held his hand in a fist, and he turned and ran back the way he'd come, his knees bouncing high in the air. As he approached the steps, Ben appeared just in time to grab the boy's shoulders. Chaddie gushed, "I did it, Ben. I told 'em. I danced the hurricane."

Ben laughed and slapped him on the back. He walked past the boy, leaving him bubbling with his elevated enthusiasm, and walked to where Chad sat next to Lou.

Chad stood, holding the clothes Chaddie had given him, and he looked at Ben with a puzzled expression. "Danced the hurricane?"

With a deep chuckle, Ben held up a hand. "He'll explain it later. Just be glad I made him get dressed before we got back. It wasn't pretty. We do have power, now. It's only five gallons, but it'll keep us lighted for a time." He looked to Lou. "Is everything all right?" He cocked his head at Chad. "Between you two?

She smiled, pulling him aside. "More than okay, Ben. Thank you—"

Just then, with a piercing screech of metal, the entire structure shifted, and the far side of the floor they were on dropped. Stinky peed herself with a yelp of fear, and Lou screamed as she crashed against Ben. Chaddie was slammed to the floor, and the clothes in Chad's hands went flying through the air. Chad's towel took leave of his body in the scramble, leaving him careening across the floor in the buff. However, no one noticed this time. The lights had gone out once again.

ONLY THE platform lights were on. Bethel Baptist was quite large, and to power up the entire array of auditorium lights was atrociously expensive. That was reserved for Sunday mornings and Christmas Eve services. The platform lights, however, illuminated the first dozen rows quite nicely.

It never surprised Bill Reinhardt when several hundred people showed up like this at a moment's notice. The call had gone out just an hour earlier, and the prayer teams had pulled together as one. That was one of the reasons he enjoyed being the senior pastor at Bethel so much. This was family to Bill, the very people who had stepped in to help raise his own after his wife had taken ill and passed on. He knew Louinda had borne much of the brunt of those hard days, but others had been there for the family, especially after Lou lost her husband and headed to the oil fields.

That was something Bill had never agreed with, but he'd supported his eldest daughter. She was strong willed, and she could express her opinions. She was just like her grandmother. Bill was the opposite. Life was water to him, and he was a duck. Bad things rolled off his back, and he continued on in spite of it. His mother wrestled with life, and people knew where she stood. His Lou was like that, and he loved her for it. His mother loved her even more.

He stood, facing the people who had gathered to pray for the two souls on Sunshine Gulf Platform No. 6. With a small movement of his hand, those in the room stood, and Bill paused. A couple opened a side door, and he smiled, waiting until they found a seat with everyone else.

"There will be no organ music this morning. I apologize. Cynda is with her youngest at the hospital in Tulsa. She left last night. This will be her seventh grandchild, and she couldn't miss it." People in the pews chuckled. Cynda hadn't been able to miss *any* of her grandchildren's births.

Bill cleared his throat to get the people's attention, and he continued. "However, Shirley and Clark have offered to sing *a cappella.* Thank you, Shirley and Clark. If you'll go ahead and come forward, Jerry has already set up the microphones, and you should be ready to go."

A rustling was heard, and then a couple in their fifties walked forward. They were both tall with dark hair, and she had on a bright red dress. Regulars on the Sunday morning program, the two could sing anything put in front of them. As they reached for their microphones, the rest of the gathered church members settled quietly into their seats.

As the reassuring vocals of *How Great Thou Art* began melting through the group of people, Bill began to talk. "As you know, a mighty storm has attacked our own United States coast. Some people would say it's the Hand of God. Others might give another more nefarious being credit." There was a spattering of laughter from his audience. They knew who this other being was.

"However," Bill continued, "the Bible says the rain falls on the just and the unjust. Does that only mean the rain of prosperity? Certainly this storm down on our neighbors' shores is showering them with rain. What does that mean? Are they just or unjust?"

Bill sighed and looked down. He had no Bible in his hand this morning. He didn't need one. He was nearly fifty-five, and he had been preaching The Word since he was fifteen, pastoring since before his eldest daughter was born. He knew The Word.

Tears were in his eyes when he looked up. "People all over the Gulf are suffering this morning, and I can lay no claim to being the only one to know worry over a loved one. However, God's Word tells us He knows every sparrow and every hair on our heads. That's the way God cares for us. We aren't a mass of writhing humanity on which He dispenses His love or wrath. No, that's not our God. Our God cares for each one of us individually, and I feel that He expects us to do the same. Haven't I read where God says that if anyone does for a brother, it's also been done unto the Father? He said, *Let the children come unto me*. He says He will give rest to the weary."

Tissues could be seen dabbing eyes as Bill paused to gather his emotions. They were running deep this day, but his flock needed to see his strength. He had to be the example of steadfastness to which they anchored their cares.

"God loves *us,* you and me. Frank, you. Your farm flooded, and God was with you. *We* were with you, and when we were there, God was there. Josh over there, and Cookie sitting at your side. When your infant angel flew to heaven, was God there with you? You know He was, because I was there, and a hundred other people from this

300

church. Everyone here, I could tell you examples of God being there for each of you, and you would know I was telling the truth. You'd *feel* it, and you'd *know*.

"Well, I know God is here today. I know because I see each of you sitting out there. I know because each of you came when I had a need. There are a lot of hurting people beyond our walls today. This storm is bad, and they say it'll get worse. However, God expects us to follow His example. If He cares about every hair on our heads, how can we not do the same for others?

"Each of you knows why we're here. Two people were left on one of those drilling platforms out there in the middle of this storm. Only God knows how or why that happened, but He has a purpose. I must believe that. My daughter is one of those people. The other man is someone she's spoken of favorably. He's a friend of hers, an older man who lost his wife on a different oil rig many years ago." Bill punctuated his message with his final words. "God cares about all the people in this storm. However, He expects me to care about just one." He smiled, and he blinked back tears. "I told Him I was willing to push it to two. I asked if that was okay with Him, and He said I could pray for both of them."

Laughter loosened the tension among those sitting in the pews. They knew this was serious, and that people died when hurricanes crashed through the Gulf. They also knew that God's hand was more powerful than any storm could possibly be.

As the soft strains of *Suppertime*, that old treasure written by Ira Stanphill, filtered from the throats of Shirley and Clark, the church members stood and gathered on the platform around Bill. Hands were raised and voices called out as one for their God to watch over the two children who had been left to battle this storm out in the wild waters of the Gulf of Mexico.

Outside the church, it was very hot already. This was August, and it was Oklahoma City. By the afternoon, it would likely be in the triple digits. As the prayers were rising to Heaven inside the building, there was a click somewhere in one of the sun-drenched flowerbeds. With a soft whoosh, sprinkler heads popped up in one section of the lawn, and a gentle spray of water fought back the rising heat. Before the prayers were finished, the sprinklers had cycled through all the stations on the church grounds, and the cooled air smelled fresh and new.

It would heat up again, and the afternoon sun would try to bake the water from the soil. Yet, when the church members exited the building, it was as if God had reached his hand down and blessed Oklahoma City to show he had heard their prayers. Even the flowers sparkled with droplets of water that the rays of the sun had yet to dry.

Bill was very pleased. He had felt God with him this morning, and he knew his daughter was in good hands. He would still worry. He knew that, but God was bigger than his worry. He knew that, also.

Chapter 17

ABRAMSKI SAT at the table, and he drummed his fingers on its surface. He could feel the engine running deep within the Coast Guard cutter, and he knew its horsepower was being tested as it fought to keep the ship steady. They were moored in the shipping channel, and while the water here was simply rough rather than violent, the ship was being battered. The skill of the pilot was the hand of God protecting this vessel. It had to be a strong hand, too, or else this vessel wouldn't be there to rescue people after the storm.

The big boat shuddered and lurched as Johnson walked in the room. He jerked, nearly dropping the cup he held in his hand as coffee splashed out onto the floor.

"Crikes! That one nearly got me." He looked up to see

Abramski at the table. His eyes were strained, and his mouth was firmly set. "Give it a rest, Abramski. You couldn't know. We'll get back out there when all this settles down."

Abramski snorted. "I did know. You know that. I lied to you when I told you those two had loaded already." Tiredness had been the cause. Still, the responsibility was his.

Johnson sat beside him. "Bram, we got fifty-eight people off. That's fifty-eight people who would've had to stay on that platform through this storm if we'd gotten there an hour later. How did we do that? Because you're the best rescue swimmer in the Guard. Remember that idiot that went in the water on that other rig, Cracker's Barrel? You saved us that hour by getting him aboard quickly. You did that, and if it weren't for you doing what you did, all those people on that last rig would still be there. Let it go, Bram. When the storm's over, we'll go get them."

Abramski's hands still danced, though. He wanted to go get them now, to prove that he hadn't left two people out there to die. Not because of him. He never let people die. He saved them. Always. That was in his records: not a person left behind, and not a life lost. These couldn't be the first.

Johnson gave him a pat on the shoulder, and he stood. At the door he met Tucker. He took a deep breath and shrugged.

"Still beating himself up, huh?"

"Yeah," Johnson whispered. "He thinks it's his fault."

"He'll be fine after we get back out there and pull those

people off. That rig'll be okay in this. Thanks for checking on him, Johnson."

Actually, Tucker wasn't so sure. He fully expected that rig to be gone when they went back. Fifty-eight people might be safe and sound, but two were already dead. He was convinced of that. Johnson might feel the same way, but neither of them would say it. Saying it made it true, and if the two they'd left out there were dead, there'd be no point in going back out, would there?

"IS ANYONE hurt?" Louinda could stand if she was careful. The floor sloped, but she could maintain her footing, and in the darkness, she reached for the person closest to her. "Chad?" The wind whistled loudly, and it was obvious the accommodations block had been breached.

"I'm fine, Lou. I'm looking for my clothes. Check on the others." She could barely see him as he scrambled away, feeling along the floor for the clothes his son had brought him.

She closed her eyes, hoping they might adjust to the dark faster if she did so. She'd been able to see fairly well before, but the lights being on even for that short time had dilated her pupils. She felt blind.

Opening them, she could just make out Ben on the floor. "Ben!" She crawled to him and put her hand on his face. "Ben, can you hear me?"

He stirred. "My head, Lou. I think I hit it hard."

"Here. Let me check." As she reached to feel, she called, "Chaddie? Are you okay?" She was relieved to hear his thirteen-year-old enthusiasm still in true form.

"That was better than a roller coaster. I've got Stinky.

305

I think she peed herself again. Lou, will this rig float?"

She whispered to Ben, "He asks the hard questions no one wants to answer."

Ben chuckled, then he groaned. "He danced with the storm, Lou. Nothing can scare him now." He went quiet, and she pressed her hand to his chest. Relief flooded her when she felt his chest rise and fall in a steady rhythm.

Chad crawled up beside her. "Is he okay?"

Without thinking, she leaned into him, hoping he would put his arms around her. "For now. I hope he is. He said he hit his head, but I couldn't find any blood."

Chad ran his hand down her arm reassuringly. "We're still safe, anyway."

Her voice was ragged as she turned to him. "This is my fault. Just like stranding you two. I should have warned everyone this was about to happen."

"The rig tilting? How could that be your fault? You didn't cause the legs to fall out from under it, or whatever made it go sideways like this."

"I saw it coming, though. After the lights came on, I saw the water running down the ceiling. These places are watertight, or at least pretty close. The water was my clue, and I ignored it."

Chad chuckled. "I forgive you, and we're still alive."

She began to sob. "What else have I missed? I missed you and Chaddie for the evacuation announcements. I missed some cue with the evac team, and the helicopter didn't wait for us. Then I missed the sign that this place was straining under the extreme pounding it's receiving. Look at it now. What else am I missing that should be telling me something? Will we die because I'm not paying attention?"

Chad rubbed her shoulder and kissed her on the cheek. "If we die, I'll know three things. I've been handed my son back. In two days, he's given me more joy than I've experienced in the past three years with him. I've also found a woman I think I could love, and she's here in my arms."

Lou leaned her head against him, brushing at her eyes with her hand. "That's sweet. What's the third thing?"

He found her hand and worked his finger into hers. "If I don't have another day left to me, those two things have given me all I could have wished for."

A deep voice rumbled up at them. "Sappy, sappy. Those words could cause love to bloom. Lou, are you okay with what he's saying?"

She chuckled. "I'm loving it, Ben."

"Are you sure?" He coughed, and it was audible even over the wind that screamed and whistled.

She reached with her free hand and patted his shoulder. "Rest, Ben. You don't worry about me." She ran her hand along Chad's leg. "I see you found the clothes Chaddie brought. You're dressed, finally."

"Almost," he chuckled. "I couldn't find the underwear, but I did get the pants and shirt on." He put his hand on hers. "At least I'm not exposing myself anymore."

She didn't say anything to that. She hadn't minded when he did that, even if she really didn't see much. However, she did shiver at the sound of the wind. It seemed to be telling her there was no question big brother had arrived, and big brother was very angry, indeed.

THE STORM battered the motel room's walls, violent

fists of wind and rain trying to force their way inside. Torch shuddered, but it had little to do with the weather. He knew he had to shoulder part of the blame for that mess with the old man. Sure, room assignments were no secret, but the old man hadn't known. He could have found out on his own, but it had been *Torch* that had told.

Then, the old fool had gone down there and made a mess of things, a royal mess. Yolanda said she'd even been forced into the middle of it. Now, she was upset that Lou hadn't gotten evacuated to the Coast Guard ship. Her friend, Ben, hadn't been on board, either.

Torch looked to where Yolanda slept on the bed. At least Galveston wasn't taking the brunt of the storm like they had several years ago during that big one that had hit. Mitch, no, Ike. That was it. Motels were at least still open. After Yolanda had broken down on the boat when she hadn't been able to find the last two people on her list, he had put his arm around her and let her cry it out.

He was going back out again. He'd told the crew from that helicopter that he was the rig's welder; and he was, even if he wasn't permanently assigned there. However, he knew the rig. If there was a problem they ran into, they'd need someone there who knew the ropes.

They'd gotten clearance to take him with them, telling him there'd be no difficulty in him riding along. Just be patient, they said. When things settled down, they'd give him a call. He could meet them just down the road by the ferry terminal. Torch didn't mind walking that far.

He sat by the phone. He wasn't going to sleep. What if he missed the call? No, he'd stay awake another day, if that's what it took. He wasn't going to sleep at all.

308

"DAD, SOMETHING'S happening," Chaddie yelled frantically. He'd danced the hurricane, but that had been outside, and he'd had someplace safe to return to. Now, the dance seemed to be coming inside, and that was a different matter altogether.

The rig had been vibrating excessively for some time. Tortured metal could be heard screaming in protest during the worst gusts of wind, and somewhere, something was broken. It banged repeatedly, reverberating throughout the accommodations block.

With the boy's words, the floor jerked, and the lower end of the structure dropped six additional inches. Then, increasingly faster, it skipped down several more times. Finally, it was still. The floor was steeper now, and at the lower end of the structure, water could be heard crashing into the metal walls.

"Dad? I've got Stinky. There's water just below us, and my feet are wet. I don't want to lose my grip and slide into it."

"Perhaps we should go up a level." Ben's voice could just be heard over the smack of the waves on the metal walls.

Lou crawled forward to lean over him, reaching a hand to touch his face carefully. "Can you move?"

He laughed, and it was soft and low. "I can drown, Lou. I'd rather move."

"I understand." She kept her hand to his face, stroking it gently. "No drowning on my watch."

"Just help me up."

"Let me get more muscle." Looking up, she called to

Chad, "Can you help with Ben? We're headed up the steps. I'm going after Chaddie and Stinky." As soon as Chad crawled over to take Ben's arm, Lou moved down towards the boy. "Chaddie? There's a door here. I'm grabbing the knob so I don't slide into you. When I reach my hand out, you grab it, and I'll hold you while you crawl up. Hold onto Stinky's collar. She mustn't be allowed to slip."

"What do I do when I get up there?" Fright was evident in his voice.

"We're heading up the steps. The upper level should still be out of the water." She grabbed the knob and stretched her arm toward him as far as it would go. "Now, Chaddie. Grab on."

She felt his hand, and she held tightly to the knob as he started to move. Once he was level with her, she asked, "Can you make it the rest of the way?"

"I'll try. You can let go of my hand, now." After he moved past her, taking several cautious steps, he began to hyperventilate, his breathing coming faster and faster. Then came barking followed by the sounds of a frantic scramble. Chaddie gasped and called, "I'm starting to slip! Help!"

"Lou?" Ben's deep voice rumbled for her attention just as a bolt of lightning crashed outside, temporarily lighting the interior of the corridor. In that moment, the water swirling at their feet was a pit of liquid terror, and no one felt safe. Stinky's whine echoed in the enclosed space, and it was clear it was up to Lou to stop this potential disaster.

"Dad!" Terror rang out in the boy's voice.

Lou grasped her door knob firmly and reached toward Chaddie, glad he'd at least made it past her precarious position; and in the dark, her hand found his backside. "Sorry, Chaddie," she said through gritted teeth. "I'm pushing, but I can't hold you long. Find something to grab."

Then the pressure was off her hand, and she called, "Chaddie?"

Chad's voice answered, "I've got him. Ben's on the steps resting. Can you make it up without help?"

She let out a ragged, "I think so."

Chaddie added, "I've got Stinky. We're okay." He could be heard moving around, and then he asked, "Lou, will it sink? The rig, will it sink, do you think, if it slips more?"

"Chaddie," his father cautioned, "some questions are better not asked."

A deep, rumbling voice called from farther up the steps. "He needs to know, Chad. He's danced the hurricane, and you won't frighten him. Trust your boy."

Lou pulled herself up to sit with the others on the bottom steps. "Chaddie, the rig as a whole can float for a time. Right now, only one side seems to have slipped on its legs. Since it's partially in the water, its natural buoyancy should keep it from slipping any farther."

"So, we're okay?" His voice was steady, but the question was real.

Chad took over. "Son, oil rigs are designed to take the worst the weather can put out. Look what this one's endured so far, and it's still here. Come here, Son." He pulled the boy over and put an arm around him, pulling him tight. "We're in this together, father and son. Whatever happens to you happens to me. What we've got to do

311

is take care of Stinky. Can we do that?"

"Yes, sir." Chaddie's voice was stronger this time. "Come here, Stinky." He whistled softly, but the dog didn't move.

"Clap," came Ben's resonant suggestion. Chaddie did, and Stinky jumped up beside him, putting her head and front paws in his lap.

"Good girl, Stinky," he said, working his fingers into the skin on her neck. "You're safe here with me. Dad, too. We'll keep you safe. Be glad you didn't have to dance the hurricane. You'd have gotten wet all over again."

Chad laughed. "What's this dance-the-hurricane thing? Ben?"

Ben's chuckle could be heard coming down the steps. "Ask your son. He's the one who did the dance."

"Chaddie, do you care to tell us what went on? I couldn't miss the excitement in your voice. Whatever it was, it must be really special."

"Listen, Dad," Chaddie said. He let the screaming of the wind and the shifting of the oil rig speak for him. That was the hurricane outside. That was what he'd danced, and he'd survived.

After a few minutes, his father said to him again, "Chaddie? You know you don't have to tell if you don't want to. Just say that, and we'll let you alone."

The boy chuckled. "I was telling you, Dad, only I let the storm say it for me."

"What does that mean?" Chad chuckled.

"Dad?"

"Hmm?"

"Are you thirteen?"

His father laughed. "You know how old I am. I haven't been thirteen for twenty years."

"That's not what I asked. Are you thirteen right now?"

"I don't know what you're asking."

Ben's response prompted him to play along. "Just answer the boy's question. It's a simple one."

"Thanks, Ben. Too simple, if you ask me."

"The world *is* simple from your son's viewpoint. Just answer it."

"Okay, Chaddie. I'm not thirteen right now. Is that the answer you needed?"

"Most of it, Dad. There's another one I need to ask, too." His enthusiasm was back in full force.

"Sure, Son. Ask away."

"Dad, can you be thirteen just for today?" Laughter infused the words.

His father took his time answering that one. It seemed just too silly. "No, Chaddie. I'm sorry. I can't do that for you."

His boy sighed, and it was a big one. "I'm sorry, Dad. If you're not thirteen, and you can't become thirteen, then you can't understand the hurricane dance. It wouldn't do me any good to explain it to you."

"Ben knows, though."

"Dad," Chaddie started, "Ben's thirteen like me. He understands." A man's deep, resonant chuckle wafted down the stairs when Chaddie said that.

"Chaddie," his father suggested, "Ben was old when *I* was thirteen."

"Careful, now," Ben warned.

Chad called up, "I don't mean anything by that, Ben.

You know what I mean."

"No offense taken. Your son's right, though. Listen to him."

Lou joined in, "Chad, just play along. I'm enjoying this." She touched his leg, letting her hand rest on the bare skin where his ankle turned to become his foot. "Go on, Chaddie. Finish what you were saying."

"Thank you, Lou. Dad, it's just that if you were really thirteen when you were thirteen, then you're always thirteen. You've got it with you always. Isn't that right, Ben? Dad, you either understand thirteen or you don't. If you don't, you'd never understand dancing the hurricane."

Ben called down, "That's about the way I see it, Chad. Your son understands the world just like it is. Maybe someday you can be thirteen, too, and then you'll understand just what your son did today."

Chad whispered to Lou, "I didn't get that."

She smiled to herself in the darkness. "Maybe you weren't supposed to. Maybe it was just between Chaddie and Ben."

"I guess," he said. "Then, maybe I never was thirteen. I thought I was. I guess I was wrong about at least one thing in my life, and I'm just now learning it."

"We're all wrong about something, Chad." She patted his leg. "I think maybe we all are at one time or another."

As she fell quiet, the group was wrapped by the raging weather just on the other side of their slightly compromised bastion of safety in the middle of the Gulf. Their gentle teasing had seemed to calm their fears over the collapse of one side of the accommodations block.

Then, a loud screech of metal against metal pierced

314

their protected space, and the drooping side of the rig fell one more time. The wind howled with a new intensity, as if they were outside in the midst of the storm, and before they could grab hold of something to steady themselves, water came pouring in right on top of their heads.

Chapter 18

"NO, GRANNY. Wrestling is on. Tummyache Rutabaker is going for the title today. This is no-holds-barred cage fighting. You can't get any bloodier than this." Willie wrapped his hands around the remote and tucked it into his lap.

"William Reinhardt. Give me that remote!" She stepped between him and the television. "That's my TV, and you can't hog it."

Willie grinned. "Possession is nine-tenths, Granny." He held up the remote then put it back in his lap.

She reached a quick hand down and slapped his where it lay, causing him to release the remote control. Picking it up, she hooted, "Possession is nine-tenths, Willie."

He was more concerned about where the remote had

been when she slapped his hand away. "Granny! That was a close call. Did you even see where I was holding that thing when you slapped my hand?"

She pointed it at the television and pushed the channel search button before turning to her grandson. "I saw where your hand was, Willie. It was there when you were three, and I slapped it away then. I never touched your male member to do it, either. You're nearly nineteen, and if you put it there again, I'll slap it away like before."

Willie laughed at that. "Granny, I already told you. I don't do that, so you just stop slapping."

As the weather channel blinked on, Granny hit the button again to stop on her station, and she turned to sit. "Grandson, I already told you, I know better. You shower in my bathroom."

Willie sank deep into the couch. He heard her words, and as his face turned red, he focused on the TV screen. Anyway, the program was on, and Granny wasn't paying him any mind. She was watching the weather again.

"Hurricane Thomas, one of the fastest moving storms in recorded history, is now losing strength and heading southwest. Property owners from Mobile to Corpus Christi are breathing sighs of relief. Tracking models now suggest a possible landfall just south of Matamoros, Mexico, where damage is expected to be minimal due to the relatively uninhabited countryside. In other weather news, transponders from three unmanned oil platforms directly in the path of Hurricane Thomas have gone dead, indicating severe damage or possibly even a total loss of the platforms, themselves. You may remember Sunshine Gulf Platform No. 6. Earlier it was thought the platform had

been successfully evacuated. That was later revealed to be inaccurate, as two crewmembers were somehow left behind when the rest of the personnel were rescued. This is our latest live footage of that rig as Ramie Zarhaire of affiliate station KHOU in Houston rides along on a Coast Guard helicopter to see how the two offshore roughnecks fared as they rode out the hurricane. Ramie? How does it look?"

A shaky view of a young woman riding in a helicopter flashed on the television screen. The wind whipped her hair about, and the sides of the helicopter were open. The noise was very loud, but the sky was bright under the cloud cover, and no rain could be seen.

"Peter, I'm here with three of the most outstanding Coast Guard servicemen I've ever had the opportunity to fly with. They were out here this morning at the crack of dawn after spending the previous twelve hours evacuating numerous oil rig workers. It's now been thirty-six hours since these men have slept, and yet here they are again, determined to get back to that rig. They've refused to let anyone else take their place, insisting that their duty to the people on this rig has not yet been fulfilled.

"I have Lieutenant Tucker piloting, although I believe his crewmembers know him as 'Tuck.'" She put her finger to her ear and paused as if she were listening to someone off screen. *"No, Peter, I do not know his first name. I was able to join this mission under the strict condition I wouldn't try to interact with the crew. I've picked up their names from clothing and listening to them interact with each other. As I said, they are very tired, and I'm lucky they let me ride along.*

"Here behind me is Lieutenant Johnson, who will remain in the helicopter at all times to assist with entering and exiting. Beside him is Petty Officer 3rd Class Abramski, a crack Coast Guard rescue swimmer, who spent time last night in the ocean at the height of the storm. That alone must have left him absolutely exhausted. If, for some reason, someone goes overboard during today's rescue, he's the one who will jump in after the unlucky person at peril of his own safety. Oh, and Peter. I have someone very special riding with me today."

"Yes, Ramie? Could you tell us who it is?"

"I have one of the actual workers who was evacuated from the rig just this morning. He's here on board the helicopter. Torch Magee. He's a welder who volunteered to come along just in case something goes wrong."

"Ramie, what an appropriate name for a welder! I'm sure there must be a story behind it. Perhaps, after the rescue, you can find out and fill us in. I certainly hope he's able to aid the Coast Guard rescue crew. How close are you to the oil platform?"

She could be seen looking off screen, and then she nodded.

"Peter, I'm being told that if my cameraman turns southeast, the rig will be in view. Be prepared, Peter. I'm told the news is not good."

The camera panned, and there in the Gulf waters appeared the stricken platform. The waves were still huge, and the wind repeatedly blew spray through the air. The platform was small in the image, and then there was a quick zoom, bringing the platform up until it filled the screen.

"My God, Peter. Can you believe this? How can any-one have survived the storm on this oil platform? If you look, you can see the superstructure. There's a large flat area that I'm told is the landing pad for the helicopter. No one will be landing there today. It's at what appears to be a forty-five degree angle, and there's a large block of what appears to be rooms just below that. Torch, can you confirm that? Yes, Peter. Torch is shaking his head in confirmation. That's where the workers would have been housed when the platform was in operation. As the heli-copter draws closer, I think you'll be able to see that one side of it is actually in the water. Waves are washing up over one end. I don't know what type of flotation devices are built into this type of rig, if any, but I cannot imagine this rig standing much longer."

"Ramie, do you see any signs of life?"

"Peter, our camera is at a very high magnification level right now. It will be several minutes before we can really tell anything."

"Ramie, we'll come back to you in a few moments for an update." The scene changed back to the studio, and an announcer in a blue suit and a yellow tie stood in front of a weather map. He smiled into the camera. *"That was Ramie Zarhaire of our Houston affiliate, KHOU. We will be back with your Forecast on the Fives just after these messages."*

"Granny, did you see that? It fell over. The storm knocked Lou's well over. Wow!" Willie no longer cared about his showers and what Granny might or might not have heard while he was inside. The images of the hurri-cane damage had his attention now.

Granny stood and watched the screen for a moment. Her voice was tired when she spoke. "Willie, I'm going to take the towels from the dryer. Tell me what they find." With a deep sigh, she walked towards the kitchen door.

"Granny," Willie called. "You don't want to see?"

She called back over her shoulder, "Willie, I want to know. I just can't watch anymore." As she walked through the kitchen to the laundry room, she felt tears start to run down her face. Her granddaughter was on that rig, and she might be dead. No, she didn't want to watch at all.

LOU WAS jarred awake. Over the course of the day, they'd been forced to work farther and farther up the steps. Each time the side of the rig had slipped, the floor had become steeper, and the water had come farther up the inside of the accommodations block. Now, the waves slamming into the rig shook it frighteningly, and sleeping on the treads had become almost unbearably uncomfortable. She was sick to her stomach, too. Despite the discomfort, that made her smile. Two days ago she had been sick to her stomach, and Ben had called it love. Now that she admitted she might be in love, she was sick to her stomach, and it wasn't love. It was seasickness.

She stood, and holding onto a protruding piece of metal step that she could just grasp, she leaned into the flooded companionway and let her stomach try to empty itself once again. She was relieved when nothing came out. She spat to get the taste of bile out of her throat. Feeling better, if only marginally, she pulled herself back into the area they'd claimed as their safety zone. It wasn't really safe. It was the spot they'd been able to reach where they could weather the storm as best as possible. The steps had given them purchase as the rig had tilted, and they'd been glad for that.

She realized with a start that she could see better than she had earlier. Each of the men with her was clearly visible for the first time since that first shattering drop that had wiped out Ben and Chaddie's efforts in getting the lights going.

The boy was curled around the dog, or the dog was curled around him. She couldn't tell. His hair was mussed, and his clothing was twisted around his thin frame. He was dirty, too. They all were. His father was sprawled over several steps. There was blond stubble over his jaw, and Lou thought it made him look touchingly vulnerable. His feet were exposed, and off to one side were the boxer shorts his son had brought him, the ones he hadn't been able to find. Somehow, the shorts had made it up the levels with them as they climbed.

Ben was the one who worried her. He had hit his head earlier, and he'd been sluggish ever since. Now, he looked pale. She hadn't thought she would ever be able to say that about him, but somehow, even his coal black skin seemed dusted with white. He was breathing, though, and that was a relief to her. She didn't want to lose this man she had called a friend since her first day on the rig.

Overhead flapped an outside door that had twisted loose in the violent upheaval of the rig's battering during the storm. It hung into the interior, and through it, she could see sky. If she could climb these steps, she could look out and see just what damage the platform had taken. She wouldn't do that alone, though, and she wouldn't wake any of her companions to do it now. Outside would have to wait.

Over the sound of the waves, she thought she heard the deep-pitched thrumming of a helicopter, but she knew that was just wishful thinking. Sitting back down, she leaned her head over and rested it on Chad's leg. At least the feel of his body was comforting to her, and with his warmth against her face, maybe she could fall back asleep for a while longer.

STINKY'S EARS began to twitch, because she was hearing the same thing Lou had heard. However, the dog didn't know what wishful thinking was. She just knew sounds that caught her attention, and this one did. It was different, it was persistent, and it was outside.

After a moment, the dog's eyes opened, and she looked around. Something was out there. She didn't know just what. When she figured that out, she'd go for it. Until then, she waited patiently, wrapped in Chaddie's arms.

"GRANNY! WEATHER'S back on!" Willie sat up and looked over the arm of the couch. "Granny!" When she didn't answer, he mumbled, "Turn your hearing aid up, Granny." Then he looked at the screen. The meteorologist in the blue suit and yellow tie was talking.

"Tonight expect a low of 82 degrees. Tomorrow our high should be 104 with a chance of afternoon clouds. There's a 30 percent chance of rain through the weekend. Our extended outlook is hot and sunny with highs in the 100s and lows in the low to mid 80s. Now back to our Weather in the News with Ramie Zarhaire of affiliate

323

station KHOU in Houston.

"Ramie, you are on a Coast Guard helicopter headed out into the storm-ravaged Gulf of Mexico. What do you see?"

The picture changed to the one earlier of the oil rig leaning askew and partially submerged. It was from a different angle, and more of the damage could be seen.

"Peter, this is the worst thing I've ever seen. The helicopter landing deck, what's known as the helipad, has been partially peeled away. As you can see, the derrick that normally extends up nearly two hundred feet is completely gone. There's no life on this structure. Behind me, I can see Johnson and Abramski just shaking their heads. I'm going to say this quietly, Peter, because I don't want to embarrass these brave Coast Guard rescue workers, but I do believe I see what seems to be tears in Abramski's eyes. This must be very hard on them to come all the way out here to rescue two stranded workers who should have never been left on this rig in the first place. Peter, do we know just how these workers were left?"

"Ramie, not with any certainty, we don't. However, I need to correct an earlier term I used to describe one of the brave souls who was on this platform. These are not roughnecks as I said earlier. Apparently these two are Louinda Reinhardt, who is the Rig Safety and Training Coordinator, and Ben Tosh, a motorman. Now, I don't know just what a motorman does, but rig safety is quite obvious. I believe these are quite high level positions, and from what I understand, Louinda and Ben were intended to be the last ones off. At peril of their own safety, they were verifying the structure was completely evacuated.

They are to be commended for the ultimate performance of their duties."

"Peter, I've been listening to the Coast Guard team behind me. They seem to have reached a conclusion that if we circle the rig twice and see no life, we will abandon the rescue attempt at this time, letting a search and rescue ship come out at a later time. Of course, that ship will, of necessity, have to wait until the seas calm down more than they have so far.

"This breaks my heart, Peter, and I know the three men here with me on this helicopter are devastated. How hard it must be to know that two people who could have been saved were left behind to weather this storm, and after hoping for their survival, we find they may have met the worst of possible ends."

For a time, the announcer was quiet, as the television showed the tilted oil platform. All that could be heard was the beat of the helicopter's rotor blades. As the camera revolved around the damaged structure, showing exactly how beat up it really was, the rotor wash began to batter the surface of the water. As the second rotation came to a completion, the announcer started up again.

"Ramie, has the helicopter noticed any movement that might suggest good news?"

"Peter, we have just completed our second pass, and as you can see, there's been no sign of life. I see Abramski sinking back into his harness, and Johnson is on the radio to the pilot. I believe they are calling off the search.

"Peter, this is indeed the saddest day of my life. My heart goes out to the families of these two people. Whoever you are out there, God bless you, and I hope your loved

ones are found safe at a later date.

"Peter, here is a final view of the oil rig as we make our exit. Back to you . . . no, wait, Peter. Don't cut the feed. My God, Zack, zoom in now. There's something there. God, Peter! Can you see it? There's a dog on that rig. It's right there. I don't know where it came from, but it's there, like it appeared out of nowhere, and I do believe our helicopter is turning around. The men behind me have come to life, and it looks as if Abramski, our rescue swimmer, is preparing to go overboard. A dog, Peter. You should be here. We just might find these people after all."

"Thank you, Ramie. We'll be back to you in just a moment." The television changed back to the man in the blue suit. *"Weather in the News will be back after these messages and your Forecast on the Fives."*

Granny stepped into the living room. Her eyes were red, and her voice was soft. "Willie, are they alive?"

He threw his head back in frustration. "Ahh! Who knows, Granny? They keep showing commercials and the Forecast on the Fives. They found a dog, though."

She walked farther into the room. "A dog, Willie? You wouldn't be teasing me, would you?" Finally at her chair, she sat heavily without bothering to adjust her position to get comfortable. "A dog?"

"Yeah, Granny. A mean-looking dog, and it was on the top of the well, the part that was floating."

She snorted, somehow finding the iron in her Oklahoma blood once again. The news of life on the damaged rig was bringing Granny back. She barked at Willie.

"Of course, it was on the part that was floating. Why they ever gave you your graduation certificate, I don't know. If that dog were on the part that was underwater, it would be dead, wouldn't it?"

Willie couldn't argue with that, but he could argue. "It wasn't a graduation certificate, Granny. It was a diploma."

She just looked at him. She knew a diploma when she saw it, and Willie didn't get one. However, she wasn't debating with him right now. He could believe what he wanted, but that didn't make it true.

"Tell people what you like, Willie. It doesn't hurt me none."

He laughed at her. "I love you, Granny."

She snorted. "If you loved me, you'd get the rest of the towels out of the dryer."

"I don't love you that much. After all, you only made me four peanut butter sandwiches today. I'm hungry." He looked at her with imploring eyes.

She looked at him hard. "You get your own sandwiches. I can fold my towels tomorrow."

"Oh, Granny," he said, and he hopped up from the couch in one, smooth move. "I'll bring you your towels. You can fold 'em while the weather's on. Can I have the pizza in the bottom drawer?"

"I don't care, Willie. No one else'll eat it."

He grinned. "Thanks, Granny!" He was gone in a flash, and the old woman just watched the television screen. She wanted to see if her Lou had survived the storm. Her granddaughter was tough. If a mean, black dog could survive, so could her Louinda. That, Granny knew for sure.

LOU JERKED awake again. She looked around, but the pounding in her head wouldn't seem to clear up. There was

327

Chaddie, and Ben was sleeping fitfully. Chad was under her head. Then she knew what had awakened her. The dog was gone, and barking was coming from outside. There was that thrumming sound, also, like a helicopter would make. It was loud this time.

"Chad," she shook his leg. "Chad! Chaddie! Wake up! Stinky is outside barking, and I think I hear a helicopter."

Chad roughly jerked his body forward and shook his sleep-filled head. "What, Lou? A helicopter? Outside?"

"Yes," she said. She saw Ben stirring, and it was obvious he wasn't doing well. "Ben, stay still, please. I think help might be here. I'm sending Chad and Chaddie up to see. I'll stay here with you." Ben just moaned.

Chad pulled his legs under him and stood. "I can hear the dog, and it does sound like a helicopter. I have to get up there. Chaddie?" He looked at his son. "Ready to climb, boy?"

His son rubbed his eyes and pulled his long limbs into action, clearly struggling to wake. "Now, Dad?"

His father reached and slapped him on the leg. "Now, Son, unless you want to spend another day or two on this rig. It's a long swim to shore."

Chaddie smiled as he ran his hand through his hair. "Without a suit, right? Lou said I'd lose Ben's."

"Right, without a suit. Come on, boy."

They looked up through the blindingly bright opening and squinted, searching a sky filled with clouds. It was a long way up, but down was even worse.

CHAD STARTED to climb. The steeply canted steps were awkward. His hands had to grasp the bottoms of treads, and he had to position his feet in places that were never meant to be climbed on. If the dog *had* gone up this, Chad didn't know how.

He glanced down to see Chaddie behind him. He was amazed at how much a man he seemed. He realized his son had grown in his eyes the past two days. He seemed to have become the adult his body was trying to make of him. Maybe it was that dance thing that had done it.

However, the open door was just ahead. Chad squinted in the brightness. It was overcast and very windy, but that didn't stop his eyes from needing to adjust after being inside so long. Then he blinked and saw Stinky balanced on the highest point she could reach. With all the energy she could muster, she was barking frantically at the sky.

As Chaddie grabbed his father's arm to pull himself up to see out, Chad saw the helicopter and pointed. It was right there not five hundred feet away, and a television camera was pointed right at them. To make sure they saw them, he raised a hand to wave.

Chapter 19

"TONIGHT EXPECT a low of 82 degrees. Tomorrow our high should be 104 with a chance of afternoon clouds. There's a 30 percent chance of rain . . . oh, forget about the forecast." The man in the yellow tie looked at someone off camera with a frown. Then he turned and smiled into the television screen. "Here's Ramie Zarhaire.

"Ramie, you are on a Coast Guard helicopter in the storm-ravaged Gulf of Mexico. When we spoke with you last, there was a dog on the top of that collapsed oil platform. I've been told that the rig belongs to Rampart Oil, and it was under investigation for improper mainte-nance. What do you see now?"

"Thank you, Peter. My eyes are filled with tears. We came out here to look for a woman and an older man, and *we found a dog on the top of the collapsed rig barking at us furiously. Now, two new people have appeared. Two men who look enough alike to be twins have climbed out of this sinking rig. They are waving at us. I don't know how they got here, perhaps lucky survivors of a boat damaged in the storm. As they say, any port in time of storm. What matters is that we've found life here.*

"Wait. The men on board with me are getting ready— Peter! Did we get that on camera? Abramski has just jumped overboard. I can see him. There's a big splash. Wait . . . yes! He's swimming towards the platform and should be there shortly. I-I-I am just overwhelmed. This is so exciting. I hope whoever's watching this, if you know these men, please call KHOU or log onto our website and tell us who these men are.

"Look! Quick, Zack, zoom in. I think it might be possible that this is a father and a son. Yes, I'm certain. Some mother out there will be very pleased today. It looks like our rescue swimmer is just about there. Oh, Peter! You can't see it, but Johnson here behind me is preparing to lower a basket. In a few moments, I'll be able to talk to one of the survivors. His story will be on screen within minutes. Peter, I'm so lucky to be here."

"Ramie, you are indeed lucky. We all feel very fortunate to be here to witness this amazing rescue. We'll be back shortly after these messages and your Forecast on the Fives."

THE SUN sparkled in the chlorine-treated water. The pool was large and circular, and it was lined with palm trees. Chaise lounges were arranged in neat rows, and on each one was a crisply rolled towel. Many had umbrellas to provide a welcome break from the sun.

A white-suited attendant walked briskly along the edge of the pool until he came to a couple lying side-by-side. They were wearing matching suits, and they both had on very dark and stylish sunglasses. Their bodies gleamed with oil.

"Ah! Here are your drinks, minus the triple sec. Your room has already been billed." As he was speaking, he set two tall glasses rimmed in salt on a table in between the two chaises. Quietly, he placed a saucer of salt and a shallow bowl of lime juice next to them. Finally, he set down an iced bottle of tequila. "Miss, would you care for a paper?"

"Oh," Diana moaned. "Chip, what do you think? Are you interested in reading anything today?"

His lips barely moved. "Is there any important news inside?"

"A hurricane, sir." The attendant stood crisply elegant in the Hawaiian sunshine.

Chip sighed. "Where? Here?"

"Oh, no, sir. The Gulf of Mexico."

Diana murmured, "Hawaii isn't anywhere near the Gulf of Mexico. Why would we care about that? Besides, I always say that no news is good news. Bring us a newspaper in five weeks."

"As you wish, miss. Will there be anything else?"

She thought for a moment. Then she smiled, "Pool boy, bring me another dry towel."

"Yes, miss. As you wish."

As he walked away, he looked down at the pocket of

his blazer. It clearly said Pool Attendant. That irritated him, but he wanted his tip. That's why he gave outstanding service, even to bozos like that.

ABRAMSKI THRUST strong arms through the churning water. He at least had daylight for this rescue, but being in the water today was little better than it had been the night before. However, this was one rescue he could not let go wrong. He had to right his mistake.

Nearing the rig, he paused to let his eyes flicker along the behemoth's exposed infrastructure, and then he turned his gaze to allow it to dance across the crest of the breaking waves. Finally, with exactitude, he studied the troughs they left behind. His mind evaluated the exact timing that would bring him to the precise place he wanted be. If he caught just the right wave, it would lift him to an exposed pipe he had pinpointed to pull himself cleanly out of the water. Treading for a moment, he waited until the pattern of swells was just right, and then he saw his chance. His arms dug into the waves. He counted his strokes, knowing by experience just how many it would take before reaching his goal.

Then, with precision, he opened a fist and grasped the exposed piping. He felt his body grow heavy as the water pulled away, leaving him high on the tilted rig. Forty feet away were the faces of the two men he had come to rescue. They weren't the ones he'd left behind on the rig that morning, but he would take who he could get.

Glancing behind him, he saw the next wave approaching, and with an explosion of bunched muscles, he threw himself up the angled wall in a quick, choreographed motion. Once again, his hand reached out, and closing it on the opening the men were looking through, he pulled himself up. He was face to face with the two, and he was surprised to find one of them was no more than a boy.

"Abramski, U.S. Coast Guard. Is there anyone else here besides the two of you?"

The older-looking man glanced down in the structure, and he nodded his head. Then, looking up, a bright smile broke across his face. "I'm glad to see you, Abramski, U.S. Coast Guard. I'm Chad Dickson, and this is my son, Chaddie. There are two others below, Lou and Ben. Ben's injured. Head, I think. We couldn't find any blood, but he seems groggy."

"The injured man goes first. Can he walk?"

Chad grimaced. "He's had to in order to keep out of the rising water."

"Take me to him." Abramski held out a hand toward the helicopter with four fingers out. In the copter, the pilot could be seen returning a thumbs-up sign. Then, Abramski followed the two men down into the stricken oil rig's accommodations block. It was his best guess whether he would come out again, but that's what the Coast Guard did. They helped when people needed it, and they never let them down.

Never.

TEARS RAN down Granny's face. There on her television was something that she would have never imagined. Two blond-haired men had been sitting on the outside of the oil well, and although one of them was very skinny like her Willie, she thought they looked very much alike. Wind had been whipping water everywhere. It seemed it was the helicopter making that happen, and that had surprised her.

Then a big, black bear of a man crawled out of the hole, and he was being helped by that Abramski man the woman in the helicopter had been talking about. The bear of a man had lain in a basket and been strapped down, and then he'd been whisked up into the air directly toward the camera.

Then the thing had happened that had taken Granny's heart away. Her own Lou had crawled from the hole, and there they'd been, four of them and that big, black dog. The dog had been barking and barking, and the skinny man had clapped his hands to get it to stop. Granny enjoyed seeing that. It was the next thing that shocked her soul. The other blond man had reached to her Lou, and he had given her a kiss on the cheek. Heaven above if her own Lou didn't put both arms around that man and kiss him back right on the mouth in front of the whole world.

"Granny," Willie called from the kitchen. "Are they rescued, yet? If so, I want to come see."

Granny grabbed the remote, and she hit a random set of buttons until a commercial for a back pain patch came on the screen. That grandson of hers mustn't be allowed to see his sister kissing a stranger in front of God and everybody.

"Yes," she called to Willie. "Lou's safe. Something else came on."

"You mean I missed it, Granny? I wanted to see Lou get saved."

"You didn't miss much, grandson. Come watch your show."

He stepped in with his pizza in his hand and flopped

on the couch. When the commercial went off, he smiled. It was what he'd wanted to watch all along.

"Thanks, Granny. It's Tummyache Rutabaker! The fight's just starting. This is going to be the best day of all!"

Granny didn't want to see it, though. She'd seen her Louinda get rescued, well almost, and that made this the best day of all for her. The man she'd kissed? That had been a surprise, but Granny did think he was rather cute. Besides, it had been five years since Tracy died. If it were Granny, she'd be kissing men by now. Heaven help, if they looked like that man on the TV screen, she wouldn't be able to stop herself if she tried.

Epilogue

SOMEWHERE IN a sun-drenched flowerbed, there was a click. With a gentle rush of air, a massive heat pump stirred to life, drawing warmth from the chilled surroundings to be redistributed throughout the massive building.

It was Oklahoma City, and it was January. Summer was a long time away. In the Forecast on the Fives that morning, the man in the blue suit had been wearing a bright silver tie. It somehow seemed very appropriate. His predictions had been for an ice storm this very night, and then blizzard-like snow conditions were expected for three days. Schools were already calling in their closings for the entire week. The man in the blue suit would be sharing them with school children all over Oklahoma City, just as soon as he knew which ones were for certain.

Inside Bethel Baptist, plans that had been underway for three months continued as scheduled. The air registers in the floor circulated the warmth of a spring day throughout the offices, classrooms, and hallways. Flowers bloomed in vases, and rose petals were scattered across the carpets. Birdseed standing in for the traditional rice was everywhere. No one had even considered letting the weather shut down the ceremonies. Today was too important for that.

A small boy ran down one hall, and he was wearing clothing he would die in if he had to wear it anywhere else. His mother had threatened, though, and he had wiped his tears and donned each item sullenly. He was cute, though. His shoes were black with polish, and his tie was a neat little bow. His jacket even had tails jutting down in the back. His hands had been the ones to scatter the flowers across the floors. Now, he just wanted to catch the little girl in the frilly dress. If he caught her, he wanted to put the snail he'd found down the back of her dress. That was exactly why tears ran down her face as she dashed away from him as quickly as she could.

In another room on the far side of the church, chandeliers sparkled and champagne flowed. Laughter danced among the attendees, and smiles were bright on winter-ruddy faces. An old woman kissed her skinny grandson and told him to pull up his pants. She cut him an extra thick slice of cake, too, telling him to put some meat on his bones.

Across the room, a petite woman in a flowing white dress was twirling in a wild dance with an oversized man who was as dark as she was light. When the music stopped, she wound her laughter down, letting the train on her dress settle at her feet. Smiling, she put her arms through the big man's, and she tiptoed to give him a kiss on the cheek.

"I love you, Ben. I love you better than you know."

His response was resonant, and it carried a warmth of meaning that only her ears could hear. "Not even a hurricane can keep us apart, Lou. I'm on Cracker's Barrel, now. You come see Torch and me."

She chuckled. "Ben, I'm in Fort Worth. At least I will be when the house in Westover Hills gets put in Chaddie's name. It's huge, too, so you and Torch come see me. Bring Yolanda, also. We'll have more than enough space." She looked around the room. "Have you seen Chaddie since the ceremony ended?" The boy had been best man, but then he was gone. No one had seen him since.

Ben smiled, and it was wide and white in his dark face. "I saw a pretty girl about fourteen who's missing, too. I understand the boy recently had a birthday. The way I count, that makes them the same."

Lou frowned. "Ben, he's with a girl? Where?" She began to search with her eyes.

Ben laughed at her in his deep, honey voice. "Look at you being a regular worry wart. He's fourteen, Lou. If he can't be fourteen now, then when will he? Let him find out what life's like. He'll never know otherwise."

"Babies, Ben." Her eyes were serious. "Fourteen-year-olds don't need babies."

He smiled, and his white teeth were bright against his skin. "He's a good kid, Lou. Don't you worry. You and Chad'll raise him right." He pointed. "Besides, he's coming in the door right there, and he has all his clothes on."

She turned to see a boy taller now than even her husband, and his blond hair was trimmed and all in place. The girl was tall, too, and she glowed each time the boy turned and spoke to her.

Lou touched Ben's arm, and she said to him, "You really are the smartest man I know, Ben, except in one thing." She looked at him and poked him in the chest with her finger.

A voice spoke over her shoulder and directly into her ear. "What's that, my sweet wife? In what mysterious thing is Ben not the smartest man you know?"

She turned and wrapped Chad in her arms. "He told me you couldn't love me. You proved him wrong."

Ben smiled at the two people in front of him. He whispered very quietly, "Thank God for that."

Chad heard, though, and he winked at Ben. Just before kissing his bride, he repeated the big man's words. "Thank God for that."

Did you enjoy this book?

Find more by this author at:

 THREE SKILLET

www.ThreeSkilletPublishing.com

www.ingramcontent.com/pod-product-compliance
Lightning Source LLC
Chambersburg PA
CBHW070307280626
47159CB00017B/394